MORTICE:
HAMMER DOWN!
MORE JUSTICE – MORT STYLE!

BOOK FOUR

Mortice: Hammer Down! © 2024 A J Wilton

All Rights Reserved. No part of this book may be reproduced in any form or by any electronic or mechanical means including information storage and retrieval systems, without permission in writing from the author. The only exception is by a reviewer, who may quote short excerpts in a review.

This book is a work of fiction. Names, characters, places, and incidents either are products of the author's imagination or are used fictitiously. Any resemblance to actual persons, living or dead, events, or locales is entirely coincidental.

Printed in Australia

Cover and internal design by New Found Books Australia Pty Ltd
Images in this book are copyright approved for New Found Books Australia Pty Ltd
Illustrations within this book are copyright approved for New Found Books Australia Pty Ltd

First printing: OCTOBER 2024
New Found Books Australia Pty Ltd
www.newfoundbooks.au

Paperback ISBN 978 1 9231 7171 8
eBook ISBN 978 1 9231 7180 0
Hardback ISBN 978 1 9231 7279 1

Distributed by New Found Books Australia Pty Ltd and Lightning Source Global
www.newfoundbooks.au

A catalogue record for this work is available from the National Library of Australia

New Found Books Australia Pty Ltd acknowledges the traditional owners of the land and pays respects to the Elders, past, present and future.

MORTICE: HAMMER DOWN!
MORE JUSTICE – MORT STYLE!

BOOK FOUR

A J WILTON

I used to work with a bloke named Mort.

A Vietnam Vet, he was a hardworking, no-nonsense bloke. Sadly, even with a loving and supportive family, Mort struggled with day-to-day life after his years serving his country.

This story is dedicated to him and all who have served their countries. Thank You.

This is an act of fiction, so please forgive me if my imagination doesn't fit with reality, my aim is to entertain not write history!

All characters and events are figments of my imagination.

*To friends and colleagues Mick & Mitch
Thanks — you know what for!*

*Special thanks to my 'Proofers',
Courtney, Shannon and Roger - Thanks!*

CHAPTER 1

It's Monday morning, the first day back at work after we arrived back from our 'holiday' in Canada and USA.

We are all taking it easy this morning, Suzie, Jenny, Maria, Pig and I really shooting the breeze as we chat about our holiday. Jenny and Maria both give Pig hugs for his efforts in the ten thousand metres at the Invictus Games, with Suzie replaying the video of the final lap for them.

Of course, Pig and I watch as well. It was an awesome effort, and we remain very proud of him.

Stacey had headed home back to Melbourne this morning, and Pig had made it clear when he got into the office from dropping her off that she would be moving up to Brisbane as soon as they were able to transfer her TAFE counselling course.

There is no doubt they make a good couple.

Pig is smitten!

That means Pig is:
- An empathic Pig
- A smirking Pig
- A loved-up Pig
- A flying Pig
- A horny Pig
- And now, a smitten Pig

Quite an accomplishment for a Pig, you might say!

The first thing I did during these casual conversations was dig out Liz's old phone and once again charge it up. Pig had taken the pen drive Midge had sent us via FBI Deputy Director Amanda Reynolds. We quickly recognised the un-synthesised voice as that of Dickie, an as-yet unrecognised associate of the Jackal bikies down in Melbourne.

The synthesised voice was used to threaten a prison warden here in Queensland, making this Dickie even more 'of interest' to us. Elevating him up the priority list!

As lunchtime approaches and we still haven't really done anything, I suggest we all head down the road to Mickle Pickle, our local café, for lunch.

Everyone jumps at the chance.

A noisy and enjoyable lunch is had by all.

Trouble is, even early in the afternoon, I can feel the drag of jetlag approaching.

It was the same yesterday, our first day home: mid-afternoon and the energy is sucked out of you.

I glance at Suzie and she responds with a tired smile, so I'm guessing she is feeling a little lagged as well.

Pig? No way of knowing and he isn't going to admit it. That would be a sign of weakness.

When we get back, it's time.

Time to see what, if anything, we can retrieve from Liz's old phone.

Liz's old phone is charged up. I turn it on, turn download back to auto and wait...

Pig is leaning over my shoulder.

No pressure!

Nothing.

Then one photo, then eight photos, then twenty-seven photos. We turn and look at each other and 'high-five' (of course!)

I turn back and now there is eighty-two, then one hundred and forty-nine.

Certainly getting quicker now.

I have no idea how many photos Liz would have in her cloud, but I do know we are very lucky to be able to retrieve them after such a long period of time.

Five hundred and thirty-one and counting.

As Pig has gone back to his desk, I decide to make us both a coffee. Of course, I make Maria a cup of tea as well.

Ever the gentleman!

One thousand four hundred and twelve.

Three thousand nine hundred and fifty-two.

Naturally, I have these being duplicated to our cloud. It is easier to review them on my laptop than trying to view them on Liz's old phone – an iPhone seven or something ancient.

The photos keep tumbling in.

I start reviewing the first ones, the most recent before her death.

This is strange. Seeing Liz in some of her selfies, some close with Kevin Clark, her 'boyfriend'.

Ouch, that hurts.

Many of various meals. She, like many these days, seems to relish taking photos of her food before eating it.

Me? I just want to eat it and enjoy it!

Then, in some of the older photos, there are Liz and I. Some of our holidays together flash before my eyes.

They certainly bring back memories.

I'm not sure if someone mentioned to Suzie that I've retrieved Liz's photos but suddenly she is behind me and intuitively knows I'm feeling sad. She places her arms across my shoulders as she watches with me.

Enough.

I stand up, giving Suzie a quick kiss and squeeze of the wrist, letting her know I'm fine, and I leave the photos to finish downloading on their own.

Work to do.

I head over to Pig's desk, sit down on the spare chair and he pulls up the list we made before we headed off to Canada where we stood in the seeking of Liz's killer.

But before we start, Maria asks: 'So don't you want to know what I've been up to whilst you've been away playing games and blowing up mansions?'

Oops. In all the chatter, we had neglected to have Maria bring us up to date.

'Okay, let's have it,' I say and she wheels her chair over to join us, placing a few folders on the edge of Pig's desk.

As you might recall, Pig's desk is always very clean and tidy, everything neatly aligned, straight and edge perfect. Messy he is not. More OCD!

Maria takes delight in placing her folders on the edge of the desk, but at a slight angle, then watches Pig as he controls his urge to straighten the folders up!

She smiles sweetly at him but doesn't get a response. He just looks at her, waiting, knowing she is trying to get a rise from him.

Maria takes a big breath, then starts. 'As you know when you left, I was working three more cases of Suzie's clients whose former partners are represented by that sleazebag Brownlow. On top of that, we now have three new cases, where the wife's lawyers reached out to Jenny who referred them to me. Only one of these is represented by Brownlow.

'Hoang's "CatchEm" is making it so easy to prove what these dumb bastards have been doing.'

You might recall our school bully victim up in Cairns, Hoang, had developed his own app that he used to identify the social media bullies who were tormenting him online. He did a bloody good job of it too. We now pay him a royalty each time we use it.

I butt in, 'Any other signs of employer complicity like Bennett Building Company?'

'Yes, there seems to be one so far. A concrete pumping company, seemingly doing the same thing.'

'Okay, how far along are you on these six cases?'

'Well, the first two, both Suzie's, the files are ready for your review.' Here, she pulls up the top two folders on the desk and pushes them across. I accept them.

'Jenny has had a read and put a couple of questions in red, you will see. I have put the answers in. Jenny thinks they should be good to file.

'The last one of Suzie's has been a bit harder. I think he is legitimately struggling financially. No doubt he is fudging his returns, but not blatantly like Mike Taylor was. I'm about a week from finishing on that one, I think.

'Then the other three are a lot newer. I haven't got too far except putting "CatchEm" to work. Haven't started analysing what it has dug up yet.'

I'm looking at Maria, having listened to her report, and can't help but admire how much she has grown in the eighteen-odd months I have known her.

I nod now, saying, 'Well done. Good job. You seem suited to this work.' Pig nods in agreement.

Maria smiles and says, 'I love it! I'm so thankful you have given me this chance to learn new skills and put them to good use. I get a real buzz out of this work.'

At over six feet tall, a proud Māori woman, she has certainly evolved from her early days as an Army grunt in the New Zealand army (dishonourably discharged for punching out an officer – who thoroughly deserved it, I'm sure!) to now being an integral part of DDS (Digital Data Solutions). Her mode of dress has also improved, now dressing stylishly instead of the casual jeans and tops of her early days. Working in the same office as Jenny and Suzie likely helped her too, as they both are always smartly dressed.

I smile at her again and say, 'I must be going soft, but I was just thinking of the first time we met, on the netball courts, when you threatened me if I hurt Suzie. And I was wondering what you would do now if Suzie broke my heart?'

I'm smiling as I say this and she smiles back before saying, 'Firstly, the words "soft" and "Mort" – or Pig, for that matter – shouldn't be used in the same sentence. On the second point, I would be quick, very quick, to tell Suzie the error of her ways!'

I smile and say, 'You do good work, Maria. No doubt I don't say it enough, but you are a valued member of our team. See, I am going soft!'

Maria blushes a little but quickly regains her composure, coming back with, 'Great, can I have a pay rise?'

Pig and I laugh and she smiles as well.

I stretch and, dare I say it, yawn. I look at Pig and say, 'I might call it a day. You okay to start the recap in the morning?'

He nods in agreement, so I head back to my desk, looking at the photos still downloading.

'Shit, thirty-three thousand six hundred and twelve and still coming!' Tomorrow.

Knowing Suzie had headed up a little while ago, I trudge up the stairs to our home.

Yes, back when I left the army and was establishing DDS, I had bought this house in Tingalpa, had the offices built into the enormous garage underneath, with state-of-the-art security (specific finger sensors for each entrance), getting plenty of eye rolls from Suzie in our early days.

But with the state-of-the-art computers and access to clients' confidential files, this level of security was, and still is, essential.

It makes it so easy to work and live in the same building. Now with Suzie running her law firm from within, makes it doubly easy!

CHAPTER 2

It's the next morning and not too early, although we did manage to go for our usual five-K run. I'm in the office putting the first pot of coffee on when Pig comes in.

After the usual pleasantries and both grousing about jetlag, we head over to his desk to start our recap.

'Shit,' I say. I forgot to see how many photos came down. I head back to my desk, wake the phone up and see it now has forty-four thousand, seven hundred and twenty-two photos.

I tell Pig whilst I check we have the same number in the cloud then say, 'Shit, I hope I don't have to look through them all.'

Pig then asks, 'Are you going to go back, say, six weeks and then start or what are your thoughts?'

I reply, 'I had thought of that but then if I don't see anything, I will have to start all over, so no, I'm going to start with the latest and just go backward from there.'

Pig puts his hand on my arm, saying, 'You going to be okay? Some will be pleasant memories, others not so.'

Empathic Pig is back!

I nod and say, 'Yep, I'll be okay.'

Have to be.

I want to find Liz's killer.

Pig brings up our list from before we went off to Canada:

It shows:

Who killed Liz? A list of what we know.

Pig updates it in bold as we read through it.

- Benson's stat dec – believed to be legitimate.

- Car tracking records clearly show Benson's car was used in a deliberate move to ram Liz. The only logical reason for this was to kill her.
- Therefore, someone should be facing a murder rap.
- Lancaster was probably not the driver as he could have done it and pressured the coroner. Would have risked injury if he had done it himself, though if this was the case, none of the recent events would have occurred, as Lancaster is dead. Absolutely. No question.
- Clearly, Lancaster set it up, paying Benson to take the heat.
- BUT why would he do that without being paid? That's the sixty-four-million-dollar question.
- WHY had they targeted Liz?
- Why no photos on her phone? Everyone has photos on their phone. The techy had told us there was no way of knowing how any photos on her phone had been deleted. It's not hard to do. Anyone could have done it – IF they got hold of her phone. **Now have forty-four thousand photos to go through!**
- Someone was monitoring Fleming and the other two bent coppers in Palen Creek Prison, we just can't find out who. Yet. **Dicky – as identified by Midge's un-synthesised voice recording**.
- Connected to Jeffy or not? Not likely now we know the caller was Dickie.
- Benson's wife didn't know anything. We were both a little pleased with how we had helped her, even if it did cause me some grief with Suzie through my mindless act. No reason she should suffer because she was married to an arsehole and bent copper!
- Benson's 'fuck buddy' Marissa may know more. One lead that needs more attention. Check the audio from her unit.
- Lancaster's old backyard MAY have something buried in it. **Continue to monitor.**
- We had not had a chance to interview Lancaster's wife. She had left the country in the days after he killed himself, using a false passport. She withdrew money from one of the Cayman Island accounts before the federal police got around to freezing it. Sloppy

buggers! With Jeffy sidetracking the AFP investigation, double-check that these accounts are still frozen. **Midge had replied that the accounts remain frozen, so no further funds have been sourced from there.**
- We also asked Midge to see if he can find out where she is living now. He had come up empty on where she may be. She flew from Brisbane to Singapore and then disappeared.
- Louie and Nico – they are likely out of the picture for a while after the beating we gave them. But we continue to monitor their phones and discussions. Something might break. **Need to check their audio feeds as well.**
- Likewise, their mate Dicky is worthy of more attention once we get back – maybe a lot more, seeing as we can't track him. Yet. Yes, identifying Dickie has to be a priority now we have him involved in the day-to-day of the Jackal bikie world in Melbourne, but also putting the hard word on a Queensland prison warden.
- Prison Warden Thomas is another open lead. All we can do is continue to monitor, but with his Joe using a voice synthesiser and a dark web phone, we aren't confident we will make much progress. Unless we catch a break. **Another one we need to check the audio on. But at least, thanks to Midge's new technology, we now know 'Joe' is Dickie of the Melbourne gangs. Not sure where he fits in, but it's only a matter of time.**

I comment, 'We are going to spend some time under our headphones over the next few days, ah!'

But coffee first!

Whilst it's brewing, we discuss how we might be able to identify Dickie. After turning the question inside out, it seems our best chance is for one of us to head to Melbourne and try a bit of foot slogging, hanging around some of the Jackal haunts and see what we can suss out. Pig volunteers to go!

I naturally tease him about being love-struck and smitten, but he just looks at me and says, 'Look who's talking!'

True.

Then my phone rings. It's *Ride of the Valkyries,* the haunting musical score from *Apocalypse Now,* the 1970s movie about the Vietnam War.

That means it's Major General Rutherford, or MGC, the boss of Section V.

I better answer it!

I do so and put it on speaker so Pig can hear:

'Sir, how are you?'

'I'm well, Mort, thank you. Trust you both are as well?'

'Yes, thanks we are all good.'

'Mort, I'm sending a plane up to collect you and Pig. After getting a call from the Deputy Director of the FBI the other week, I have been watching the news and I suspect I could plot your journey from the news stories!'

I smile but don't say anything, thinking, *Well, some of the best parts didn't make the news!*

When I don't respond, he continues, 'Yes, so I would like a debrief on your exploits but also, we have a developing situation of suspected domestic terrorism and I would like you to both sit in on the briefing meeting being held here in Canberra in the morning.

'We will have dinner at my club tonight, so I can debrief – unofficially, of course – then the meeting is set for nine in the morning. Bring sufficient clothes for a few days.'

'Certainly, Sir. Jacket and tie tonight, Sir?'

'Yes, of course.'

Pig pulls a face across the desk!

'Weapons, Sir?' I ask.

'No, not at this stage.'

'No worries, Sir. What is the ETA of the plane?

'ETA Archerfield, four p.m. your time.'

'Okay, Sir, we will see you tonight.'

'Yes, Frank will collect you and bring you to the club directly from the airport.'

'Confirmed. See you later, Sir.'

'Well, that buggers up our plans on taking it easy this week,' I say to Pig.

Maria, who had listened to the call, pipes up, saying, 'More action for you guys, eh!'

After a bit of grousing about having to wear a tie, from both of us, Maria adds her two bobs worth in, asking for us to send photos, 'so I know what the defendants look like,' but I quickly remind her that description is reserved for Kiwis wearing a jacket and tie.

Pig and I agree; he will head home shortly to grab his 'go bag' (a duffel we both keep packed ready to go for occasions like this so we can mobilise within minutes of getting a call such as this.)

Whilst there is no urgency to get to Archerfield (a small airport in Brisbane's southern suburbs) at present, it makes sense for him to shoot home, collect his duffel and come back here.

I will go up and get mine whilst he's away, then we will both be right to head to Archerfield in time for our four p.m. flight.

As he leaves, I wander into Suzie's office to let her know I'm off for a few days.

CHAPTER 3

It's a little after six-thirty p.m. that night as we exit the RAAF (Royal Australian Air Force) VIP Falcon 7X at Canberra Airport, but at the private terminal, away from the main passenger terminal.

Frank is standing beside the Land Cruiser 300s just outside the terminal. We shake hands all round and mount up.

Pig and I had changed and put our ties on loosely on the plane, so we only have to do up our top buttons and pull the tie tight once we get to 'the club'.

No sense being uncomfortable any longer than we need to be!

It's only a short drive to the club, which Frank explains is the 'Commonwealth Club', adding he has booked us rooms there for the next few nights, as well.

Pig responds, 'Shit, hope we don't have to wear bloody ties for breakfast!' getting a grin from me, whilst Frank answers thoughtfully.

'Well, I'm not sure. Never stayed there, so can't say.'

We exit the Cruiser at the front entrance. We grab our duffels from the back and as we say goodbye to Frank, he tells us he will be collecting us around 8.15 in the morning to take us to the potential domestic terrorism session at nine a.m.

After being shown to our rooms, where we drop our bags, we are then escorted to the dining room, where we find MGC sitting at an isolated outdoor table. Fortunately, it is one of those rare occasions – a pleasant evening in Canberra!

As we approach, he stands up, smiling, and comes forward to shake our hands, saying, 'As always, good to see you both!'

Almost in unison, Pig and I respond, 'Likewise, Sir!'

As soon as we sit down, the waiter places a glass of beer in front of Pig and me whilst refreshing MGC's glass of whisky. Top shelf, no doubt!

Menus are sitting on the table and with the waiter hovering, we order quickly and settle down.

After a few minutes of chit-chat, the General says, 'All right then, let's hear the details of your exploits over there. Off the record, of course. I'm keen to know what you two have been up to!'

Pig and I then take turns in recounting the high points of our recent trip, and I start by showing MGC the video of Pig's last lap of his ten thousand metre race at the Invictus Games. He is engrossed and, of course, has to ask if he made it. When Pig shakes his head in the negative, he still leans across the table to congratulate him and say, 'Bloody good effort anyway.'

I can tell Pig is chuffed by this and I think, *Well, we need to now add 'chuffed Pig' to our list!*

We explain how we had run into Hunter and Campbell there at the Invictus Games and what we agreed to do for them.

The General is really intrigued and impressed, I guess, with the little plan we – or in truth, Pig – had come up with and how we enacted it, flawlessly.

He knows the FBI caught Diego Garcia in New York and had assumed we had been instrumental in this. Such a high level of expectation on us!

We then fill him in on the middle parts of the story around Washington, the car chase and our escape, and also how we had provided the FBI with full and live access to the Garcia cartel's intranet, thus all their financial records, their bank accounts, the full box of tricks.

As he already suspected our involvement in the explosion and deaths of the top five of the Garcia cartel's West Coast operations, we confirmed this for him.

After telling our little tale and enjoying a decent feed, he gives us a briefing on what is suspected to be a domestic terrorism threat to the water supplies of a few cities. And the suspicion someone is only 'testing the water' so to speak, ensuring their plans work on a small scale before their likely aim of a mass attack potentially on all our major cities.

Before we leave the table, he also updates us on changes within Section V, where they are now operating 24/7, with duty officers manning their phones and all communications. Apparently, the three duty officers report to Robert who updates the General immediately of anything critical.

He also confirms, 'We now have small teams in both Melbourne and Sydney on the ground as well. Ready to swoop and assist if anything comes up. These are experienced police officers, seconded to Section V, but continue to perform their usual duties, able to drop anything in an instant, when need be.'

We nod in acknowledgement. This seems a logical step for Section V, with the apparent ever-growing risks to our nation. Seemingly more from within than outside.

As we move out of the dining room, he assures us this evolving situation is a serious threat that needs an urgent solution.

We shake hands as he heads out the door, where we can see Frank waiting patiently. Pig and I head to our rooms, grabbing a coffee to go on the way!

CHAPTER 4

As promised, Frank is right on time collecting us the next morning and MGC is already sitting in the cruiser.

The General explains the meeting, which is to be chaired by the Department of Health but attended by senior representatives from Federal Police, ACT and NSW Police, NSW EPA (Environmental Protection Agency), DCCEEW (Department of Climate Change, Energy, the Environment and Water).

But he doesn't elaborate other than saying that I, and we in Section V, have oversight if and when it is determined to be a domestic terrorism threat.

Mmm, should be interesting seeing how all these bureaucrats jockey for positions!

Frank delivers us to the Federal Department of Health. After clearing security and being issued with temporary visitor passes, we are escorted to a large meeting room up on the fifth floor.

There are already ten to fifteen people sitting in the assembled chairs, or helping themselves to the coffee, tea and water set out down either side.

Pig and I head down the left side as MGC heads to the head of the room, and we watch as he shakes hands with two, I assume, senior bureaucrats already sitting at the top table.

Having surveyed the room, neither Pig nor I see anyone we know. What we expected, so we make ourselves comfortable on the edge of a middle row, close to one of the coffee pots!

An older man in a white shirt and tie, with a nod from MGC, taps on the podium asking for everyone to take their seats.

Once quiet, he introduces himself as Sir Owen Mansfield, Director

General of the Federal Department of Health, and acknowledges, 'My colleague Michelle McMasters, Director General of the DCCEEW.' (Yes, he used the acronym rather than the full name – and who can blame him.)

He then starts the meeting by saying:

'We have asked you all to come this morning, as we suspect there is a deliberate effort being made to sabotage the water supply to some of our cities and towns. Whilst so far the instances that have been flagged are only minor, with no more than twenty to thirty people having been affected, we are concerned, very concerned, that someone is, so far, at least, only testing their processes before one or more of our major cities are attacked.

'As you might appreciate, a debilitating disease, delivered via our water supply, would be very hard to stop. It could have disastrous consequences for our country if they are successful. As Covid proved to everyone's satisfaction, unfortunately, our medical – and more specifically, our hospitals – simply could not cope with a major epidemic of this potential size.

'Imagine, if you will, the relatively small town of Gosford being shut down by a water-supply-based disease. Multiply that for the towns of Geelong, Campbelltown, Greater Sydney and Greater Melbourne. The effect would be catastrophic.

'That is why you are all here today.

'We need to nip this risk in the bud before it becomes a full-blown attack on our nation.'

He stops and takes a couple of minutes to slowly run his gaze over the assembled throng.

Satisfied everyone is taking him seriously, he continues:

'I will now ask Paul Cummins to step up and give you all a brief on what has happened to date.'

At a nod, a short, balding man hustles up to the front and sets up his first slide on the large screen on the front wall.

It has on it:

Gosford, NSW. Monday 17th – 19th 12 reports, 4 hospitalised

Campbelltown, NSW. Wednesday 26th – 29th 18 reports, 8 hospitalised
Geelong, VIC. Tuesday 8th – 12th 25 reports, 12 hospitalised
A total of 24 hospitalised so far.

He stands at the wooden lectern, hands clasped behind his back. He continues, 'To date, all cases have been explained away as food poisoning and local authorities are busy trying the identify a central point – i.e., a restaurant or supermarket or take away shop, some point that connects with each case.' Using a pointer, he taps each city, reinforcing his points.

'Alas, to date, there is no connection in any of the locations.

'Within DCCEEW, we have a national monitoring program and every Health Authority is required to submit a report on any food poisoning or suspected water contamination. That is how we have identified these incidents.'

I speak up. 'You might need to add Stanthorpe in Queensland to your list. I read in *The Courier Mail* the other day they had a case of eight suspected food poisoning cases.'

This creates a few murmurs from the assembled meeting but Paul, up on the podium, looks my way before he says rather dismissively, 'That's unlikely. All health authorities know what is required and that all instances of suspected food poisoning must be reported.'

He appears to be dismissing my suggestion and moving on, but MGC interrupts, saying, 'Please have the Stanthorpe angle checked out.'

Paul, perhaps not knowing who he is addressing, turns and says, again rather dismissively, 'As I said, all water authorities know they must report any instances of suspected food poisoning.'

The General's reply of 'I am not asking' is accompanied by a fierce glare. Pig and I look at each other, smiling, having both been on the wrong end of that look more than once in our lives!

Paul, now a little uncertain, glances at his boss Michelle. Getting a small nod from her, he responds, 'Very well, we will reach out to Stanthorpe, or their local water board, to double check, but I am sure our report will be proven correct.'

I think, *I hope so for your sake, buddy!*

After a bit more background with an explanation, it is suspected that arsenic is being added to the water supply somehow, but only in minute quantities. It is stressed also that this may be happening accidentally, but it has been agreed this is highly unlikely considering the widely spread affected areas.

When asked for any questions, someone in the crowd who identifies himself as Lawrence with 'Federal Police specialist services' asks, 'How can arsenic, or any other substance, be added to our water supply?'

Paul, who still has the podium, answers, 'If it is being done deliberately, we suspect that somehow they must be perhaps drilling into the water supply pipes to inject the poison.'

Lawrence then asks: 'What quantity of arsenic would need to be added to create a major incident?'

Paul and a couple of his colleagues waffle on without answering the question. Perhaps fairly, as it would depend on where the arsenic is injected, the size of the pipeline and the volume of water it is carrying. But the takeaway from the conversation is, not very much.

A pretty scary situation.

This leads to a follow-up question from the floor. 'Surely then you have pressure monitors on these pipelines that would show there has been a lowering of pressure that would indicate an intrusion?'

Paul and a few of his colleagues huddle down discussing this before he straightens and says, 'We don't believe so. Most water pipelines run at such a low pressure it wouldn't be noticeable and, in fact, most water lines have regular leaks, so another one, even if deliberate, wouldn't raise any flags.'

This again creates a few murmurs and Pig and I look at each other, thinking, *Shit it sounds like it would be bloody easy to inject poisons into the water supply.*

I suspect we aren't alone in our thinking.

Pig then asks, 'From the dates you have listed, it is taking them roughly ten days between each new site. It's now the eighteenth. Any new incidents being reported or suspected?'

Paul shakes his head. 'No. We have been anxiously watching for any new reports but none yet. We are hoping if it is, in fact, deliberate, they have not finished their testing yet. I can't stress enough how dangerous it will be if we have a large outbreak of arsenic poisoning in one of our major cities, let alone two or more.

'One thing we all learnt from Covid, is that our health system and hospitals, in particular, are not set up to handle emergencies the size that this could be.'

MGC then stands and without introducing himself, says, 'I want to stress to you all this is a live and potentially disastrous situation and no risks, I repeat, no risks, are to be taken. Do not assume. Please, report any discrepancy or concern so it can be investigated.'

With a nod, he sits down again.

On that sombre note, the meeting is closed with all attendees advised they will receive regular updates as the investigation proceeds.

With Pig in tow and fresh coffee in hand, I push through the crowd, keen to identify Lawrence from the Federal Police, sensing he knows a little more than most of us about water supply.

I find him toward the back talking to a couple of his colleagues, these two in uniform, whereas he's in jeans, an open-neck shirt, work boots and a light jacket.

They sense us waiting and turn, eyeing us as their conversation petters out.

'Lawrence?'

He nods so I reach my hand out introducing myself and Pig as Mort and Julien of Section V.

We shake hands as his two colleagues drift off, but not before one of them gives me a dirty look. *Odd,* I think.

We move Lawrence away from another nearby group and I ask him, 'You seem to know a bit more about water supply than others so thought I would see what we can learn from you.'

He smiles but pulls a face before saying, 'Not really, but I had a need in the past to use a small company up in Brisbane who seemed to know almost everything to do with pipes and how to cut them and anything else you might want to do with pipes or pipelines.'

'Okay, what was their name?' I ask.

He pulls his phone out saying, almost to himself, 'Can't remember, but I'm sure it started with pipe or piping or something.'

We wait patiently – yes, we are good at it!

After a couple of minutes, he says, 'Yes, this is them, "Piping Machine Tools." The owner is Alex.'

'Why don't you call him and ask what would be involved in injecting a substance into a water supply pipeline?' I prod.

'Sure, why not?'

He pulls the phone number up and dials it, putting it on speaker so we can hear, and we move away, finding a quieter corner.

The phone is answered with, 'Alex speaking.'

Lawrence responds, 'Hi, Alex, it's Lawrence from the Federal Police. You might recall a few months ago you were able to assist us?'

'Yes, of course, Lawrence. I have your phone number still in my phone, so I knew it was you. Can we help you?'

Lawrence. 'We hope so, I have you on speaker with a couple of colleagues and want to know how easy it is to add or inject a substance into a water supply pipeline.'

Alex replies, 'Shit, I hope this is a theoretical question?' When Lawrence doesn't reply, Alex continues. 'Okay. In reality, if you know what you are doing, it is not difficult at all. You can use a "hot tapping machine", which is a fancy name for a big drill, but with the difference you can "tap" into a live line, even pipelines full of gas, so water is relatively easy with its low pressure. Once the tap is completed, you can then feed a line into the pipeline for as long as you like.

'The hot tap machine is usually used to add a junction to an existing pipeline, so for gas supply to a new subdivision or something, you tap into the main line and then you have the smaller line coming off that then goes into the new subdivision.

'What type of pipe is this waterline? Well, it doesn't matter really, as the hot tap machines we sell are suitable for both steel and HDPE lines. HDPE stands for high-density polyethylene, more commonly called poly pipe. Most main water lines are concrete lined steel pipe, so this wouldn't be an issue.'

I jump in, asking, 'So you sell these machines, do you?'

'Yes,' he replies, 'we are one of the biggest dealers for these machines. We rent them as well.'

I look at both Pig and Lawrence before asking, 'Alex, could you set up a demo for us, say, this afternoon?'

I'm getting a shocked look from Lawrence, but Pig is nodding in agreement.

'Well, yes, I guess. Maybe not a full demonstration but we can certainly set a machine up and show you how it would work.'

I look at my watch, noting it is not yet nine-thirty a.m., so I calculate quickly.

'Great, so if we can be there, say, by twelve-thirty p.m. today, you can have it set up?'

'I'm getting a sense of urgency from you, so yes, I will make it happen.'

'Thank you, Alex. Unless you hear from us to the contrary, we will see you this afternoon. Thank you.'

Lawrence ends the call and I'm already on the phone to MGC, not sure if he is still in the room.

He answers on the first ring and I say, 'Sir, can you get us to Brisbane by midday today? I want to see how a machine that can be used to inject substances into pipelines works.'

A slight pause. 'Let me get Frank on it. Give me five minutes.'

I hang up and Lawrence is looking at me, at us, and says, 'Shit, who are you – that you can pull a plane out of thin air like that?'

We both smile at him and Pig says, 'Can you be ready to join us?'

Before he is finished, Lawrence is nodding his head. 'Certainly, not going to miss this. Even if I have to sleep in my clothes, I'm good to go!'

My phone goes beep and I have a text from Frank. *'Flight confirmed, departing Canberra ten forty-five a.m. I will collect your bag from the club and pick you up from MGC's office at ten-fifteen.'* I send a thumbs-up emoji.

I look up and smile. 'We do have good logistics; we leave at ten forty-five a.m. Can you meet us at the airport, Lawrence?'

He nods before saying, 'I'll head off now then. Better tell the boss I'm going to be away for maybe a day. Can I tell him who I'm with? As he sure will want to know!'

So, we re-introduce ourselves, as he clearly had not taken our details on board, from Section V and he replies, 'No idea who Section V is, but I'm guessing you're important if you can rustle up a plane in ten minutes!'

Pig and I smile as we shake hands, and I see MGC heading our way through the thinning crowd.

CHAPTER 5

The logistics work. We pull into the yard of Piping Machine Tools and there is an older, portly gent coming out to greet us.

As he approaches, I think, *Living the good life, not the hard life,* judging by his size and shape.

Still, he is keen and has a certain energy about him you can sense, as he introduces himself to us as Alex before leading us into the warehouse.

Of course, we had to don hi-viz vests and safety glasses and sign the prerequisite visitors log first.

Inside the warehouse, they have set up what looks like a twelve-inch (three hundred millimetres) steel pipe sitting up on oversized plastic cones. Beside it, in a long box nearly three metres in length, lies a long, odd-looking tool.

Alex then introduces us to Lee, I'm guessing the senior storeman (there was another one zipping around on a forklift) and Philip as their senior salesman.

After the introductions, Philip takes over and explains in some detail how the hot tapping machine works, how it is called a hot tapping machine as it can and is used to 'tap' (i.e. drill) into live lines, carrying gas, water, sewage, you name it.

'You usually tap in when you want to add a junction, T junction or Y junction,' he explains.

Anyway, whilst they didn't set the machine up fully, Philip has a video to show us on his laptop sitting on an adjacent table.

At the end of the video, it's pretty clear how this machine works.

I start with the questions:

'If you wanted to add something like a fluid of some sort into a water pipeline, you could tap in using this sort of machine to inject this substance into the line?'

There is a pause as both Philip and Alex contemplate what we weren't saying before Philip, after looking at Alex, answers, 'Yes. No doubt you could do that.'

Alex adds, 'I hope your question is theoretical?'

I shake my head in the negative. I decide I need to clarify something.

'Alex, Philip, I need you to understand we are talking about a current, developing situation, so whilst we don't have time to sign you up to the Official Secrets Act, we do request – that is, insist – that you treat what we are discussing in total confidence.'

I finish and take a moment to give them both a hard stare, to reinforce the seriousness of the situation. Pig pipes in, 'Besides, we know where to find you.'

And, standing together, we are big, imposing bodies. Doesn't hurt when you are trying to ensure they keep quiet about our discussions.

They both nod, looking a little intimidated.

Pig asks, 'What is the smallest line you could add into a larger waterline?'

Alex comes back with, 'What size water pipe are you talking about?'

I look at Pig and Lawrence, thinking, *Shit, hadn't thought to ask that.*

Pig grabs his phone and walks away to give MGC a call, coming back a couple of minutes later, saying, 'He will check and get back to me in a few minutes.'

Lawrence starts asking some technical questions of Philip and they wander back toward the machine and whilst I can't hear what is being said, I see Philip using his hands, motioning what he is explaining. They then head back to join us.

Alex nods and continues, 'The smallest machine we sell and rent has a minimum of four inches or one hundred millimetres. As random as it might sound, these machines and even steel pipe are often still referred to in inches.'

Pig persists, 'Okay, but if you only wanted a small tube.' Here, he is holding his fingers together, reflecting a tiny tube size of approximately one centimetre (roughly half an inch).

Again, Alex and Philip look over at each other before Alex says, 'Well, it wouldn't be hard to use a reducer, although to reduce from one hundred millimetres to ten millimetres is quite a reduction.'

Then Philip adds, 'I'm sure it can be done. If you push the feedline through almost to the junction, and this is pressurised, you know the fluid you are injecting is pushed through by some form of pressure – it would work.'

After a pause, he then adds, 'Well, thinking about it, you would definitely need to pressurise the feeder line, otherwise it wouldn't work.'

I nod as this makes sense.

Pig's phone rings, so he moves away to answer it and I ask Alex, 'How many of these smaller machines have you sold recently?'

He replies, 'It's not a fast mover so we don't usually carry stock. We do or did have a rental unit.'

He stops and looks over at Philip who is fiddling with the hot tap machine.

Then he continues, 'We actually sold it a few weeks ago.' As he says this, Philip looks up and comes over to him, saying, 'The Irish brothers?'

Alex nods back at him.

Pig re-joins us, saying, 'Of the three confirmed locations, they range in size from 450 millimetres to nine hundred millimetres.'

Alex and Philip both nod, with Philip saying, 'That's the sizes I would expect, and it wouldn't impact on the use of the machine.'

Alex can't resist. 'So you have three cases of this happening?' I give him a hard stare and he retreats, smiling and saying, 'Okay, okay I understand, but you can't blame a bloke for being curious!'

I relent and say, 'Potentially. We haven't located the where yet, but you may well have explained the how.'

I continue:

'The Irish Brothers? Tell me more, please.'

Philip responds, 'It was...' Here, he looks at Alex, who answers, 'Maybe six, seven weeks ago,' before Philip resumes.

'I took an inquiry for a small hot tap machine. Would have to check my notes to get his name but long story short, Paddy, that was his name or nickname I guess, asked for a demo, so we set up very similar to what we have done here for you.

'He and his brother Declan then turned up and we showed them how it worked. We actually did a tap with them, with Paddy using the machine.

'They ended up buying the rental unit as they said they had a contract which they wanted to start straight away so couldn't wait for a new machine to arrive.'

He certainly has Pig's and my attention now, Pig taking notes on his iPad.

'Okay,' I continue, now addressing both Philip and Alex. 'Can you provide details of these two? How did they pay for the machine – credit card?'

Alex answers, 'No. We don't accept credit card payments for major machinery sales. Too risky. We insisted on EFT payment.

'We will have their full details on file. If I remember correctly, we recorded their licence details as well. There was just something about them that seemed fishy. We even referred to them as "the dodgy brothers",' he finishes with a smile.

I can see he is thinking about something, so I wait patiently – yes, we are good at it.

Alex finally recalls what it was he had been thinking about, saying; 'It was also a bit strange because there was also an older Asian man involved. I'm pretty certain he was the one who paid for the machine, not the Irish boys. He cruised into the yard a couple of times during the demo and Paddy would go out and seemingly give him an update.'

Another pause before he continues, 'Not sure how relevant this is, but this bloke had a chauffeur and was being driven around in a black BMW735. I remember wondering if the chauffeur was a bodyguard in fact because he was a big burly bloke.' Then, looking from Pig and back to me, he adds, 'Well, not compared to you two, but on a general scale he was.' Again, he finishes with a small smile.

Shit, we may have struck lucky here. I look at Pig and judging from the smile hovering around his mouth, he is thinking the same thing.

Not only do we now know how the arsenic can be injected into a water pipeline, but we also have two likely suspects. Bonus.

'Okay, Alex, we need to follow up on your dodgy brothers and NOW. Can you please get all the info you have on them – copies of their licences if you did copy them. A copy of the EFT receipt as well, plus if your accounts people can see if your bank records detail any other info, whatever you can find please.'

He nods, saying, 'On it,' and heads off to the office. I notice him stop and have a word with Lee the storeman on his way, who is back at the machine, and it looks like he is packing it back up.

After about ten minutes, Alex comes back holding a sheaf of papers. Lee stops him as he approaches us and hands him a couple more pages, then accompanies him back to where Pig, Lawrence, Philip and I are standing, having been shooting the breeze.

Alex starts, 'They are down in Tasmania. In Mount Field National Park at present.'

Shit.

'You mean your dodgy brothers? How do you know that?' I quickly ask.

'Yes. Well, not sure they are, but the machine is. We have GPS trackers in all our rental machines and in the rush to sell this one, the tracker wasn't removed. We can trace them from here to Stanthorpe. They spent a few days there, then down to Gosford. More time spent there, into Campbelltown in Sydney. A week there. Then another week near Geelong before heading to Tasmania.'

'Awesome. Bloody bonus!' I smile and nod to Lee, as I suspect he is the one who forgot to remove the tracker.

Alex then hands me the paperwork he had brought from the office, saying, 'Here, these are photocopies of their licences. This is the rego of their ute. It was a rental from one of the smaller hire companies. I'm trying to remember the name of it. And this is a copy of the remittance advice. The money came from an overseas bank, I think they said a Hong Kong bank, and I now remember the girls telling me even though we had the remittance advice because it was coming from offshore the money wouldn't hit the account for one or two days. I remember debating whether to release the machine or not. In the end, I decided to risk it.'

Pig nods his acceptance as he takes all the documentation, looking first at the two licences: one for Patrick Joseph O'Donnell, the other for Declan Conor O'Donnell, both with the same address here in Brisbane in Highgate Hill.

Pig hands Alex his business card, asking, 'Can you email all this and also how to track the GPS with the machine?'

Here, Lee pipes up, saying, 'I will send you the login details and the ID number so you can log in, twenty-four seven, and check where it is and the exact locations it has been to.'

'Cool,' replies Pig.

We are pretty pumped.

A real breakthrough on our first day.

BIG bonus.

Then Alex pipes up, 'I remember now, CSTHire was the name of the rental company. I remember as I wondered what the initials stood for.'

I write the name on the back of his card, not sure, at the moment at least, what benefit this will be.

Neither Pig, Lawrence nor I can think of any more questions to ask, so we shake hands all round and whilst I express my appreciation for their help, I finish off by stressing the importance of not sharing our discussion 'not even over dinner with your family, please.' I'm tempted to say, 'No pillow talk, either,' but decide not to!

We head back to the rental Camry Frank had organised for us from Archerfield. As we leave their yard, I realise we are just around the corner from Nikkalatte, one of our favourite cafes. Alas, they are just closing up, so whilst they do make us all a coffee, we have to forgo their yummy banana bread. But we do sit outside under their umbrella to enjoy the coffee and ponder our next moves.

Being curious how Lawrence knows of this company Piping Machine Tools, I ask, 'Lawrence, how do you know Alex and his company?'

He replies with a smile, 'They helped us out a few months ago. We needed to cut through a large 450-millimetre cylinder, and they supplied the equipment and operator. He did such a good job, he didn't even spill any of the "contents"!'

'Drugs?' asks Pig.

Lawrence nods in the affirmative.

After chatting for a few more minutes, I move away and ring MGC.

He answers, 'Mort.'

'Sir, we have had a real breakthrough.'

'The company Lawrence took us to had recently sold one of their rental hot tapping machines. Two brothers, Irish apparently, were the purchasers. Pig is sending you and Robert the buyer's licence details now.'

'The added bonus is, they sold them one of their rental units, which all have GPS trackers, so we know the machine and therefore likely the two Irish brothers are currently, right now down in Mount Field National Park in Tasmania.

'The tracking history shows they have spent time in Stanthorpe'—here MGC grunts in annoyance—'then Gosford, Campbelltown, Geelong and now Mount Field National Park in Tassie. Judging by what we can google, Hobart's water supply comes from Mount Field National Park.'

I stop for a breath!

Then continue, 'Additionally, Sir, they believe "an older Asian man" actually paid for the machine. Pig is sending through the remittance advice as well, the money coming apparently from a Hong Kong bank. This Asian gentleman stopped by a couple of times whilst they were having the machine demo'd and was being driven by a big burly chauffeur, or bodyguard.

'No ID or description though, but hopefully you may get a connection from the bank account.'

Major General Charles Rutherford (MGC) is silent for a few minutes, digesting all I have told him. I wait patiently.

Eventually, he comes back with, 'That is excellent news. Well done. As usual, you have clearly asked the right questions to elicit this information. Your next steps?'

Pig has come over and is now standing next to me, so I put the phone on speaker and say, 'Sir, we believe we will need a third pair of hands, particularly as Mount Field appears to be quite rough terrain and, well, with Pig not being as dexterous as he would like, we believe a third person will be necessary.'

Pig is nodding his agreement, as we had discussed this before I rang MGC. In fact, it was Pig who suggested he may find the going difficult. I would never voice such a thought, as he has never let us down. And his admitting this did raise a question in my mind about his artificial leg.

MGC replies, 'Do you have anyone in mind?'

'Sir, yes. We suggest we ask Maria to join us, she maintains a high level of fitness and we know she still trains with her pistol, as we have been to the range with her.'

'Remind me again of her background,' he replies.

'First NZR before a DD for clouting an officer with wandering hands, Sir. She is proving herself very handy and helpful in our business.'

'Very well, sign her up as part of your team and add her time to the charges. I expect at a lower level than you two.'

'Yes, Sir, we will check she is available but am confident she will be. We will also stop and collect our weapons, Sir.

'Also, if it is alright with you, I would like to stop at Stanthorpe on the way back to Canberra to drop Lawrence off, as we are keen to see how they have fitted and left the device they used to inject the arsenic into the water supply. It would be reasonable to assume that they would use the same method for the other locations. You won't need our expertise to disarm these, and I want to get down to Hobart ASAP tonight. Don't want to lose this break or push our luck, Sir.'

Phew, again a big speech for me.

Silence as once again MGC ponders this. 'Yes, that all makes sense. I will advise the pilots to follow your instructions and let them know you will be going on to Hobart this afternoon. I will have Frank organise a vehicle for you at Hobart as well.'

'Make that two 4x4 work utes, please, Sir. Mount Field looks rugged so I'm sure we will need a 4x4 and we will then fit in. We may have to go in separate directions, hence the need for two utes, Sir. We will be grabbing our hi-viz, so we look like workers.'

'Very well. Accommodation?' he asks.

'Let's leave that, Sir. I expect the two brothers are staying at a local hotel somewhere and I'm sure the tracker will tell us this once evening approaches.'

'Very well. You seem to have covered everything as usual, so I will leave you to get going.'

'Good-o, Sir. Thank you.'

I hang up and Pig and I fist bump.

I pull Maria's phone number up from favourites and give her a call.

She answers on the third ring, saying in a joking manner, 'Hi, don't tell me you need a hand already?'

I answer, 'Yep, your time to shine! IF you're up to it, of course.'

'Shit, seriously?'

This time Pig pipes up, as once again I have it on speaker. 'Yep, hi-viz uniform and all. We are "loading up"'—soldier speak for fully loaded weapons!–'as well, so do you have a preference between an EF88-16 sixteen-inch barrel assault rifle or an EF88-16 assault rifle?' he asks.

'Shit, you make it difficult. I have shot both the EF88 and the EF88, so I guess I will go with the EF88. I will bring my own handgun as well though.'

I conclude the discussion by saying, 'Okay, get going. Can you be packed and meet us at Archerfield airport in, say, one hour's time? We have places to be. Pack for three to four days. We will be in rough terrain so make sure you wear solid comfortable walking boots.'

'Awesome! I'll need to shoot. Need to arrange for Mum to pick the kids up and get sorted. I do have a "go bag" already packed so should be okay time-wise.'

'Okay, see you there.'

We ask Lawrence if he minds making his own way back to Archerfield as we need to go back to the office and 'load up'!

On the way, Pig tells me he has sent all the info on the Hong Kong bank account and even the two brothers' licence details to Midge as well, now there is possibly an international connection.

'Good idea,' I tell him.

CHAPTER 6

Lawrence is already sitting in the Archerfield Terminal when Pig and I get there. As are the RAAF crew, sitting quietly drinking coffee. As I head in their direction, I randomly think, *I bet the coffee isn't as good as the brew they make on board the plane,* which looked like a fancy unit – and the coffee was great.

As I approach, the senior pilot stands and we head away from his crew to talk. I smile and say, 'We will be ready to go in a few minutes, just waiting on a new team member. We also have some luggage and tooling to be loaded. We then want to make a short stop at Stanthorpe before heading on to Canberra, but then we need to go straight on to Hobart. Ideally with no delay.'

He nods before replying, saying, 'Yes, a message along those lines has come through and that I was to take instructions from you. We will have hit our daily hours by the time we get back to Canberra, but a replacement crew will be waiting for our arrival, so you should see minimal delay before heading on to Hobart.'

I nod and we shake hands. He seems about to add something, I suspect why the Stanthorpe stopped and why heading urgently to Hobart tonight, even about the 'tooling' I mentioned!

Instead, he says, 'Looks like your new team member has arrived.' I glance back and see that yes, Maria has arrived with her duffel.

I reply, 'Let's load and get going, please. Can you also give me an ETA to Stanthorpe so I can arrange transport?'

'Will do as soon as we file our flight plan.'

I nod as we separate.

As requested, Maria is dressed in hi-viz workwear. The trouble is the shirt must be her husband Ronnie's, as it is very tight across the bust. A glance at Pig and the half-smirk on his face, I can tell he is dying to say something. But it will have to wait. I say, 'Okay, grab your gear, we are loading up, want to get to Stanthorpe before everyone out there knocks off for the night.'

In discussion with Robert and MGC, we have confirmed the Southern Downs Regional Council is responsible for the water supply for Stanthorpe. Robert had been in touch requesting two 4x4s meet us at the airport for an 'urgent security assessment' of their water pipeline.

I go over and grab my gun case. Pig does the same. Maria hoists her duffel onto her shoulder – army style – and we troop out to the RAAF VIP Falcon, with Lawrence bringing up the rear. His eyes grow like saucers when he sees the gun cases Pig and I are carrying.

Once on board, having stashed the luggage in a rear luggage compartment, Maria can't resist saying, 'My, my aren't we a bit flash,' as she takes in the plush interior of the plane and the uniformed steward standing waiting to be of service.

I nod and say, 'Total contrast to the old Hercules transport, ah, Maria!'

She turns and looks at me, nodding and smiling as she settles into one of the large armchair-style seats.

Once airborne, I confirm to the others that we are first heading to Stanthorpe so we can inspect the actual location of what we suspect is the drilling into and contamination of the water pipeline. 'We will be met by staff of the Southern Downs Regional Council who are responsible for the local water supply. We will give them the location so they can drive us there.'

As I'm talking, the co-pilot pops out of the cockpit and looks over to me, saying 'ETA Stanthorpe thirty-five minutes.'

I nod and quickly text Robert so he can inform the Southern Downs water crew. Yes, we have full Wi-Fi on board!

I now look up and continue, 'We want to inspect the actual line tapping, to understand it is being done as Alex and co told us. Then of course we can close it off, so they cannot contaminate the water again.'

Maria, still a little in the dark, comes back with, 'Shit, are you saying someone is deliberately contaminating Stanthorpe's water supply?'

Pig answers, 'Yes and Gosford, Campbelltown in Sydney, Geelong in Victoria and now they are down in Tassie, we suspect working on Hobart's water supply. So far, twenty-four hospitalised but no deaths yet, so keep your fingers crossed.'

Lawrence then pipes up, saying, 'I got a text earlier to say that one of the hospitalised victims at Campbelltown has passed away this morning. An older lady, not in the best of health, but her death is being attributed to the waterborne disease.'

'Shit,' I respond and we all look rather gloomily at each other.

Pig says, 'We need to make sure we put an end to this. Take these arseholes out quickly.'

Further nods all round.

Silence settles on us as we all contemplate what lays ahead.

But not for long.

Pig can't resist.

Turning and looking at Maria, who is sitting in the same row but on the other side of the plane, he says, 'So, Ronnie isn't as big across the chest, ah?'

'Shut up!' Maria flashes back, slightly embarrassed, I suspect, from the flush around her neck. But Pig is not to be put off.

'I reckon that top buttons are only hanging on by a thread – it could become a lethal weapon should it burst!'

It's not appropriate to laugh and I notice Lawrence is trying hard to hide his smile, as am I.

Maria feels compelled to explain. 'Shut up. I have never got around to putting my hi-viz through the wash – they are still wrapped in their plastic. I've never needed it before coming to work with you guys. I thought I would fit in better in a well-worn uniform.'

Pig responds, 'Well, yes you would, except for the top button.'

Before anyone else can add to the banter, the steward announces we are descending into Stanthorpe and will be on the ground in five minutes.

CHAPTER 7

We land and taxi off to the side of the small terminal. Once stopped, the stairs are lowered and we descend. Pig and I had agreed we would leave our weapons on the plane, not expecting to encounter any baddies here. We are confident they are down in Tassie.

As requested, there is a Prado and Hilux 4x4 Dual Cab parked off to the side of the Apron with Southern Downs Regional Council logos on them.

We head over and an older gent dressed in casual 'office gear' – i.e. not hi-viz – introduces himself as Walter and his colleague Lou.

I explain we need them to take us to this specific location along the water pipeline from Storm King dam and give him the coordinates of the location but he, Walter, is clearly not conversant with these, so Pig silently shows him his iPad with a Google Maps overlay. He nods and he and Lou confer.

Walter then says, 'Okay that will take approximately fifteen minutes.' He looks at his watch before adding, 'We normally knock off in twenty minutes,' looking at me.

I reply, 'You're going to be late today.'

I hold his glance and he doesn't question me; instead, he nods and heads to the Prado. I follow him as does Lawrence, with Pig and Maria following Lou.

Once underway, I explain to Walter why we are here and what we anticipate finding at the location we have given him.

He doesn't say anything but a look of horror flashes across his face followed by a look of determination.

We discuss pipeline security and he explains they do have a contractor who runs a drone survey of the pipeline every three months. He stresses they are looking mainly for leaks, not interference with the pipeline.

As we crest a rise, he says, 'The location is about halfway down this hill. There is a gate off this road and the location is about one hundred metres into the paddock.'

I ask him to stop where we are, saying, 'I want to check to ensure they don't have any surveillance cameras or system in place. Stay here please until I wave you forward.'

He nods his acceptance. I get out and move off to the left of the track. Lawrence has also gotten out but I ask him to stay, nodding for Maria to do the same as she and Pig join us.

Using my binoculars, I sweep the fields below, using the gate ahead as a focal point. Sure enough, the water pipeline runs about one hundred metres in the paddock to the left of and roughly parallel to the road, sitting high above the ground, supported by concrete supports every twenty metres or so.

The location we are focused on appears to be in the middle of a clump of scruffy scrub, which is hiding the pipeline for about ten metres.

Certainly, there is no one around, so Pig and I jump the fence and walk directly toward the pipeline, staying over one hundred metres from the actual location. Once we get to the pipeline, we take a close look at and along the pipeline in both directions. Nothing stands out – it is, well, a pipeline!

Using the binoculars again, I study the trees surrounding our spot. They are hardly worthy of the name trees, just scrub really. No sign of any surveillance cameras. There are no other trees or elevated positions nearby that could be used for cameras either.

I bend down, looking at the underside of the pipe. Nothing different, so I reach up putting my hand on the top. It's a large pipe and whilst I'm pretty large myself, I am wondering how can I get over this bloody thing?

Pig seems to be thinking the same thing, saying, 'You can try first,' giving me a smile!

Challenge put down – I don't have a choice, do I!

I stand to the side putting my left hand up and launch myself up trying to jump it, sort of like a high jumper (sort of, I said!)

I don't make it, landing in a heap on the ground.

I quickly look at Pig, saying, 'Don't bloody laugh because you have to get over it too!'

I can hear Maria laughing in the background, yelling something I can't hear properly.

Pig turns and yells back, 'Would be interesting viewing seeing you try in that top of yours!'

Her reply is her middle finger.

I stand again, looking at it. With a shrug, I then stretch up, placing both arms as far over the top as I can reach. I can reach just past the apex, so I have some leverage and I haul myself up, at the same time pushing off with both feet and end up spooning the pipe, laying over the top.

I let myself slide down the other side, ending up face-first on the ground. Very gracious.

Lawrence yells out, 'They have a ladder here if you would prefer.'

Very funny how they waited until I made it over before offering.

I look back and see Maria is bringing the ladder over to Pig.

I leave them to it and walk along the pipeline toward the location of interest.

I'm walking about three metres away from the line, in case there is some sort of sensor.

I'm being ultra-careful for no apparent reason. But we are alive because we do just that.

I now bend down and study the contraption. It is almost exactly like Alex and Philip had suggested back in their warehouse. The hose has been tied back on itself, no longer connected to any foreign chemicals. But in place if or when they come back.

It is also on the bottom half of the pipe, so not easily visible from above (i.e. unlikely the drone survey would have detected it and being on the opposite side of the pipe from the access point, again I'm sure the Southern Downs boys don't bother climbing over the pipe for no reason.

I busy myself taking plenty of photos.

When Walter and Lou arrive, having driven both vehicles through the gate and up to the pipe and used the ladder, they actually have one in each vehicle, so they put one on either side of the pipe. Easy access now!

As we discuss the location and purpose, I ask Walter, 'How often is there an "in person" survey of the pipe done?'

He pulls a face, saying, 'Rarely, and then we are only looking for leaks. Whilst we are supposed to get out and walk beside the pipe, one each side, we do tend to drive along checking it out as we go.'

Nodding at the location, I follow up, 'Realistically, you think you would have noticed this?'

He looks at Lou who shrugs with Walter, saying, 'Being honest, not likely.'

I check my watch and decide not much else we can do here. We have places to be.

I say to Walter, 'Okay, I want you to leave this in place. Engineers from DCCEEW will be up to inspect. Can you come back tomorrow and put a twenty-four hour camera on the gate as I'm sure they won't bother walking with the gate so handy. This needs to be monitored or alarmed so you or the police can act immediately. At least daily drive-bys, or even better, get your drone survey to do two patrols a day until you hear from me.'

He pulls a face saying, 'That's going to blow our budget.'

'Better that than having some of your residents dying,' I reply.

CHAPTER 8

We land in Hobart, Tasmania after the quick change of crew we had been promised in Canberra. Lawrence left us there, wishing us good luck as he departed.

We had a lengthy phone conference with MGC and Robert once airborne and heading to Hobart.

Pig had received an encrypted email back from Midge earlier, giving details of one Ahmed Badour, an Indonesian national and known terrorist financier or middleman. Apparently, the nephew of the 'Bali bomber' Umar Patek who killed 200 back in 2002, he is listed on Interpol's most-wanted list. He is suspected of being associated with the bank account from which the payment for the hot tap machine was made.

Bugger, high-level global terrorism connections. This is becoming serious shit.

We discuss the ramifications of everything we have learnt with them. And how much more we need to find out. Confirming the connection between the Irish brothers and Badour will be critical. Finding Badour will be the icing on the cake.

It also confirms the big picture here; now there is no question this is a very serious, planned and orchestrated terrorist plot.

Midge had said in his encrypted message, 'Shit, boys you do have a knack of finding serious arseholes to chase down. Badour hasn't been sighted for eighteen months. Last known location was in Indonesia. I have flagged his possible involvement there in Australia. You will have many agencies watching your progress.'

Then Robert brings us up to date with what they have found about the O'Donnell brothers. They are qualified plumbers who arrived three years earlier having been sponsored by a small Sydney-based pipeline construction company.

After working for them for two years in Sydney, they moved up to Brisbane and set up their own business called 'P and D O'Donnell Plumbing'. They worked mainly for a smaller civil construction company, specialising in subdivision developments. The brothers apparently laid all the sewer, gas, and water lines to new subdivisions. They live together at the Highgate Hill address and neither of them has a police record or even traffic fines.

MGC then finishes off our chat, saying, 'Mort, Pig and Maria, this is a genuinely serious domestic terrorist threat, now with global ramifications. If they succeed in poisoning the water supply to any of these cities, let alone all of them, it will shut Australia down. Cripple us. We can't afford to have that happen.

'Good luck grabbing these two. But that is only the first step. We have to hope they can lead us to this Badour so we can capture him as well. Keep me posted, please.

'Maria, you will be learning from the best. Clearly, they have total faith in you, so, so do I. Good luck.' And he signs off.

Maria appears both excited and a little apprehensive about what we have suddenly got in front of us. Calm, reassuring words from Pig seem to settle her down though.

A soothing Pig! Another for our collection of special Pigs!

The GPS tracker on the hot tap machine now shows, and we therefore assume, the brothers are at the National Park Hotel adjacent to Mount Field National Park, an hour or so out of Hobart.

We disembark and, as promised, Frank has arranged for the delivery of two 4x4 utes. These are sitting in the private airport car park with the Hertz man standing beside them. Fortunately for him, it isn't raining but a chilly wind is blowing.

I sign the paperwork. The utes are Isuzu D-Maxes, but beggars can't be choosers.

He watches with interest as we load up our gun bags. Pig and Maria in one ute, I'm solo in the second.

I punch in the National Park Hotel, having booked two rooms there whilst in the air.

The GPS says it's just an hour's drive, so good, we should get there before dark. Being summer, sunset comes quite late down at this latitude.

Just over an hour later, we pull into the hotel car park. Pig and Maria are leading, I'm trailing a bit having spent most of the drive on the phone. Yes, I have been chatting to Suzie. Not answering her inquisitive questions but chatting anyway. On Bluetooth, so don't tut-tut me.

They pull in beside another ute, two guys leaning on the ute tray, smoking and drinking.

I suspect they are Paddy and Declan, our targets.

As Pig and Maria exit their ute and head past the pair on their way to the hotel entrance, Pig gives them a nod and Paddy says, in his broad Irish accent, addressing Pig, 'Oh, matey, aren't you the lucky one? Having her as your assistant. Why don't we swap? You can have my brother Declan here. Good worker but not a patch on the princess here. She would be worth turning up to for work each day!'

Then turning his attention to Maria, with a leery grin in place, he says, 'Hi, lovey. Wouldn't you like a change of scenery? Come work with me! Can I help you with your top button maybe? It looks like it's barely holding on.'

Pig smiles at this, whilst Declan joins in. 'That top must be Irish linen. It's doing a great job holding those in.'

Maria stops and walks right up to Paddy, not saying a word. She looks him up and down, still not saying a word, then shakes her head dismissively and walks on.

Paddy does an imitation shudder coming back with, 'Ooh, what a way to go. I would go with a smile on my face for sure.'

I have caught up with Pig and Maria now. Maria has stayed silent, now smiling. As I stop at the end of their ute, I can see the black hot tap box in the ute tray, the same as the one we had seen back at Piping Machine Tools in Brisbane. Tick.

As I join them, I ask Paddy, 'You staying here?'

'Yes, matey,' he replies, looking at his watch before adding, 'If you want a feed, you better hurry, the kitchen shuts at nine. Promptly like.'

I glance at my watch and see we have five minutes. No time to waste.

We go inside, having to ring the little bell on the reception desk and an older lady comes out of the bar, placing a tea towel over her shoulder as she comes in.

She looks at her watch as I say, 'Hi, you have two rooms booked for Ireland.'

She glances down at the old-fashioned day book and ticks our names off before addressing us. 'Yes, I do. If you want dinner, the kitchen is about to close so you need to order before you go to your rooms.' She hands us each a menu.

'Yes, we do want a feed,' I reply.

'Okay, leave your bags behind here,' she replies, indicating the reception desk. We each take turns dropping our duffels where indicated, in the confined and cluttered reception and wander into the main bar.

All our weaponry is securely locked in the utes.

We move into the bar, take a seat and quickly review the menu, steaks for both Pig and me with Maria choosing the chicken parmie. I go up to the bar, order the meals and grab three beers. Random as it is, with Tassie having two good brewers of their own, the beer on tap is 'Great Northern' from up Cairns in North Queensland. Weird, ah!

We click glasses in a toast and relax. It's been a busy day. Started out in Canberra, back to Brisbane, then Stanthorpe, Canberra, Hobart and now here we are in Mount Field National Park!

The receptionist then brings over the booking forms, asking me to sign. When I offer the credit card for payment, she simply says, 'We will sort that out in the morning,' and hands over two room keys.

'One a twin?' I ask, not wanting to share a bed with Pig!

'Yes, room five is the twin. Seven has a double bed.'

After the receptionist leaves, Pig can't resist, saying to Maria, 'Shall I tell Paddy out there you will be all alone in a double bed tonight?'

Her middle finger is her reply and I add, 'Maybe wear your own top tomorrow, ah.'

She smiles and says, 'Don't worry, I will be!'

I then remind them, 'Don't forget even though we know their names, we haven't been introduced so if we see them again, don't use their names. They left here around eight this morning, back here just after three p.m., so fair to assume will be around the same time tomorrow, so let's let them head off in the morning before we surface.'

'Typical tradie hours,' Pig comments.

Nods all round before Pig asks, 'What time is brekkie served?'

Good point. I flick the menu over and it shows breakfast is served seven a.m. to eight-thirty.

'They better not be late leaving then,' Pig replies.

CHAPTER 9

Next morning, it's dull and overcast. It's also a bit of a drag not wanting to engage with either Paddy or Declan but having been up since five-thirty, Pig and I do take a wander down through the car park just to get some fresh air and stretch our legs, but steer clear of the pub. We do slip a GPS tracker onto their ute as we pass it, so we can track it separately to the hot tap box.

A little after eight a.m., we hear Paddy and Declan talking as they walk past our room, and then watch out the window as they jump in their ute and head off.

Time for breakfast. We knock on Maria's door as we walk past. She immediately opens it, clearly as keen to get out as we are. Yes, she is wearing a brand new hi-viz top and yes, it fits her much better. Should avoid any more leery comments.

'Sleep well?' I ask as we walk down the hallway back toward the dining room.

'Yes, thanks,' she replies.

'Paddy didn't find you then?' Pig, of course, again getting the middle finger but with a smile.

Over a full breakfast – can't have anything else in these country pubs, after all – we discuss our plans.

I lead, saying, 'We will leave a little after nine. They should be in place by then. We can confirm both trackers are in the same location and no reason they should leave before we get there.'

We have viewed the area where the hot tap is on Google Maps. It is fairly hilly and rugged. Seems to be a 4WD access track along the route of the pipeline but it is cut across the side of a hill with the pipeline approximately sixty metres below the track at the point they are set up.

There seems to be a gate across the track at the top of a ridge, approximately 1200 metres from their location, so we agree to stop there.

Breakfast finished, ablutions completed, hand the keys in, settle up the account and we are good to go.

Both trackers show approximately one hundred metres apart, we are off.

It is an easy twenty-five-minute drive to our designated gate and we pull off the track on either side.

As we had agreed, Pig is going to stay here and block the track if either of them makes a run for it. Bloody sure they won't get past me and Maria but always have a backstop.

Armed with our EF88 assault rifles, Maria and I head off walking across country, staying above the track and as much as possible in the tree line. It's a national park so it's not like we are crossing paddocks or anything but there are fences running above the track. Maybe the pipeline is right on the edge of the national park?

We make good, silent progress until we are directly above the brothers. We know this from the radio they have blaring as they work. They can't see us as we are well hidden in the scrub.

Their ute is parked just off the track about sixty metres above where they are working on the pipeline. There is a ridge running down past them to our left. I suggest I will follow this down whilst Maria heads back fifty metres or so and will make her way down to the track, then work her way quietly down to within fifty metres of their worksite. We are already mic'd up with ear plugs, with Pig tuned in as well.

We discuss plans and we agree we will confirm when on station by saying 'one'.

Then I will say 'two' when we want to make our presence known.

Ten minutes later, Maria says, 'One.'

I'm a little slower, having had to work my way down the steeper slope. I crest the ridge and find I am only thirty metres from the brothers. Good.

'One.'

I can't see Maria through the scrub but she knows once I say 'two', she will come out into the open, as will I. We are both armed with our EF88 assault rifles, so will be rather intimidating when they see us.

Before I move out into the open, I video them working on the pipeline.

'Two.'

I move to within twenty metres of the brothers. I can see Maria now coming out of the scrub in my peripheral vision.

Snick.

I arm my assault rifle, a very distinctive sound.

Snick.

Maria does the same.

Paddy seems to have sensed the different noise and looks around, seeing me and uttering an expletive. I'm not sure what he says as it is drowned out by the music blaring from their little Bluetooth speaker sitting nearby.

He says something to Declan who now looks up as well. They stand there together watching me. They haven't seen Maria yet. I say loudly so they can hear me, 'Turn that off.'

Declan looks at Paddy and then moves over to the speaker and turns it off. As he turns back around, he notices Maria, saying to Paddy, 'She's here too,' causing Paddy to jerk his head around to watch her as well.

Perhaps sensing we're distracted, Declan makes a break for it, rushing the short distance to the fence, placing his left hand on top of the fencepost and starting to vault the wire fence.

Bang!

I fire. I don't miss.

Fortunately for Declan, I'm not aiming at him, rather the timber fence post he is leaning on.

It splinters under his hand. He crashes down onto the fence, screaming.

The top strand of the fence is barbed wire and whilst his face and head go over the wire, his torso and shoulder get ripped on the barbed wire as he goes down.

He is now caught in the barbed wire; it's holding him up.

He is still screaming. This eases to a whimper as he regains his feet, taking the pressure off his body caught on the wire.

I'm now only ten metres away from them, still uphill from them and Maria has positioned herself between them and their ute.

We remain silent, waiting for Declan to extract himself from the wire.

He does this, pulling his clothes up to show multiple cuts and scratches, plenty of blood flowing, so more than mere surface scratches.

Maria remains focused on Paddy, her finger sitting gently on her trigger. It's clear he is aware any move and she will fire.

'Morning, boys,' I say. 'You, Paddy and Declan, have been rather naughty boys. Poisoning people. Twenty-four people hospitalised, one dead. Domestic terrorism carries a life sentence. Now we can add murder as well. Any more silly moves like that and we won't miss. If you survive, you will be in plenty of pain.'

They look astonished, looking at each other.

'Down on the ground, both of you. On your stomachs, arms and legs spread,' I order.

'Why? We aren't dangerous. We aren't criminals, just plumbers earning a quid.'

'Yeah, right. You are domestic terrorists, far worse than criminals. Now, down on your guts. I won't ask again,' I say, motioning with the gun at the same time.

I'm close enough to be really threatening but not too close for them to try an attack.

They look at each other and start to comply, getting down on their knees and then leaning forward.

When on his hands and knees, Declan complains, 'I'm hurt, I can't move my shoulders properly.'

'No one else to blame but yourself is there. Down you get. Now,' I reply.

He then flops down onto his stomach with a whimper.

Paddy, of course, doesn't bother spreading his arms or legs.

'Paddy you're not getting the message. Do as you're fucking told, or you will feel my boot. It's a size thirteen and I know how to use it. I can inflict pain like you have never experienced. Now spread them.'

He does so, adding, 'You don't look like police. Who are you?'

'Your worst nightmare,' I reply. (I know, I know. Corny but I couldn't resist.)

'No, we aren't police. We are a specialist anti-terrorism task force. We don't play by any rules. If you piss me off, I'll just shoot you and roll your body down into the gully. No problem. The wild animals and birds will have a feast.'

Now they are both face down on the ground, I tell them, 'Empty your pockets and place everything on the ground beside you.'

After a bit of grousing about how difficult it is, they comply. I'm really only interested in their phones and potential weapons.

With this done, Maria leans her gun against a tree nearby, kneels down and frisks them. Paddy, persistent to the end, says, 'Now, if you had come and done that last night, it would have been much more fun.'

She ignores him. Once satisfied they aren't armed, she forces their arms behind their backs and uses zip ties to secure their arms behind them. I smile as I watch her tighten Paddy's zip ties extra tight until he complains. She then says, 'Hope you're comfortable, arsehole.'

She then collects their personal effects, handing their phones to me.

Once they are secure and Maria has grabbed her EF88 again, I walk down and inspect the work they were doing. I see the hot tap machine has done its job and has been removed. They are now in the process of fitting a little bottle of chemicals to the waterline. There is no label on the bottle, so I clamp the tube and tie it off, removing the bottle and placing it in a small zip lock bag, one of many I have in my pocket and put it into another pocket for future analysis.

I use my phone to take numerous photos.

I say quietly to Pig, who is listening in through our specially encrypted app, 'You hearing this?'

'Loud and clear.'

I walk back, stand in front of them and start.

I tell them, 'Okay, sit up. I have some questions for you.'

They struggle into a sitting position. This is a rather awkward manoeuvre but we aren't offering any help.

'As I said, whether you live or die is of no consequence to me. Answer my questions honestly and you have a chance of surviving. If not, a bullet to the gut. You will die a slow and agonising death out here; the animals won't wait for you to die before they start eating you alive. We will take your ute back to Hobart. No one knows where you are, you will simply disappear without a trace. No one gives a shit. But the ones you have put in hospital might feel a little better for the pain and anguish you have caused them and their families. And for those that you have killed, well, it will be an eye for an eye.'

Phew, quite the speech for this 'man of few words'.

I pause to let this message sink in.

It's Tasmania, so of course it starts to rain. Not heavy rain like we often get in Queensland, just a persistent drizzle, or ironically, what the Irish call 'soft rain'.

None of us have coats on, so we are all getting wet. No matter, more important issues to resolve here.

'Paddy, you seem to be the leader. Let's start at the beginning. How did you become terrorists?'

He exclaims indignantly, 'We aren't bloody terrorists, just plumbers earning a quid.'

'What, by killing people? Putting over twenty people in hospital? We have you tracked from Stanthorpe, Gosford, Campbellfield, Geelong and now here caught red-handed, tampering with Hobart's water supply. You must know what the consequences of adding arsenic to these cities' water supply were going to be?'

'Arsenic? He told us it was a harmless chemical they wanted to secretly test in various environments on behalf of a major chemical company that hoped it would be a breakthrough and economically prevent antibacterial infection of the water supply. We didn't know it was bloody arsenic. Bloody hell.'

I glance at Declan, whose mouth is hanging open after I mentioned arsenic. His face flushes at the thought of what they had been doing. Or maybe because they had been caught.

I continue, 'Who is he?'

'He called himself Muhammed. No idea if that's his real name or not.'

'How did you become acquainted?'

'He rang me one day out of the blue. Said we had been recommended to him and he wanted a two-man team he could trust, for a secret project.'

'Who recommended you?'

'He wouldn't say but as a show of good faith, he said he could make my gambling debt go away.'

'Gambling debt? How much were you in for and who to?'

'Just a local bookie. Liam O'Brien.'

'How much?'

He pauses before answering, making me immediately suspicious about his answer. 'Just over eighteen grand.'

Declan growls in frustration, his eyes piercing as he glares at his brother.

'Eighteen grand just disappears, ah? How much are they paying you for this job?'

'We share fifteen grand for each insertion. That's sixty grand we have made so far.'

'How do you get paid?'

'In casino chips. After each job, we come back to our hotel room and there is a briefcase full of casino chips. So far, we have forty-five grand in Star casino chips and fifteen from Crown in Melbourne.'

'How many have you spent?'

This time, it's Declan who answers, 'None. I won't let him near a casino and I control the chips. Not fucking letting him waste my money.'

Casino chips. That's different, I think. *Another way to avoid paying tax, I guess.*

'An Asian man named Muhammed asks you to secretly add an unknown chemical to our cities' water supply, and you say sweet, seventy-five k to share and none of this raises the question – is this legit?'

The scorn in my voice is clear, and the brothers have no answer for me.

I let it lie.

For now.

'How do you contact Muhammed?' I ask.

Paddy replies, 'We can't. We don't have any way of contacting him. We sometimes get a text message from an anonymous number but if we reply, it bounces back.'

'Show me these text messages,' I demand.

Silly question; he's sitting with his hands tied. Paddy can't do that.

I pull their phones out of my pocket (luckily, I have many pockets!), confirm which is Paddy's and scroll through his messages.

I ask, 'When did you get the last one from Muhammed?'

'Yesterday,' he replies. I find a text from yesterday reading, *'Book into the Wrest Point casino when you have finished.'*

I take a photo of the message and the number it came from.

'What about previous messages?' I ask.

'They all come from different phone numbers.'

Of course they do, I think.

With the rain continuing to fall, I decide that's enough out here.

'Okay, we are going to leave now. On your feet.'

Having had to practice getting up from a sitting position with my hands tied behind my back, I know this is a difficult proposition, so I watch as they manfully try, falling over and getting quite muddy.

I look at Maria, motioning for her to stand watch, and I go over, offering Declan my arm. He grabs hold of my forearm and I pull him to his feet. He whimpers with the effort. Sniff sniff.

I wait for him to move further away, so he is no threat, then I help Paddy up as well.

If I'm honest, and whilst they were either deliberately naive or bloody stupid, I am inclined to believe they thought what they were injecting was harmless. I see them as gullible and greedy for a quick quid, not hardened blokes who would risk killing people for a bit of extra cash.

Not going to let on to them though!

'Okay, we are going to walk to your ute. You two are getting in the back.

One either side. Try anything stupid, you will be hurt.'

I nod at them to lead the way.

It's only a short walk to their ute and when we get there, I say, 'Paddy, you first in this side,' opening the passenger rear door.

Clearly, it is uncomfortable sitting with his hands tied behind his back. Tough. Keeping one hand firmly on his chest, I lean in and do up his seatbelt, not that I am concerned for his safety but this will make it even more difficult to try to escape or attack.

Once he's in, I move Declan round to the driver's side rear and do the same with him.

I say to Maria, 'I'll drive. I'll drop you at our ute and you can follow me.' She nods.

I turn the ute around, slipping a little on the now-wet grass, even in four-wheel drive. The track is now muddy and rough, so I take it easy up to the gate, move through it and wait for Maria to get organised in our Dmax. We had turned it around before leaving it. You never know when you might want a quick getaway.

I move away from the ute and join Pig standing next to his ute with Pig saying, 'What do you think?'

I pause before answering, regretting not grabbing a coat before leaving the ute, as it is now raining a lot heavier.

'To be honest I don't see them as terrorists, greedy and unscrupulous yes, but not intentionally wanting to kill or injure anyone.'

'Yes, that's what I got from what I heard as well,' he replies.

I say, 'I'm getting wet, so we will head back to the hotel, clean up and have a word with MGC whilst there and he can decide next moves. Maybe you can give him a call on the way in and brief him. You go on and wait at the start of the access track, in case something goes wrong.'

'Okay, will do both. Good luck.'

I grunt acknowledgement as I walk back to their ute with Paddy and Declan still sitting inside, knowing Pig will still hear anything that is said or goes down as we are still mic'd up.

On the way in, the boys don't say a word, even to each other. They sit silently, shoulders slumped. Contemplating a pretty dismal future, I guess.

Still, the silence lets me contemplate, mulling options over.

We are driving in convoy, Pig leading, me in the middle with the two prisoners and Maria bringing up the rear.

We pull into the pub's car park, the rain now quite heavy. I wait for Maria to bring my raincoat from our ute, which she does but only after putting her own on first. This looks like it might have been her New Zealand Army issue, camo colours and all. If so, I'm sure it will keep her dry, but fashion statement it is not.

I pull mine on which is a fashionable hi-viz fluoro yellow. But it will keep me dry and warm.

Pig is similarly dressed in his fluoro yellow coat, waiting by his ute. He has left his guns in his ute, so I pass mine out to Maria and she takes it back to our ute and locks it in its case. Out of sight and secure.

The brothers are still strapped into their seats. I open Declan's door, lean in, left hand firmly holding his chest.

'Ouch,' he exclaims as I press on some of the cuts and abrasions from the barbed wire. Oops.

I undo his seatbelt, then quickly undo Paddy's as well. Pig, realising what I am doing, opens Paddy's door and signals for him to get out.

I line the two brothers up in front of the ute, still without coats in the now-heavy rain.

I tell them, 'We are going back to your rooms now, Pig with you Declan, Paddy with me. You will have ten minutes to shower, get changed and be ready to go. Anything you haven't got ready in ten minutes will be left behind. Enjoy your last private shower, your next one will be in prison, with hundreds of eyes savouring the "fresh meat".'

We escort them back to their rooms. Fortunately, the reception is empty, so we don't have to explain to anyone what's going on.

I take Maria aside and ask her to check the boys out and find out how their rooms have been paid for, getting all the details she can. She nods. Our gear is already in our utes, having checked out this morning when we left.

Ten minutes later, Paddy has packed his case, showered and is ready to go. I zip-tie his hands together behind his back, then escort him to Declan's room, where Pig has done the same thing.

'Down on the floor, boys, like you were before. Now.'

Maria has re-joined us, handing me copies of their booking including credit card receipt. I silently signal her, asking if she has her Glock, using my fingers in the fashion of shooting. She nods in the affirmative, pulling it out of her waistband.

'Can you stand guard here whilst Pig and I confer please?'

'No problems. I'll shoot either of them if they move,' she responds, arming the Glock with its distinctive snick.

Pig and I head outside and move along so we are just outside their room, close enough so we will hear any commotion, but not close enough for them to hear us. But still under the eaves as the rain continues to tumble down.

Pig nods to me, saying, 'Spoke to MGC and Robert. They are waiting on our call.' As he is talking, he is dialling them up again, putting the call on speaker.

MGC answers, 'Mort, Pig. Any update?'

'No, Sir,' I reply. 'We have them at the hotel, packed ready to go.'

'Well, I have arranged for a plane to come down and collect you. It will bring you all back here to Canberra where we can hold them securely. Under domestic terrorism laws, we can hold them for fourteen days. This will give us time to make further inquiries and decide what to do with them.'

After a pause, while Pig and I look at each other, I reply, 'Sir, with due respect, why don't we take them to the Wrest Point Casino where they have been told to check in and see what plays out? With three of us, we have the manpower to keep them close and secure. Hold off locking them up for a few days and see if Badour makes contact. We have a number of phone numbers he has sent texts from, and we will share these shortly. Hopefully, you might gain a lead or location from these.'

Pig nods positively to me whilst we wait for MGC to mull over what I have suggested.

Silence for a couple of minutes as this suggestion gets a thorough mauling in his mind.

It must have survived, as he comes back saying, 'Very well. I have total confidence in your ability to keep them secure and silent, so let's do that. How will you handle the logistics?'

'Haven't thought through to that extent, Sir, but we will book a twin room for the brothers and two separate rooms nearby for us to use. We will take turns keeping them on close watch in their room most of the time. Won't be too hard. We can work in two-hour shifts, so on for two hours, off for four. We should be able to stay awake and alert, Sir. One of us will always be available to follow any sniff of a lead that comes up as well,' I finish with a smile.

'Alright, that makes sense. Do you want Frank to book rooms or anything?'

'No, Sir. I will use Paddy's phone and credit card to make their booking, just in case there are eyes or ears watching. We will take care of ours, then we will ensure we get rooms adjacent or at least close by.'

'Alright, let's do this for seventy-two hours, then review if there has not been any movement.'

'Righty-o, Sir. We will move out in ten, fifteen minutes.'

'Confirmed. Please report in hourly until you are all settled at Wrest Point.'

'Yes, Sir. Out.' And I hang up.

I hand Pig his phone back and without asking, he googles the casino.

I dig out Paddy's phone and do the same as Pig says, 'I will let you book their room before I book our two. I will need my laptop to then access their system and ensure the rooms are at least close by.'

I nod and proceed to book a room in Paddy's name using the same credit card as he had used here at the National Park Hotel. I decide to book a Tower Executive Suite, not to give these two a luxury stay but as there are going to be three of us in there most of the time, this will give us a bit of extra space. But I do make it a twin!

Once done, I nod to Pig and he gets his booking underway.

I text Maria, *'All good?'* Thumbs up comes straight back at me.

I then text her saying, *'Will update you in a minute. Staying in Hobart for a few nights, watching and waiting.'*

This time I get a question mark reply.

It's only a few minutes and Pig says, 'Booking made. I'm going to go into the bar to use the Wi-Fi and log into their website so I can ensure our rooms are close by.'

I nod, saying, 'Okay. When you're finished, go and relieve Maria, please. I need to bring her up to date.'

He nods and I decide to stay where I am. Yes, it is cold, blustery and wet, but fresh air is good for you!

Whilst waiting for Pig, I text Suzie to say hi and let her know we are likely to be away for a few more days yet.

Sad face followed by a red heart is her response.

CHAPTER 10

Once all is sorted, we load up, Pig with Declan secured in the back of his ute, Paddy in the back of mine and Maria following us as 'first response' if anything goes askew. Maria is included in our secure app, so she will be hearing anything Pig or I say.

We had taken pity on Declan, using my first aid kit I always carry in my duffel – as does Pig – to cleanse his wounds. These are largely superficial, so plenty of iodine (yes, it stings, so we used plenty!) and a couple needing plasters.

Done and dusted.

As we are about to leave, I say to Pig, 'Hold up, remember "Devil" always used to brag about that bakery in Richmond was the best in the world? Let's see how far it is.' ('Devil' is a former colleague, so called for no other reason than he comes from Tassie, i.e., after the 'at-risk' Tasmanian Devil.)

Google Maps tells us it is just over an hour away. Hobart another twenty-odd minutes further on.

Good, feeling a little famished!

We head off in our little convoy.

When we arrive in Richmond, after a detour to drive over their famous convict-built bridge, we pull into the bakery's car park. It's actually a pleasant morning here and I say to Paddy, 'Mate, this place is meant to have the best pies and pastries. I'm going to let you out, without your constraints, but one false move and you won't know what hit you. Clear?'

He nods silently. He hasn't said boo on the drive in, no doubt contemplating his dismal future.

I undo his seatbelt and he slides out. Once out of the ute, I use my pocket knife to slice the zip ties.

Pig, watching, realises what I'm doing and does the same for Declan. With the same warning, I'm sure.

Maria comes over raising a quizzical eyebrow and I simply say, 'We will let them have one last coffee and pie before they are incarcerated.' Loud enough for them both to hear, of course.

The pies and pastries live up to their reputation. Maybe not the best in the world, Pig and I agree, but worthy of the detour.

Whilst sitting outside at one of the numerous tables set up, I explain the plan to Paddy and Declan.

'We are booked into the Wrest Point casino, you two in a twin room and you will have one of us'—I indicate Pig and I (not Maria)—'for company at all times. We have booked high-floor rooms, not for the view, but to make it difficult for you to escape. We are hoping you will get contacted by Muhammad, as he is a known terrorist, and just so you know, on Interpol's most-wanted list.'

Now Paddy and Declan share a look of defeat, with Declan shaking his head in apparent frustration, making me think it might be worthwhile having a chat with him on his own. I continue:

'I will have your phones and you will spend most of the days in your room. We might let you out for some fresh air occasionally and of course, if you try anything, you will get hurt. Eventually, we will fly you to Canberra where you will be charged with domestic terrorism, and we will hand you over to the Federal Police. The more you help us, the better it may go for you. You might get off lightly and be deported back to Ireland.'

I notice a look of concern flash across Paddy's face, making me think, *Another reason to have a quiet chat with Declan.*

They don't have any questions, so we head back to the utes to resume our journey after zip-tying their hands behind their backs and securing their seatbelts. I then ask Maria to swap utes as I want to talk to MGC again.

We head off; this time I'm tail-end Charlie. I dial up MGC, knowing

Pig and Maria will hear the conversation, and after giving him our ETA (estimated time of arrival), I say, 'Sir, what did you find out from the Irish authorities about these two?'

'Hold on, I will bring Robert into the call.' Silence for a couple of minutes before I hear them both come back on to the call. Robert answers my questions, saying, 'Mort, neither of them has records in Ireland.'

'Well, clearly, Robert. They would not have got a visa to come to Australia if they had records. But what about digging deeper? Surely you have done that. Checked with the Irish police, see what they have been suspected of, or what they know about them? Seems highly likely if Paddy has a gambling problem here, he may well have run away from the same problems back in Ireland.'

I let my annoyance show in my tone.

Silence.

Then MGC says, 'Mort, it appears this hasn't been done. I apologise. It will now be done as a priority.' The tone implies he is as annoyed as I am, as I'm thinking, *Very poor effort. We are looking at a major terrorism threat and they haven't dug any deeper than the headlines. I might say typical bureaucracy, but Robert has learnt better than that.* Or so I thought.

After letting the silence continue for a minute or so, I then say, 'Sir, I'm also thinking maybe we should put out a little news story saying Hobart health authorities are looking into a small food poisoning outbreak? Maybe just online, as I'm pretty sure Badour won't be down here in Tassie. We need him to think the boys have been successful down here.'

It's Robert who comes back quickly, saying, 'You can't do that. That's spreading rumours or falsehoods.'

I ignore him. He isn't in my good books.

MGC then responds, 'I don't see any harm, if we keep it to *The Mercury*'s online edition'—(*The Mercury* is Hobart's daily newspaper)—'it can be retracted in a couple of days, if need be, but you are right – if it leads to Badour, it's worth a little disinformation. I will get Sir Owen to make this happen.'

(Sir Owen Mansfield, Director General of the Federal Department of Health).

'I will let you know when this is up but I will be stressing the urgency, so expect this to be up in a few hours,' he continues.

'Good-o, Sir,' I reply.

With nothing else to say, we sign off with Robert closing the conversation, saying, 'I apologise, Mort. I will get back to you as soon as I have a more detailed explanation from the Irish police.'

'Before you go, what have you learnt about the bookie, Liam O'Brien, up in Brisbane?'

Silence.

Robert replies, 'I didn't realise we had to. What do you hope to gain?'

As MGC has kept quiet as well, I suspect he hasn't thought of this either.

'Well, Badour found out about the brothers through the bookie. He paid off Paddy's gambling debt. Which I suspect was more than the 18K he claims. There is, therefore, some link that needs to be explored. A good place to start is a little backgrounding. Then in a day or two when we get home, we have a running start.'

I let that sink in then add, 'It would be really handy to know if he is a legit bookie or a backyarder.'

Pig pipes up. 'I couldn't find him listed as a legitimate bookmaker.'

Silence again.

'Mort, I'm sorry I missed this possible connection as well. But you are dead right, of course. I am rather embarrassed I didn't see this. I will make this a priority as well. What sort of connection do you think we will find?' responds MGC.

This is something I have been mulling over all morning.

'Sir, I suspect the bookie has sold his bad debt – Paddy's debt – to a debt collector of some description. If as Pig suggests he is a back yarder, then he may have laid off his debt to bikies or some other gang. Someone who Badour has connections with.'

MGC replies, 'Understood. We will come back to you quickly and update you on what we find.'

Once the call is finished, Pig pipes up, saying, 'Good idea. Getting the story out, that's what he or they will be looking for. Seems Robert might need a kick in the arse though.'

'Yeah,' I reply, 'we need to give ourselves every opportunity here and yes, I agree Robert needs to lift his game. Maybe now he's got underlings he doesn't think he needs to think!'

I let a little silence settle.

Knowing both Maria and Pig can hear me, but the brothers can't, I then add, 'Maria, Pig and I will be taking two-hour shifts watching over the boys. I will need you to spend a lot of time in the foyer somewhere as our "first responder" if we do get any contact. You okay with that?'

'Sure, Mort, no problem,' she replies with a sense of excitement.

'Okay, this is what we will do,' I continue, knowing I need to explain it in a way they can answer questions in front of their prisoners without giving away what we are planning.

'I will take the first shift as babysitter. Pig, you and Maria can check into our rooms. Please get three room keys so we each have access to both rooms. I will do the same for their room. Pig, if you can swap with me after two hours, please.'

He grunts acknowledgement.

I continue, 'Once settled, Maria, can you go back down to the lobby, find yourself a quiet spot where you can see the entrance or entrances if more than one? Whilst I don't expect anything to happen quickly, we need to be ready in case something does pop. I will relieve you in two hours or so.'

'No worries,' she replies.

'Okay, Maria, we will swap utes again before Hobart. Can you self-park at the hotel, please? Pig and I will valet, that way we have one ute available for use immediately and don't have to wait the mandatory fifteen minutes for the valets to bring our ute up.'

Two grunts confirm we are all on the same page.

CHAPTER 11

The rest of the journey passes in no time, and it is now evening. It has been a busy day!

On the drive in, Pig asks, 'Don't Cadburys have a large factory down here?'

Maria answers, 'Yes, they do. Pity we don't have time for a factory visit! Mind you, Tassie is also famous for growing lavender and mint of all things, and also opium poppies.'

'What, the drug opium?' I ask.

'Yes, it is grown under licence for medicinal purposes. I watched a TV program on it once.'

'You are a fountain of useless information, aren't you?' is Pig's teasing reply.

We stop on the edge of Hobart, in a layby off the motorway, and remove the zip ties from our prisoners, so we/they do not stand out on arrival at the hotel.

Maria and I swap places again with her, saying, 'What? You don't think I can handle Paddy, ah?'

I smile and reply, 'Not taking any chances, is all.'

Check-in is easy. I accompany Paddy to check in for their room, then Declan joins us and we head up to their room on the tenth floor whilst Maria and Pig check into our rooms. Yes, Maria gets a room to herself, whilst Pig and I share. We won't both be in the room at the same time anyway, as one of us will be always with the brothers.

With only hand luggage, Paddy, Declan and I head up to the tenth floor.

I open their room, well, it's a suite, truth be told. I ordered this so there is sufficient room, with twin beds in the bedroom and a separate lounge area. It is going to be a boring couple of days, whilst we wait to see if there is any contact.

I let them choose their own beds. The couch seems comfortable enough and with a TV in both rooms, there won't be any fighting over the remotes!

As I get a chance, I place secret mics in both rooms as well as the bathroom, so no matter where they are, we will hear what they are saying.

Declan and Paddy aren't saying too much.

They remain in the bedroom and turn the TV on.

Time for dinner. I text Pig to see what he wants, and we agree on a works burger each, with cheese, bacon and chips, of course!

The brothers then decide to have the same.

Four big burgers, easy order. I call it through, adding three pots of coffee. Twenty-five to thirty minutes, I'm told.

Pig and the meals arrive almost simultaneously.

We sit down in the lounge area with the brothers accepting their coffee and burgers, retiring back to the bedroom.

I raise an eyebrow at Pig, asking the obvious question, 'Any news?'

He shakes his head in the negative before confirming Maria is on station in the lobby.

We chat for a few minutes and suddenly, I hear the brothers having a quiet conversation. I don't try to listen; rather, I keep chatting to Pig so they think we don't realise they are talking.

But, of course, it is being recorded and we can listen at our leisure.

I give Pig a thumbs up, so he knows the rooms are mic'd.

Licking our fingers, we agree the burgers, too, were very good. Tassie is renowned for its good food, although I'm sure they don't normally mean pies and burgers!

Once they have finished conversing, I take my leave and head to our room to freshen up. And to listen to what they had to say.

In the privacy of our room, I replay their conversation. It starts with Declan asking, 'What will happen if we get deported back to Ireland about your gambling debts?'

Paddy doesn't answer for a little bit, then says, 'I don't know. Nothing good, for sure. I don't want to think about it. They will know as soon as we arrive back and no doubt send the heavies knocking.'

Declan replies, 'Yeah, that's what I thought. Trouble is, they will come after me as well, not just you. I reckon we are both fucked if we are deported.'

Silence, then I hear me say goodbye to Pig.

A few minutes later, Paddy adds quietly, 'Yeah. No future back there for sure. We have to do all we can to avoid being deported.'

Declan responds also in a whisper, 'Spending the rest of our lives in prison here isn't any more attractive though.'

Then continues, 'We have to offer to help them trace Muhammad. It's our only chance of getting out of this shit. I should never have agreed to help you, you dumb bastard. Getting yourself up to your eyeballs in gambling debts. You dumb fuck. Now we are both fucked.'

Not surprising to see this growing tension between them, considering the future they face.

CHAPTER 12

The night passes uneventfully. The brothers don't engage with us but quietly get into bed and turn the lights out in the bedroom.

I'm on duty at the time, so I turn the TV volume down and dim the lights. Respectful as always!

Pig and I agreed to extend the shifts to four hours each, so we both have a chance to get some rest, if not sleep.

My phone beeps around two-thirty a.m. with a message from Robert saying, '*Story up on Mercury website.*'

Naturally, I have to check. It is a short note saying, '*Department of Health And Human Services, Tasmania are investigating a small suspected food poisoning outbreak in Hobart and surrounding suburbs. Five people have reported to hospital emergency departments in the last twenty-four hours with suspected food poisoning.*'

That's it.

Should be all we need, if Badour is in fact watching, waiting.

Pig and I swap at four a.m., so my turn to rest. I even manage a couple of hours' sleep before my phone rings just after six-thirty.

It's Robert with the grim news that 'Liam O'Brien was killed in a hit-and-run accident ten days ago. The police say it is a suspicious death and they are investigating.'

'Shit,' I reply then let the silence linger as I think this through.

'Tidying loose ends?' I say to myself as much to Robert on the other end of the phone.

A pause as he seems to be thinking about this before he comes back, 'Well, I hadn't thought of it that way but it does make sense, I suppose. I will send you what I have here, which is just the police news release so far. As soon as the officer in charge responds, I will get you more detail.

'Have also heard back from the Garda, the Irish police, who confirm there have been stories swirling about Paddy owing twenty-five thousand Euro to bookies. Apparently, shortly after he left for Australia, there was a flurry of activity as a few heavies were trying to hunt him down. I'm sending you the email we received from the Garda now as well.'

I reply, 'For that amount, I'm surprised some of them haven't come out here to chase him down. Thanks, Robert. Let me know when you get more info from Queensland Police on O'Brien. Maybe tell them of this possible angle as well.'

'Will do,' he replies and hangs up.

I think you know by now that we don't muck about, so I glance at my watch. It's still not seven a.m. yet, but I pull up DS Chris Morris's phone number and give her a call.

She is possibly the only Queensland cop we trust.

She replies, 'Hi, Mort. You're obviously back from your holiday. Did you have a good time? How did Julien go in the Invictus Games?'

I smile as I answer, 'Yes, we had a good time, had a bit of excitement and yes, Pig – sorry, Julien – did really well. When we catch up next, I'll show you the video of his final lap of the ten thousand metres. It's so cool!

'Anyway, we are back in harness, currently interstate on a domestic terrorism case and the suspicious death up there of Liam O'Brien, the bookie may be connected. Can you share any background on the investigation?'

Silence. I know from past experience, Chris takes her time, considering her answers well.

'Okay, for a start, how do you know he is or was a bookie? We hadn't publicised that?'

'One of our DTs'—(domestic terrorists)—'owed him supposedly $18k and the debt was repaid if he did some work, which has now landed him and his brother in deep shit. Without knowing any of the facts, I suspect O'Brien's death may be this terrorist organisation, which has global links, cleaning house or tidying up loose ends.'

I again wait patiently for Chris's reply. 'Well, that is a new angle we will need to consider. I'm not involved in the investigation. It is being run by DS Shirley Bryant, a friend, so let me give her a buzz and see what she has to say. Knowing her, she will want to interview and get your comments on record.'

'Chris,' I reply, 'you understand how and who we work for, so please save your friend and me the trouble of a pissing match. As I mentioned, we are interstate, running an active DT investigation, so I do not have time to waste sitting down with her or her team, as what I told you is only my surmising, we have no facts to back it up. But any info she has gleaned from his bookie records may be useful as we try to track down the kingpin of this DT ring. There will be an official approach today from Section V, so all I want is what you suspect, not necessarily what the facts prove so far.'

'Okay, okay, let me give her a call now. I'm sure she will be in already so give me a few and hopefully we'll come back to you.' And she hangs up.

Bloody politics and bureaucracies – I hate them. Mind you, I spent fifteen years living in one of the biggest, least efficient bureaucracies in the nation, so I should know.

Whilst I wait, I text Pig to see what he and the brothers want for breakfast. Suddenly, I think, *Shit, better check in with Maria and give her a call.*

'Hi, boss. Everything all right?' she says on answering the call.

'Yep, all good. How about you? Bright-eyed and bushy-tailed?' I suddenly think, *Where did that come from? It was a saying Mum used to say to me growing up. A bit random.*

In reply, Maria laughs, saying, 'I haven't heard that for a few years!'

I laugh in response, saying, 'Yeah, I was just thinking the same thing. My mum used to say it. Are you up and about?'

'Yes, I'm down in the restaurant, just sat down to breakfast. Still have a good view of reception though. Also, whilst no one was around last night I stuck a little mic under the reception counter, so I can hear what everyone is saying. It's quite amusing as the desk staff are quite rude and uncomplimentary about their guests!

'Cool. I'll come down and join you, bring you up to date. I'm just waiting on Pig to tell me what he – or they – are doing for brekkie.'

As I hang up, a text comes back from Pig, saying all good and he is about to order three big breakfasts. I text back, telling him to go ahead and I will relieve him at eight a.m. as planned.

A thumbs up is the reply.

Good, breakfast.

I head down and see Maria in the Boardwalk café and realise there is a full breakfast buffet. Cool, I can help myself, which I do after giving Maria a little wave.

But before I can load my plate, my phone rings. An unknown mobile number. I move away and answer, 'Mort speaking.'

A female voice answers, saying, 'Mort, this is DS Shirley Bryant. I have you on speaker with Chris Morris. I understand you know Chris?'

'Hi, Shirley. Thanks for calling back. Yes, have met and worked with Chris on a couple of occasions.'

'Well, I was part of the clean-up squad rounding up the corrupt politicians and bureaucrats and again last year in the mess at Newstead, so whilst we haven't met, I'm aware of your work.'

As there is no inflection of blame or disapproval in her voice, I take this as a good sign.

'Thanks, Shirley. Not sure what Chris has told you, but we are currently interstate working an active DT case, where one of the DT's had his gambling debt to Liam O'Brien forgiven, or repaid, whatever, by the DT lynchpin, who we have identified as a known international terrorist. He is here in Australia. We are trying to thwart his efforts and, I suspect – and I stress, we *suspect* as we have no proof of this – that Liam's death may be connected, as this terrorist mob tidies up loose ends.'

Silence, as I suspect Shirley finishes writing down what I have just told her. Either that or she follows Chris's philosophy of carefully thinking her answers out before responding. Maybe both!

'All right, what we know is Liam finished his nightly ritual of having a couple of beers at the Morrison Hotel on Stanley Street on his way home.

He left the bar and headed out into their car park and was run down as he walked across the car park to his car.

'A hit and run. Driver didn't stop. At first, we thought maybe they had one too many and feared the consequences but we have the car – a BMW X5 SUV, stolen, of course – on CCTV sitting idling in the driveway of the car park, seemingly waiting. Then, when O'Brien came out, it took off, accelerating until it hit him, even ran over him, and sped off. We tracked the car back over the storey bridge and out along Lutwyche Road. Then found it burnt out the next morning in Marchant Park, Chermside. It was stolen a couple of days before from Geebung Railway Station. As we say, the investigation is ongoing. Confidentially, we don't have any suspects. Yet. Your thesis reinforces our view that this was deliberate and therefore murder.'

My turn to pause and ponder.

'Thanks, Shirley, for being open and honest with me. An official request will come through channels today as well, but good to know there are more tentacles to this terrorist web than we knew. Which, of course, is a bugger.'

I pause as another thought hits me. 'Shirley, I don't want to tell you how to do your job but if you have an accountant, go back through O'Brien's books and bank account. You should find where he was paid the eighteen grand to settle Paddy O'Donnell's debt. This might be a good start for both of us. By the way, I suspect Paddy's debt was much higher than the $18k he claims. So don't just look for this amount.'

This time there isn't much of a delay before she comes back with a sense of excitement in her voice, 'Right, Mort. I will get someone on that straight away and will update you if we learn anything. Thanks.'

We say goodbye with Chris chiming in with her farewell as well. I promise to let them know if we learn anything else that may help their case. I add Shirley's phone number to my contacts.

Breakfast. I go back into the restaurant, respond to Maria's smile and head for the buffet.

I fill my plate – you never know when you might get a chance again.

Well, that's what I tell myself!

When I sit down at Maria's table, I see she has also chosen the full-cooked breakfast, telling me, 'Eat your bacon first. It's basically cold.'

I grouch, saying, 'You know, it can't be that hard to keep bacon – and scrambled eggs, for that matter – hot but it is very rare for hotels anywhere to achieve this. It's as bad as having to put a piece of bread through their toaster two to three times. My record is five times – it's ridiculous!'

Maria looks at me saying with a slip of a smile. 'Well, well, who hasn't had enough beauty sleep then!'

I have to smile. 'Yes, first world problems, ah, if all we have to complain about is cold bacon and eggs.'

I hoe in and whilst not exactly hot, it is nourishing and filling. The waitress seems to sense I like my coffee and stops by regularly to top my mug up.

I decide to finish off with a couple of Danishes to go with my coffee. And I ask for another coffee to go – make that two.

Whilst I'm eating, Maria gives me a summary of what she had seen and heard overnight. None of which is relevant to us. She seems amused by a couple of the male staff, giving each female guest a rating. 'The best I've heard so far was an 8.5 and she was pretty young, I thought.'

I can't resist and say, 'Why don't you go up and ask a question? I'll sit here and see what they rate you as!'

I get a smile, but she doesn't raise to the bait.

'Now, what's with the big, long phone conversation? What have you learnt?' Maria now asks me.

I give her a brief overview that the bookie is dead, and it looks like a hit-and-run murder and that Paddy had run away from a twenty-five Euro gambling debt in Ireland. I add also that the brothers are dead scared of being deported back to Ireland, Declan convinced the heavies will come for him as well, if they have to go back.

'Shit. They are arseholes for what they have done, but they are sort of nice arseholes, aren't they?' she replies, looking at me.

I smile and nod. 'Yeah, they are harmless and easy-going guys, caught up in much bigger goings-on than they realise.'

I glance at my watch. Shit, already 8.15. I better get going – need to clean my teeth, et cetera before relieving Pig.

As I get up, I tell Maria, 'We might take the boys out for some fresh air this morning, allow housekeeping in to clean the room. I will want you handy as well but still able to hear, if not see, reception.'

She nods and waves her teacup in acknowledgement as I head off. I text Pig, saying, *ETA 5. Much to talk about,*' with a smiley face. That will get him wondering!

CHAPTER 13

I get up to their room and let myself in, noticing the housekeeping cart is just down the hall.

Pig is sitting on the couch watching TV, looking bored shitless. No sign of the brothers so I raise an eyebrow and he motions to the bedroom. I stick my head in so they know I'm there. They both look at me and nod. They both look pretty miserable.

I go back to Pig and we move over to the balcony door, so the noise of the TV is between them and us. I whisper, 'The housekeeping cart is just down the hall. What say we take these two outside for some fresh air? Maria can help whilst I bring you up to date.' I smile as I can see he is dying to know what about!

He nods so I go back to the bedroom door and say, 'Righto, boys, we are going to take you outside for some fresh air so be ready in two minutes, please.'

They both nod and Paddy picks up the remote and switches the TV off.

We exit the room and head to the lifts. I detour and find the housekeeper (a guy, not a lady. Must be an equal-opportunity employer!) and tell him we will be back in an hour or so if they can clean our room, please.

He replies with a smile and a nod.

Plenty of smiles and nods this morning, ah!

In the lift, I text Maria to join us if she can still hear the mic.

On the ground floor, we exit the lift and head to the side entrance, to the lawn overlooking the Derwent River. Maria comes over to say, 'Sorry, I need to stay inside to get audio but I can stand here and watch, so I can respond if they try anything.'

'Okay, thanks. You tuned in?' I reply.

She points to her ear and gives me the thumbs up. Yes, she will be able to hear what we all say.

The two brothers sit on the riverbank, legs dangling down over the river.

It is a pleasant morning, although a cool breeze is blowing.

Pig and I move a few metres away so we can converse quickly and in private. I bring him up to date with what I learnt overnight and from talking to Chris and Shirley about the O'Brien murder.

He doesn't have much to add, so I say, 'Let's go and chat to the boys, see what else we can find out.'

He nods as we head back to them.

We sit down either side of them.

I let the silence linger.

'Right-o, boys,' I start. 'How well did you know Liam O'Brien, Paddy?'

He shrugs non-committally, so I continue. 'He's dead. Run down last Thursday in the car park of the Morrison Hotel.'

A gasp and look of shock on Paddy's face as he turns toward me, hoping I'm joking.

I shake my head. 'No, I'm not bullshitting you, it's true. Police are investigating it as a suspicious death. There is every chance it is your mate Muhammad cleaning house, getting rid of loose ends.'

I pause for effect.

'You two could be next, now you have finished your taps.'

'Shit.' This comes from Declan as he looks at Paddy in shock and, no doubt, fear.

Paddy puts his head in his hands, shaking it to and fro. No doubt wondering, *What have I got myself in for?*

Again, I let the silence linger.

'Yeah, so whilst we aren't your friends, I still might shoot you and dump your bodies out at sea, to save the hassle of the bloody paperwork. We are your best chance of surviving this. You might even get off lightly and be deported back to Ireland.'

I have floated this deliberately, knowing they do not, cannot, go back to Ireland. A painful death and humiliation await them there.

It's Declan who cracks. 'We can't go back to Ireland. He'—he points at Paddy—'owes the bookies twenty thousand Euro. We won't survive a week there. They will kill us, use us as an example to anyone else thinking of running away from their debts. What if we help you find Muhammed?'

I don't rush my response, taking my time. 'How will you do that?'

He looks at Paddy. When he doesn't get a reaction, he continues, 'If we help you, you need to help us. No deportation and only limited prison time. Surely you understand we didn't know what we were doing was harming people. Shit, our ma will kill us herself if she knew what we have done. For sure, she will have us in the confessional for weeks. No, make that months.

'Please, we aren't criminals. Sure, we got greedy, but you know we had to do this otherwise'—he again points a finger at Paddy—'his gambling debts would have got us both beaten up badly. Maybe even killed. Please. You have to help us.'

Quite an impassioned plea.

I watch them both intently, not showing or saying anything. Pig and Maria also remain silent.

The silence lengthens.

Eventually, Paddy cracks, saying, 'Muhammed had a driver and bodyguard as well. East European, we think. His name was Gregor. We heard Muhammed call him that. We saw him again, leaving our hotel in Gosford. When we went in, he had left our casino chips in our room.'

Declan pipes up. 'He drove a black BMW 7 series, sort of like a limo. Muhammed always sat in the back. In Gosford, I followed him back to the car park. Not so he would see me, mind, but he was driving the Beemer. He was alone though, no one else was in the car.'

Again, I let the silence do its work.

Used correctly, you can get more answers by using silence than beating the shit out of people. Guilty people seem to have to talk! Mind you, I have had success with both options.

It's Declan that breaks first again. 'You see, if you ask us questions about what you need to know, we may even be able to help you more. Please.'

I look over at Pig. He raises an eyebrow, code for okay. I look over to see Maria learning against the door frame, arms folded across her chest. Her eyes dart between us, clearly engrossed in what is being said. Sensing I'm looking for her input, she gives me a little smile.

It seems we are all of the same opinion then. Whilst what these boys have done is unforgivable and they do need to be punished for it, if they can help find Badour and also this Gregor, maybe their punishment won't need to be too severe.

Again, I let the silence linger. They are both now on edge, unsure of what is going to happen to them next.

'Okay, what happens to you is way above our pay grade. BUT if you help us find Muhammed and this Gregor, we will certainly put in a good word for you. Do not think you will get away scot-free, though. One person is dead as a direct consequence of your action. That is manslaughter, if not murder. That can't go unpunished.'

Their heads drop as if in shame. Randomly, I think, *Maybe we should let their mother know what they have done. Maybe she will straighten them out!*

'Paddy, Declan, we are staying here a couple more days. We want to see if Muhammed contacts you at all. Pays you the next instalment of $15k. We want to be here when they do that. If they do that. Ideally, if your Gregor drops by with your chips, we can nab him.

'But equally, we are using you as bait. For all we know, Muhammed may plan on having you killed. You are two more loose ends to him. In this case, we are your bodyguards. You will be safe in our hands.

'For us to put in a good word for you, you will need to be on your best behaviour. Any attempt to escape, you will get hurt AND that will be the end of our efforts to help you. Got it?'

They both look up from their naval gazing and nod at me in acceptance.

'I need a coffee. What about you two?' I ask, including them in our ritual. Inclusive, that's me!

You know as well as I do, Pig is never going to turn down a coffee.

'Yes, please. Long blacks for both of us, please. He takes two sugars,' Declan answers. He seems to be taking over as chief spokesman.

'No sugar in prison, so he might as well learn to go without now,' Pig replies as he heads inside to get the coffee. And Maria's tea, of course!

Whilst waiting for Pig to come back and knowing he can hear anyway, I ask, 'How did Gregor deliver the casino chips to you in Gosford?'

Declan answers quickly. 'In a leather briefcase. It was locked but they texted us the combination so we could open it.'

'Do you still have the briefcase? Also, where are all your casino chips?'

Paddy jumps in. 'Yes, we have left them at the Crown Hotel in Melbourne. We stayed there the night before we came over on the ferry. We left all four briefcases in safe deposit boxes at the hotel.'

I look at Declan and say, 'That was a bit risky.'

He half smiles, saying, 'It was a bit of a test for him. But he never suggested even going into the casino from the hotel.'

Here, Paddy pipes up, saying, 'I know I have a gambling problem. It has got me in dead shite twice now. I am determined to stay away from casinos and bookies from now on.'

I look at him intently and there is no doubt about the look of determination on his face as he says this.

Pig comes out, handing Maria her tea as he passes her before bringing out the four long blacks. And, bless him, four muffins!

CHAPTER 14

Of course, the little new information the brothers have told us has formed new questions.

I let them enjoy their coffee, as do I, for a moment then ask, 'What is the set-up at the Crown Hotel for the safe deposit boxes?'

I get two questioning looks, so I elaborate. 'Do you have keys, finger scans or combo locks? I need to know as we need to get these cases and the chips ASAP. We need to fingerprint them, swab them for DNA even, knowing your Gregor has been handling at least one of them.'

The brothers look at each other, then in consternation, Paddy says, 'Shit, the two keys are on the keyring of the ute. Where are they?' looking from Pig and back to me.

I pat my pocket and retrieve the keyring for their ute. Yes, it has a couple of extra keys on it. I remove them from the keyring, showing them to the brothers who both nod to confirm these are the keys needed.

Declan clarifies, 'We have two safe deposit boxes as they are only big enough for two briefcases each.'

'You understand these chips are proceeds of crime and you won't get to keep them, don't you?' I say, sounding unkind even to my own ears.

Again, they look at each other before nodding. I remind myself of the lady who has died and the twenty-plus others hospitalised because of their actions, just to ensure I don't feel sorry for them.

I look at Pig and say, 'We need to get these keys to Melbourne and have someone retrieve these cases for testing.'

'Declan, what day was it you saw Gregor in Gosford?'

'Awh, geez, I don't know. It was the last night before we drove down to Sydney. I would have to look at the hotel receipt to see what the date was.'

'Where are your receipts?' Pig, getting in first, asks.

'Stuffed in the glovebox of the ute, with all the others.'

I nod to Pig, get up and head to the car park. Thinking about it as I walk, I realise we haven't checked out their ute either. A slap for us. But I will do that now.

I get to the ute, unlock it on the passenger side, open the glovebox and out tumble a whole lot of receipts, dockets, you name it. Typical tradie filing cabinet!

I find an empty Coles plastic shopping bag on the floor in the back and put all these dockets in there.

Putting this on the driver's seat, I then inspect the ute, looking under the seats, behind the rear seat, in the toolbox, under the tray, but nothing interesting – just this pile of dockets.

As I head back, I think, looking at the keyring, I will need to let the company, CSThire up in Brisbane, know they need to recover their ute down here in Hobart. *A nice drive for someone*, I surmise.

Getting back to where the two brothers and Pig are still sitting, I show them the Coles bag, saying, 'When we go back up to your room, you can sort through these and confirm what the date was you saw Gregor.'

I pause here before continuing, 'I want to understand about all your interactions with Muhammad. Each time you talked to him, met him, et cetera. We will be recording this; it will become part of your official statement. We best do this back up in your rooms, so let's go.'

They both look at me but don't respond, other than stand up and start heading back into the hotel, Pig and I trailing. I quietly say to Pig, 'You go on and get them started on the receipts so we can get MGC or Robert to organise the pickup of the safety security box keys. I need to update them with the probable connection to the O'Brien murder too.'

Maria heads back into the foyer, out of their way. They take no notice and head directly to the lifts.

We head up to the tenth floor and I let the three of them go on. Pig will be listening in to my conversation anyway.

There is a little foyer by the lifts, so I stay there and put a call into MGC.

'Morning, Sir. We have a bit of an update for you.'

'Morning, Mort. Hold on, Robert will join the call and record it.'

A minute later, Robert says, 'Morning, Mort. Good to go.'

'Sir, I have spoken to a DS Shirley Bryant who is leading the investigation into Liam O'Brien's murder. They aren't actually calling it murder yet, but once I briefed her with our suppositions and suggested she go back through his accounts, she may identify where the money came from to settle Paddy's gambling debt.

'Now, we have got a bit more info out of Paddy and Declan this morning and they say Muhammad has a driver-cum-bodyguard by the name of Gregor, who drives a black BWM735. That is a match with what Alex from Piping Machine Tools told us. Declan saw him down in Gosford at their hotel and he was driving the Beemer then. The assumption is he had driven down and left their gambling chips in their room. Sir, all their gambling chips are in two safe deposit boxes at the Crown Hotel in Melbourne. We have the keys to these boxes here. Not sure if you want to arrange collection of the keys or whether you just get the Victorian Police to request the contents.'

I take a breath, letting MGC ponder what I have told him.

It doesn't take long before he comes back. 'Mort, it will be far easier to access these safety deposit boxes with the keys. I don't want to weaken your team, so I will have one of the Melbourne team jump on the next flight to Hobart. He can come to the hotel and grab these keys off you.'

'Right-o, Sir. That makes sense. We have also got a pile of dockets and receipts – all filed in the ute's glovebox, just like most tradies! The brothers are currently going through these to confirm what day it was they saw Gregor in Gosford. Once we have that date, we will access the hotel's CCTV files, hoping they keep two-three months before overwriting them. If we are lucky, we may get a rego of the Beemer. In my opinion, this Gregor has got to be in the frame for O'Brien's murder too.'

I'm now met with more silence before MGC comes back. 'Alright, I can see that. No proof, of course. Yet. I can't see what we are likely to get out of these dockets, but we can certainly review them. We will get back to you with contact details of our Melbourne man and what flight he will be on.'

'Good-o, Sir. One more thing. Can you make a priority in getting a copy of the boys' phone logs from their phone carriers, please? I am about to sit down with them and work up a timeline of all their connections with Muhammad. They say each phone number they have received messages from, reply messages have bounced. But deep in the bowels there, I am hoping you have a techy capable of either identifying these phone numbers or at least their location when they sent these texts!'

I then read out the two phone numbers and a list of four phone numbers they received messages from Muhammad.

MGC replies, 'We will see what we can do, Mort, and get back to you with any developments.'

I reply, 'Thank you, Sir. We will keep you posted if anything else breaks this end.'

I hang up.

I need a piss, so I head to the brothers' room and let myself in. And use the bathroom!

Once I have relieved myself, I come out and see the brothers are sitting at the coffee table, collating their dockets, with Pig watching from a distance. Pig informs me: 'They are putting all the dockets into date order. It looks like they left Gosford on Wednesday nineteenth, which matches the dates we have for the Gosford outbreak. That, in turn, means Gregor visited their hotel on the Tuesday. Declan reckons it must have been around seven-thirty to eight p.m. that he saw him.'

He nods his head toward the bedroom, so the two of us quietly head in there, where I stand near enough to the doorway that I can still see the brothers. They certainly look up and watch us, but when they see I am still watching them, they go back to working on the dockets.

Before Pig can say anything else, Maria comes through our app, saying, 'Shit, the cleaner has just found the mic under the receptionist's counter. She looked at it funny and threw it into the rubbish. Shit. I will have to get another one on there as soon as I can. Will let you know when back up. Out.'

Pig and I look at each other and shrug.

He then in a quiet voice, says, 'Now you're here, I want to log into the motel – the "Gosford Inn Motel", by the way – to see if I can see the Beemer or even Gregor walking around. He must have gone into reception to get their room number, so here's hoping.'

I nod, saying, 'Good luck!' and before he heads back to our room, he adds, 'I have sent those phone numbers to Midge as well. He does have the best and newest technology of everyone we know, so here's hoping!'

'Good idea!' I reply as he heads out the door back to our room to get to it.

I go back into the main room of their suite and say, 'Right, we are going to sit down now and make a timeline of dates and locations of each time you have had an interaction with Muhammad – either by phone or in person.'

Declan says, 'Okay, I will make us all a coffee on this little machine here.'

I look and sitting above the mini bar fridge is a small Nespresso coffee machine. Bonus!

It takes quite a while to work up the timeline. The brothers aren't being difficult but theirs is a simple life, and it appears after working together all day, they have separate social lives. Declan certainly didn't seem to realise Paddy was gambling again and gambling badly.

Once we have the semblance of a timeline, we're able to cross-match it against both the dates of the various outbreaks of 'food poisoning' and also the dates we know they had been at Piping Machine Tools. In fact, I have to prompt them to mention these interactions, as they don't bring them up. I use this to highlight we know a lot more than they realise. (Not necessarily true but no harm in them thinking that – might keep them on the straight and narrow.)

The long and short of it is, Paddy got a phone call, inviting him to meet Muhammad late last month at the James Squire Brewhouse in Grey Street near the Brisbane Convention Centre. He didn't tell Declan about it. He reluctantly went along and met Muhammad who explained that he had bought his gambling debt and he, Paddy, now owed Muhammad $26750, and the interest was accruing at one hundred dollars per day. He then explained what he had to do, in effect, to survive. Travel to Stanthorpe, Gosford, Campbelltown, Geelong and Hobart to do these hot tap tests, all expenses paid. His debt would be forgiven, and he would even have seventy-five thousand dollars in cash! No tax, no record.

No wonder he thought he was onto a good thing.

He also realised, in hindsight, once he had seen Gregor a couple of times, he was sitting at the next table whilst he met with Muhammad.

Both brothers agree to sit with a composite artist to get images of these two. But that will wait until we take them to Canberra. Of course, they don't know, that we already know that his Muhammad, is one Ahmed Badour. One of Interpol's most wanted terrorists.

Suddenly, Maria comes through our app, 'Shit. Six. Excuse me,' and we can hear Maria running – or I guess that's what the sound is – then she continues, and I envisage she is running after someone, 'Are you a bike courier?'

I hear a male voice say something I can't catch.

Action time.

'Six' is an unofficial soldiers' warning, a request for help. Immediate help. I had to use it once before when calling Maria to come and look after Suzie.

I'm up, heading to the door. Before I leave, I turn to Paddy and Declan and say, 'Something is up. I must go. Now. We have laser beams across both the doorway and windows, so if you try to leave, we will know. You won't get away. You will be hurt. We will throw the keys away, so best you stay put and keep working on your receipts. Comprenda?'

They nod as I rush out the door. I don't wait for the lift. Down the stairs, two, three at a time. I'm ten floors up.

Maria, in the app again. 'I have some legal documents I need to get to my solicitor in the city. I thought you might be able to take them for me please?'

A male voice I don't recognise says, 'Sorry, we aren't allowed to do casual jobs. You will have to call the office to book a new job. Here, this has the office number on it. Sorry, but I'm already late for my next pickup.'

By now, I'm out of the foyer, running toward the car park as Maria comes on saying, 'Mort, Pig, a bike courier just dropped off a briefcase at reception. I couldn't be sure but I'm pretty confident he said it was for Paddy O'Donnell. As you heard, I tried to stop him.'

'Quick thinking, Maria,' I respond as puffing heavily, I near the D-max, key in hand. No remote entry on these, so need to put the key in the door lock, turn and open. I key it; it starts. I'm in first and already heading to the car park exit.

'Describe him,' I say.

'Sorry. Skinny, Lycra-clad guy. Blue bike helmet, blue bike pants and a yellow-greeny hi-viz windbreaker. He didn't say where he was heading.'

'I'm assuming he is headed back to the CBD. Not sure of my chances of catching him in this traffic,' I finish as I head out onto Sandy Bay Road toward Hobart CBD.

I'm in pursuit of a bike!

Suddenly a bus pulls out in front of me, billowing black smoke. Randomly, I think, *Glad I'm in a ute and not on a bike.* I slip back into second gear and give the ute a boot full as I pull out to pass the bus. Cars coming the other way flash their lights and give me a blast of their horns, needing to come to a stop to let me squeeze in front of the bus. I acknowledge them with a 'sorry about that' wave before, bugger, coming to a stop at a red light at the next intersection.

This is going to be bloody hard, I contemplate before hearing Pig come through the app.

'Got him with the drone.'

(Of course, this is highly illegal but we aren't telling – are you?)

'He's four, five blocks ahead of you but in typical bike fashion, he isn't stopping for red lights, slips onto the pedestrian crossing and keeps going. You can back off now. I suggest you get off the main road as after that move to pass the bus, I'm sure more than one local will have reported you to the police for your reckless driving.'

'Will do,' I respond, taking the next left and away from the main thoroughfare. Still headed toward the city though.

'Maria, I had to leave the boys unattended. I told them we had laser alarms across the door and windows so not to try and escape, so can you go up there and babysit them, please? Would be good to know if the briefcase is for them too,' I request.

'Will do, boss,' she replies.

'You still armed?' I add.

'Sure am. But pretty certain I can keep those two boyos in check without needing it,' she replies.

I don't doubt that!

Pig keeps us appraised of the courier's progress until he says, 'Okay, he has propped his bike up against a bus shelter in Elizabeth Street, just after the intersection with Macquarie Street. He's gone into an office building. Hold on. It's twenty-two Elizabeth Street opposite the post office. You can't miss his bike – pretty old and tatty, a pannier bag either side over the back wheel.'

I respond, 'Thanks, I'm coming down Macquarie Street. now.'

And Pig replies, 'Grab a park on Macquarie Street as no parking on Elizabeth Street.'

'Will do.'

Fortunately, as I approach Elizabeth Street, a car pulls out of a parking space, so I get to practise my reverse parallel parking! Still pretty good, I conclude and quickly head around the corner into Elizabeth Street. I see the courier's bike exactly where Pig told me.

'I can see the bike now,' I state.

He replies, 'Yes, I have vision of you. How are you going to play this?'

'Not sure. Play the official line, I guess, and hope I can persuade him to tell me.'

No more time for idle chit-chat as I see the courier exit the building, still putting an envelope into the satchel slung across his shoulder.

As I'm closing in on him, Maria comes through. 'Hi, just letting you know the boys are cool and yes, the briefcase has been delivered.

No one has touched it here.'

I don't have time to respond, as the courier is reaching for his bike, pulling it up from leaning against the bus shelter frame.

'Excuse me,' I start. He pauses, not quite ready to mount his bike, waiting for me as I cross the last few metres. I already have my official Section V ID card in my hand and I show him this. I introduce myself. 'I'm Mort of Section V. We are a high-level government anti-crime authority. I need you to quickly confirm who gave you the briefcase you delivered to Paddy O'Donnell out at Wrest Point a few minutes ago.'

He looks at me for a few moments, then at his watch and sighs. On the underside of his right wrist, he has a small tablet-like device (similar to what courier drivers use, come to think of it.)

He taps a couple of buttons then says, 'It was booked and paid for online by a Sally Smith, with the pickup address of The Tasman Hotel, just down the road a bit.'

'Who did you collect it from?' I respond.

'A woman met me as I arrived and handed it to me. I confirmed the booking confirmation number was correct and that was it.'

'Are you able to give me the credit card details it was paid for with?' I ask.

'Hold on.' He then fiddles with his device before confirming, 'Here you go, a Visa,' and rattles off the sixteen digits, expiry date and CCV numbers from the credit card. He looks at me strangely when I don't write these down. No need – all being recorded.

'Thanks. Can you describe this woman?'

Another sigh as he again looks at his watch. 'Medium height, I guess. Dark hair under a baseball cap, dark sunglasses, grey shapeless hoody and jeans. She had a small backpack slung over her shoulder. Not much to go on, I guess, but she did have a cute arse. I remember watching her as she went on out into the street.'

Good to know, I think!

'Did you see if she got into a car or where she went?'

'She headed down toward the waterfront. I passed her on my way out to Wrest Point. She was walking toward Salamanca Place.'

'Thanks. I need your phone number in case we need any further info, please.'

He pulls a face again, saying, 'Mister, I've told you all I know. I'm a bike courier – I don't have time to watch everyone and everything. Hard enough to avoid the dickhead drivers on the road without watching out for anything else.'

'Understood. Your phone number, please.'

He sighs and recites his number, which I punch straight into my phone and call it. I hear it ringing and give him a nod. 'And your name?'

'Howie. Howard Smart.'

I hold out my hand. We shake and I say, 'Thank you, Howie. Appreciate your help.'

'What about if I remember something else? How can I get in touch with you?' he asks. I slip out one of my DDS business cards and hand it to him.

He nods, mounts his bike, punches a button on his device and is off.

I need coffee. I look around. Yes, there is a café on the corner.

Pig comes through. 'I've logged into The Tasman Hotel. It's a fancy joint, part of the Marriott group, but their digital security is lousy. I'm accessing their CCTV footage from this morning now.'

I head into the café and order a large coffee – long black, as always – and take a seat whilst I wait for an update from Pig.

I then notice I have a text from Robert of Section V saying, *'Frank is coming down for the keys. Was easier than getting one of the Melbourne team involved. He is on QF1561 ETA 15.05. He is then booked on to Melbourne Virgin departing at 16.50. Does this suit?'*

Instead of replying, I decide to give them a call and update.

I take my coffee outside, Franklin Square, a large open-air park is across the road, so I head over there where I will be able to talk privately.

When MGC answers, I say, 'Sir, might help if you add Robert into the call. We have a bit of an update.'

'Hold a minute. Okay, proceed.'

'Sir, a bike courier delivered a briefcase to Paddy at the hotel this morning. We haven't opened it yet; we assume it holds their fifteen thousand dollars in casino chips.'

'Or a bomb,' MGC butts in.

'Or a bomb,' I agree as I hear Maria, listening in via the app, mutter, 'Shit!'

I continue. 'We haven't touched it. I have not seen it yet but will thoroughly inspect it and remove it into open spaces before we open it.'

Again, I hear Maria, over the app, say, 'Paddy just got a text with the code for the briefcase padlock. Came from one of the previously used phone numbers.'

I continue, saying to MGC and Robert, 'Paddy has just received the passcode to the padlock now as well. We managed to grab the bike courier after a mad scramble. He confirmed the pickup booking was made online by a "Sally Smith" and paid for by the following Visa.'

Here, Pig prompts the numbers for me to recite, knowing I wouldn't have written them down. We are a good team, remember!

'We have a very vague description of her, dressed very well to be unrecognisable on any CCTV footage. The pickup address was The Tasman Hotel here in Hobart. Pig is inside their CCTV footage presently checking to see what he can find. Hold on, he is giving me an update now.'

I mute the call so I can hear Pig tell me what he has found.

'Hold on,' I tell him. 'I will patch you into the call as well. Sir I have patched Pig through, he has an update.'

Pig comes through, 'Afternoon, Sir. The woman, let's call her Sally, appears from nowhere, enters the hotel foyer from a side door from the footpath and hangs around there for six, seven minutes, I suspect keeping an eye out for the courier.

'As soon as she sees him heading toward the entrance, she makes a beeline toward him. She shows him what I suspect is the booking confirmation. He signs a document for her and takes possession of the briefcase. He heads back outside, slides the briefcase into a rear pannier bag on the bike, mounts his bike and takes off. He did tell Mort he saw her heading to Salamanca Place, so I am now searching for external CCTV footage, street and local business cameras to see if I can trace her any further. Sir,

I suspect she is a pro at this. The way she was dressed, she never once lifted her head and with the shapeless hoody, dark glasses and cap, there isn't a much better way to hide your identity.'

I add, 'We will give Frank the briefcase as well as the keys, Sir. But we will check it isn't a bomb first.'

Silence as MGC puts all this new info through his filters.

'Pig, it might be worthwhile checking the CCTV footage for your Wrest Point Hotel as well for this woman. They had to know somehow that they had checked in there,' MGC comes back.

Mmm, fair point, I think. I then add, 'Sir, the other way they would know that is by having access to the credit card Paddy is using. We used this to book their accommodation. Has anything come back on that card yet?'

It's Robert who answers, 'Hi, Mort. Nothing yet. I will now add this new number into our search and see what comes up.'

Pig then replies to MGC, 'Right-o, Sir. I will do that this afternoon.'

I add, 'Sir, I need to head back to the hotel and check out the briefcase, so it is ready for Frank when he gets here. I'm not sure what else is likely to happen down here now, so I suggest we give it until the morning and if nothing else comes up, perhaps you can send a plane down to collect us tomorrow morning, Sir?'

Silence as he contemplates this.

'Yes, Mort, I agree. Don't see what benefit there is of you staying down there any longer. We hoped for a contact but they have been smart enough to use one, or maybe more, cut-outs, keeping their distance. So, yes, if nothing changes, I will have a plane down there to collect you around ten a.m. tomorrow.'`

'Good-o, Sir. I will give you an update after I have opened the briefcase or, worst case, Pig will need to call you, Sir!'

A bit of black humour to end the call on!

We all say our goodbyes and I head back to the ute.

Bugger, I have received a parking fine. In the rush, I didn't bother feeding the meter.

CHAPTER 15

I get back to the hotel, park, and head up to the boys' room, letting myself in. Having warned Maria, I'm on my way up.

Pig had told me on the drive back that he is still in our room, checking any CCTV footage he can find that may shed any light on the mystery Sally.

The briefcase is sitting on the coffee table; everyone is looking a little intimidated. Declan asks the question on everyone's lips. 'Do you really think this is a bomb?'

I look at them both, then include Maria in my glance and say, 'In truth, no I don't. But we aren't going to take any chances.'

He replies, 'But why would they try and bomb us?'

I look at him, at them both, and say, 'Your Muhammad is a world-renowned terrorist. Killing people, innocent people, is their goal in life. If it suited their purposes, they would not hesitate to set off a bomb to kill you. Any others killed or maimed are insignificant collateral damage as far as they are concerned. Don't forget they have had you poisoning water supplies to five different cities, so far. Now, you are going to stay here and I will take this outside, away from everyone and inspect it. What is the passcode?'

Maria replies, 'One, two, three. But what about you, Mort? If it is a bomb, and it goes off, what will happen to you?'

'We have to hope it isn't, don't we? But I have had experience in disarming explosives, including full training on disarming bombs like this.'

'Well, I don't want to be the one who has to ring Suzie and tell her you're no longer with us,' she replies with a hint of a smile.

'Don't worry, Maria, I'm going to go and hold his hand, so nothing bad is going to happen,' Pig comes through the app.

'If you both get blown up, I'll just shoot these two and head home then,' she says, watching Paddy and Declan as she says this.

I say to Pig, 'See you downstairs in five,' and head over to have a close look at the briefcase for the first time.

Nothing seems out of the ordinary. It is a pretty standard, black briefcase. It certainly doesn't look like an expensive one either.

I ask Paddy and Declan, 'Does this look the same as the others you have?'

They both come over, making sure they don't touch it or get too close to it, before nodding and saying almost in unison, 'Yes, looks exactly the same as the others.'

'Okay dokey then,' I answer as I pick it up by the handle and gently carry it to the door, down in the lift and then wait outside for Pig to join me.

Once he arrives, I nod with my head to the open grassy space in front of the hotel, on the banks of the river. We head that way.

We position ourselves as far away from the other groups sitting or wandering around the lawn, after agreeing a maximum blast range of one hundred metres is likely to be safe.

I look at him and say, 'You don't need to be here. No sense both of us being in jeopardy.'

'Just get on with it,' he growls. My reaction would have been the same if the boot had been on the other foot.

If it is a bobby-trapped bomb, the trigger will be the locks. Click them open and kaboom!

Therefore, instead of opening the briefcase as you would normally, I pull out my penknife and, using one of the little tools on it (it's like a Swiss army knife but smarter!), I manage to break the hinges on the back of the case. This splits the case in two, now only held together by the locks.

I slide my hand inside the case – gloves on, of course – sliding it all the way around on the bottom half, then repeat the movement on the top half, being particularly careful around the inside of the locks.

Nothing. No wires or anything out of the ordinary. Just packs of chips or, I suspect, chips from the shape of them and what seems to be scrunched-up paper, presumably to stop the chips (or whatever) from rattling around.

I give Pig a nod and then force the case open from the bottom. The locks give way with a bit of a screech but nothing other than paper and casino chips inside. These are in packs of ten, wrapped in Glad Wrap. Most are black one hundred dollar chips, wrapped in tens, making each pack one thousand dollars, a few lavender five hundred dollar ones and two shiny blue one thousand dollar ones, all wrapped together. I total them all up and yes, they total fifteen thousand dollars. Pig picks a few up and confirms, 'Crown Casino.'

Maria pipes up from the balcony, 'Good to know I don't need to ring Suzie and Stacey, ah, boys!'

I glance up and see her standing on the boys' little balcony and give her a smile and wave.

I tuck the broken case under my arm and we head back up to their room.

They, of course, are also relieved it wasn't a bomb, because if it was, they were the intended targets. Meaning Muhammad had finished with them and considered them a risk.

Pig peels off and heads back to our room to keep up his search for the mysterious Sally.

Back with the boys, I let them know unless something else develops overnight, we are all headed to Canberra, where we will hand them over to our boss. Their future is in his hands. As part of this discussion, I ask, 'Do either of you remember any mention or see a woman with Muhammad or Gregor? It was a woman who gave the chips to the courier here in Hobart.'

They look at each other and shake their heads in the negative.

Bugger. Disappointing but not unexpected.

With Frank inbound, I decide it will be quicker if I take the safe deposit keys, and now this briefcase, out to the airport to ensure he doesn't miss his flight back to Melbourne.

With the broken briefcase tucked under my arm, I stop at the concierge's desk in reception and grab some tape off them, so I can hold the briefcase together. Yes, duct tape – now with 1001 uses!

A bit bodgy but better than having it fall open!

I leave Maria once again in charge of the boys and Pig seemingly chasing shadows on the local CCTV footage and head to the airport.

Frank's flight is on time and I meet him as he exits the plane.

He takes one look at the briefcase and says, 'I'm not carrying that around, so let's find a shopping bag or something.'

To which I say, 'Good luck. I'll sit over there and order you a coffee.'

The coffees are served quickly, so I am enjoying mine when he comes back with a large 'Australian Way' shopping bag, looking rather smug!

I help him place the briefcase in the bag, hand over the safe deposit box keys and after a brief chat, I leave him to it and head back to the hotel.

I head to our room so Pig and I can have a chat.

When I let myself in, he is sitting at the small desk, headphones on. I lean over his shoulder to see what he is looking at and he says, 'CCTV footage from Hobart Airport since she dropped off the briefcase. Nothing even remotely dressed like Sally was, but that's not surprising. This does seem a pretty professional set-up.'

He continues, 'Best possible match I have is for a blonde woman, similar build, now dressed in fashionable slacks and black jacket, boarding a Sydney-bound Virgin flight ninety minutes after the handover. No backpack but a large fashionable handbag. I've sent the footage from the hotel and airport to Midge to check the gait, as that is what brought her to my attention, a similar purposeful walk. Next, I'm going to watch the flight arrival into Sydney and see if I can trace her to another flight or out of the terminal.'

I clap him on the shoulder in support and we discuss dinner and tomorrow's journey to Canberra and hopefully onward home. He suggests he will stay at it, hoping to find the woman exiting the plane in Sydney, and we agree room service will again be best for dinner.

Maria is, of course, listening so I say to her, 'Check what the boys want for dinner, please. Might be their last dinner in freedom.'

I head up to the boys' room with Maria organising our dinner.

When I get there, they all agree to a repeat of last night's burgers, so we place a simple order of five works' burgers and add a dozen James Boag beers – good to support the local Tasmanian brewery!

When Pig comes up to join us for our burgers, he quietly tells me he had followed the woman that we hope is Sally from the Hobart flight and onto another virgin flight to Brisbane, pointing out she now had replaced the black jacket with a red one. Same Michael Kors oversized handbag, though!

Maria comes over and asks, 'What was that about a Michael Kors handbag? I've dreamed of owning one of those but do you know how much they cost?'

Yes, I do, having paid for not one, but two on our recent holiday in the States. Part of my penance, you might recall!

Then, on arrival in Brisbane, Pig had followed Sally to the airport pickup point, where she was collected by a black BMW735. Yes, he had managed to get the number plate and is waiting on ownership info to come back.

Boom and boom. Link closed!

We fist bump and I tell Pig, 'Bloody good job, looking through all that airport traffic in Hobart, Sydney and Brisbane to track her all the way. Awesome effort!'

It seems our Badour has a support team of one 'Gregor' and a female we will call 'Sally'.

We enjoy our dinner of burgers. Maria had added desserts all round of Pavlova and cream, so we are a bit spoilt!

Of course, I warn the brothers the two beers might be their last for a long time.

After dinner, I tell them we will be heading to Canberra in the morning, where they would be taken into custody by Australian Federal Police but held in isolation as we try to capture their Muhammad.

A text from Robert confirms our plane's ETA in the morning at ten.

Gentleman's hours!

Before taking the first shift of the night babysitting the brothers, I head downstairs for some fresh air and to call Suzie.

Alas, it is now raining and blowing a gale so I have to stay inside but do have a nice chat. We both giggle like teenagers and she promises a lovely dinner tomorrow night – assuming we do make it home!

I ponder as I head back up to the brothers' room, *Maybe there is substance to the old saying, 'Absence makes the heart grow fonder!'*

Yeah, yeah, I know I've only been away a few days!

CHAPTER 16

Our plane arrives as scheduled and Frank and Robert once again meet us at Canberra Airport with their trusty Toyota Land Cruiser 300s.

Through the night, a text had come through to Paddy's phone, saying, *'Well done. We will be in touch when we are ready for stage two.'*

Paddy didn't see this, as I had his phone. I immediately forwarded it on to MGC and Robert, letting Pig know when we swapped shifts.

I take Paddy with me to Frank's car, whilst Pig and Maria take Declan to Robert's. At Frank's suggestion, we leave our luggage and gun cases on the plane, as he says it has been booked to take us home when we are all finished with MGC.

Good to know.

Surprisingly, instead of going to MGC's office, we head out into the suburbs of Canberra, eventually pulling up at a nondescript house in Queanbeyan, an outer suburb, which is actually in NSW.

As we pull into the drive, MGC appears at the front door, coming out to meet us, followed by a young lady I haven't seen before.

We exit the vehicles, with both Paddy and Declan looking around a little uncertainly. I must confess, I am somewhat surprised as well and judging by the looks I get from both Pig and Maria, I'm not alone.

MGC comes forward, greeting me, Pig and Maria by shaking our hands and saying, 'Let me introduce Lieutenant Rebecca Styles, my assistant and a new member of our team.'

We dutifully welcome her with Pig saying, 'Hope you know what you've got yourself in for!' Smiling, of course.

MGC then pulls us aside, saying, 'I didn't bother letting you know beforehand as I would be seeing you shortly, but after the text you sent through early this morning, I have decided to hold these two in secret, so if or when they are contacted for stage two, we can let them play along. Comments?'

'Seems like a good idea to me, Sir,' I respond, whist Pig and Maria give affirmative nods.

MGC nods, pleased, I suspect, saying only, 'Good.'

We now take him over to meet Paddy and Declan, who Frank and Robert had been holding back by the vehicles.

Here, MGC addresses them, saying, 'Paddy, Declan I have decided to hold you here under guard rather than put you into the prison system just yet. There is no doubt you have been played by some seasoned professionals, working on a much larger terrorist plot, so I want to keep you out of the prison system a while longer. You never know where the tentacles of these gangs may be. You will be under armed guard and as no doubt Mort and Pig have warned you, any attempt to escape will only jeopardise any prospect you have for a future.'

Surprisingly, it is Declan who responds, 'Sir, I hope Mort has told you since being captured we have tried as best we can to help. We certainly did not know we were poisoning people. Sure, we were greedy, thinking our little jaunt was easy money. But of course, that has come back to haunt us, big time. We are very keen to help in any way we can. We do want to have a future. A future here in Australia as was our dream.'

MGC watches and listens in silence before nodding and leading the way inside.

Frank shows the two boys to separate bedrooms off the hallway to the right; neither the main bedroom, judging by the size, but I note all windows do have steel bars across them and the front door also had a full security door. A fairly secure house by the look of it. He tells them they have the run of the house but there will be two armed guards with them at all times.

I see there are two armed men sitting out on the back lawn.

One stubs out a cigarette and they both come in. With a nod to MGC, they take up positions in the lounge. One checks that the front door is locked first. Watching them, I am satisfied they appear professional and I, suspect, they are army rather than police.

With a nod of his head, MGC invites us outside, where we find he has a table set up as a desk out on the patio, away from prying eyes and ears.

I take a look around the back lawn. High six-foot-high fence and bushy hedge on all sides. Very private. I peer over the back fence, straight into another back lawn, similar size to this one. Both side properties also appear similar. Frank, who has been watching me, comes over, saying, 'Both adjoining properties are police service houses, so no nosey neighbours.'

Lieutenant Styles (call me Becky, please!) is well trained it seems, already pouring coffee from a coffee pot, with another on the go. Not saying that in a sexist way but as the junior officer, no doubt she understands her role as MGC's personal assistant.

We sit down around MGC's desk and recap everything we have learnt. Really nothing new to tell him. Whilst sitting there, I realise I haven't heard an update from DS Shirley Bryant on the O'Brien murder, so I send off a text asking for an update.

After nearly two hours of discussion, MGC wraps it up, saying, 'Well, there isn't much else we can do for now. With this Sally woman back in Brisbane, it seems this viper nest is headquartered up there, so you boys'—he takes a quick glance at Maria, so she knows this includes her!—'will be on standby in case we come across any further leads.'

He looks at his watch, saying, 'Frank will take you back to the airport shortly. The plane is waiting, so once you are on board, they will be ready to take off. Home for dinner tonight!'

* * *

Next morning, back in the office nice and early after a good five K run – I pushed myself to make up for the lack of exercise whilst away, so I am feeling good.

Dead keen to get into you-know-what.

I have nearly forty-five thousand photos to review.

Fresh coffee and I press start!

I start at the latest and head backwards from there.

I have to admit, seeing Liz in many of these photos – and particularly those where she is with Kevin – is a little difficult. But I am tough. And in love!

Suzie actually beats Pig in, coming over and giving me a lovely big kiss. Not sure if it's because of what I am doing, going back through my former wife's photos, or a reflection of the thoroughly enjoyable evening we had last night. Again, making me think, *I need to spend more time away to enjoy these homecomings!*

I'm damn sure she wouldn't have kissed me like that if anyone else was in the office but hey, I'm not complaining.

After rearranging herself in the aftermath of the kiss, she asks, 'Found anything yet?' with her arm still around my shoulders.

I shake my head. 'No, plenty of meals, some with both of them in various locations, some even with his three kids as well. Nothing of interest.'

With a squeeze of my shoulder, she heads off to her office. I calculate I have only looked at nearly 250 photos in the nearly forty minutes since I started. *Shit, this is going to take a while,* I think.

Well, time for a fresh coffee anyway.

Pig and Maria come in around the same time, both later than normal but hey, that's fine. We have been away for a few days!

Maria is clearly pleased to be home with her family, but immediately grousing about how disorganised the kids are when it's time to head to school. *Same as households across the country. Well, make that the world,* I think!

Pig makes us both a coffee and comes over, sitting down and saying he is going to take a few days off at the end of next week to go down and bring Stacey home. I offer him the van, and he accepts as this should get all 'her junk' in.

Once that is sorted, we discuss the projects we have on the board. Yes, we have a large whiteboard where each project we have on the books is listed with current status. We had received two more acceptances of proposals whilst we were away in Tassie. One of these we agree is urgent and he will get stuck into this. Maria has her own section of the whiteboard, being dedicated as she is to hunting down delinquent fathers.

I keep plodding away. I pull four images at a time onto my screen, review and move on. I even try putting four on each screen, so I'm reviewing eight at a time, but then realise I'm not giving each full focus. So, back to only four.

After lunch, I decide I need a break and get back into working a data breach review I started before heading off to Tassie. This is boring shit but it has to be done, and it pays the bills well.

* * *

A couple of mornings later, Suzie and I are sitting finishing our breakfast when Pig yells up the stairs, 'Are you two decent?'

I am, dressed for work, but Suzie is only in a house coat, covering her 'essentials' – bra and panties.

She sinches the belt tight and gives me a nod.

I reply to Pig, 'All good.'

He comes up the stairs, gives us a nod and heads into the kitchen and helps himself to a coffee before coming over and sitting down at the table.

He clearly has something to say.

'We're pregnant.'

I can't resist. 'We?'

'Well, you know. Stacey is pregnant. I'm going to be a dad! I can't believe it!'

I'm watching Suzie closely, looking for any sign of disappointment. You see, we have been talking about starting a family. Well, truth be told, we have been doing more than talking about it!

Suzie jumps up comes around and gives him a big hug, offering, 'Congratulations, that is so exciting! How does Stacey feel about it?'

'She's over the moon, as am I.'

I too get up and give him a hug – a man hug, that is.

Pig continues, 'You know, with the life I've led with George and that, I have never seriously considered becoming a father. Now I'm going to be a dad!'

He's smiling from ear to ear.

'How far along?' I ask.

'Just over twelve weeks. She went and got a proper test yesterday. I didn't know until I got home last night. Shit, I'm going to be a dad!'

I do the maths in my head. 'Washington?'

He nods and smiles again, 'Yeah, we reckon.'

Again, I look to Suzie, and she has a wistful look on her face.

'That's so exciting. I'm going to ring Stacey and congratulate her!' Suzie says as she pulls her phone off the table and disappears into the lounge to call Stacey. I yell out, 'Hold on when you're finished so I can talk to her as well.'

She is already out of the room, but I'll assume she heard me.

I smile at Pig and say, 'So, whilst I was supposedly snoring that night, you were conceiving! Awesome! Any wedding plans then?'

He shakes his head. 'We have discussed it but don't feel the need for vows, so no, we won't bother.'

I'm now smiling as much as Pig. Well, almost.

Suzie comes back holding out her phone, so I grab it and pass my congrats on to Stacey as well.

All very exciting.

We settle down quickly with Pig and I heading down the stairs. There is work to do.

When Maria arrives a little later, I greet her by saying, 'You need to take a seat in case you fall down when you hear Pig's news.'

'What? What do you mean?' she asks, looking at Pig.

He is smiling and says, 'I'm going to be a dad!'

Maria lets out a squeal, surprising me as I didn't have her tagged as a squealer! (You see, it is not only Pigs that squeal!)

She goes over and gives Pig a hug, saying, 'I need to call Stacey. How is she feeling?'

Pig shrugs. 'She's fine. Hasn't been feeling nauseous at all.' Implying he didn't know what all the fuss was about.

Maria cuffs him around the head, saying as she smiles at him, 'You better look after her good; otherwise, I'll sort you out!'

Then I hear Maria talking to Stacey about baby clothes, organising a baby shower and they start going through a list of all the baby furniture they are going to need. She's apologising, saying she had thrown out or given away most of her baby furniture, knowing she would not be needing it again, then looking at Pig, she adds, 'You might have to look at any overtime available to pay for all this stuff.'

I decide I will shoot up the road and grab a little celebratory cake.

* * *

It's three days and some four thousand plus photos later when one shakes me awake. It's pretty boring looking at old photos, but this one is different.

Very different.

'Come and look at this,' I say.

Pig looks up and comes over. As does Maria.

I have enlarged the photo of interest to full screen.

It shows a meal in the foreground, baby barramundi with potatoes and red cabbage is my guess, but what is of interest is the couple at the top of the photo, clearly not the intended focus, but captured clearly in the photo all the same.

The man is looking intently directly at the camera, whereas the lady is looking adoringly at her companion, so her head is side-on in the image.

'Where is that taken?' is Pig's question.

'No idea, yet,' I reply.

Then, looking at the date on the image, it looks vaguely familiar. I pull up the files of Liz's receipts I had scanned and sure enough, it's the same date as her meal at Rick Shores down at Burleigh Heads on the Gold Coast.

'Shit, looks like it's at Rick Shores – you know, where we had dinner after the Gold Coast half marathon.'

I move the focus of the image, highlighting the beach and ocean views in the background and we agree, we can remember seeing similar images when we ate there.

I lean back in my seat.

Shit.

The date was just over six weeks before Liz's death. I shake my head, almost in admiration.

To identify Liz – an innocent member of the public – set up a 'hit' and make it look like an accident all within six weeks is no mean feat.

They would definitely have needed help.

Bloody Lancaster.

'Why would they, whoever they are, want to kill Liz because she captured them in a photo?' asks Maria.

'That is a bloody good question,' I reply.

'First guess is they are not married and don't want their relationship known. But, hell, it's bloody extreme to kill someone just to ensure no one sees a photo of you with your lover.'

As I'm talking, I am editing the image, taking a full headshot of the man and separately of the woman. First step, identify them both.

I flick between the full-sized shots of them both. At full screen the image is rather pixilated, so I reduce the size to improve the clarity of the photo.

There is something about the image of the woman that is vaguely familiar. I can't put my finger on it, so I say to Pig, 'I'm sure I haven't seen the man before, but there is something about the woman. What do you think?'

I continue to move the image of the women, looking at it from different angles.

No, not triggering anything.

Pig responds, 'No, don't think I know her.'

I have saved the images and just as Pig goes back to his desk, Suzie comes out, again placing her arm along my shoulder, Maria having let her know we had found something.

I say to her, 'This is taken at Rick Shores. See, do you recognise the view in the background?'

'Okay, yes, I see that. They must have been sitting further to the left of where we sat.'

Pig advises, 'I've sent both images to Midge and Robert and am going to put them into our usual databases as well.'

Hopefully, something will pop up.

With the excitement dying down, I keep going, seeing if there are any other images taken on that night and yes, a few more. Once again, they have this couple in the background but nowhere near as clear.

Somehow this seems right. This photo is the reason why Liz was killed. Way, way over the top, murdering an innocent lady simply because you are in a photo of her food. Mean, vicious, callous bastard. He doesn't know it yet but his days are numbered.

CHAPTER 17

With the photo now identified and over coffee, Pig and I set our priorities on hunting down our other leads.

We now know why Liz was targeted – not that it makes sense to any rational person. Now to find out the who.

We decide we need to focus on:

- Dickie – of the Melbourne gangs, but also monitoring the three bent coppers in prison here in Queensland. Sophisticated enough to use a phone on the dark web and a synthesized one at that. We are coming, Dickie.
- Warden Thomas – he still has some explaining to do, but we remain reluctant to proceed yet, as that will likely spook him and therefore Dickie, in his phone as 'Joe'.

Also, we agree Pig will continue to identify all major transactions through Lancaster's numerous bank accounts prior to and after the killing of Liz, in case he made any other payment that might be relevant.

It continues to be a major bugbear. Why wasn't he paid to arrange for her murder? Just doesn't ring true.

We can put a line through Marissa now as it appears Jeffy and Benson were schoolmates and seemed happy to share their 'fuck buddies'. It seems that Jeffy was already aware of the scam Lancaster and co were running, making it easier for him to step in and take over.

* * *

As a follow up, I put a call into DS Shirley Bryant, keen to know how the O'Brien murder investigation is coming along.

She suggests a catch up over coffee, surprisingly at Mad Cuppa the next morning.

Ten a.m. finds us there and we see Chris Harris coming toward us with a colleague. Sure enough, Chris introduces us to Shirley. We order coffee and take our usual seats outside.

After chatting about this and that – it's summer so Chris doesn't have her usual vent about the Broncos – Shirley briefs us.

'We still don't have any leads, concrete ones anyway. We have traced all black BMW 7 series and there are a surprising number. Most we have eliminated but there are maybe a dozen owned by rental car companies and leasing companies that, so far, we haven't been able to identify who they are renting or leasing these to.'

Pig pipes up, 'Let me know the regos and companies that own them. We may be able to assist – unofficially, of course.'

This gets us an appraising look from Shirley as she looks between us and more than once glances over at Chris, who sits there silently.

She doesn't bite and we don't offer twice. She will come back to us one day if they don't make any progress.

'Still no ID on the driver of the stolen SUV used to run O'Brien down either. Nor have we seen any eighteen thousand dollar deposit paid into any of the bank accounts he had, that would match what you suspected.'

Shirley, having finished her summary, now finishes her coffee and it is Chris who asks: 'What happened to your two domestic terrorists? Did you capture them? I haven't seen anything in the news about them.'

I nod, as Pig goes back in for fresh coffees, Chris joining us for another one, whereas Shirley declines.

'Yes, we caught them both. Now in federal police custody. Higher levels will decide what to do with them now.'

We come back from our chat with Shirley and walk into the office to find two ladies sitting talking to Maria, Suzie and Jenny.

Both tall ladies of, I suspect, Fijian descent. One I'm guessing early twenties; the other, similar age to Maria, and she looks familiar. Whilst looking at her, I realise she plays netball with Suzie. I even remember her name as Alitia, so I nod to her and say, 'Hi.'

The atmosphere is tense and there are tears in their eyes, Suzie and Jenny both clutching tissues.

Something is amiss.

It's Maria that starts, 'Mort, Pig, this is my friend Alitia and her niece Tia. Mort, you might remember Alitia plays netball with Suzie and I?'

I nod and reach out to shake their hands, as does Pig.

Suzie again dabs her eyes and I raise my eyebrow – what?

But it is the young niece, Tia, that starts.

'I've been raped. And the bloody police don't seem to be doing anything about it.'

I sit down. I look around the group, at Hoang, who is now living here in Brisbane studying a Bachelor of Commerce at ACU (Australian Catholic University) and is working part-time for us. He has grown up in the months since we met him; he is fit-looking, running daily and lifting weights he had proudly told us, something he had never done at home. He looks and sounds much better for it. Much more self-confident too. His CatchEm earns him a little licencing fee, for those we authorise to use it. Much of which goes back to his mum and dad to help keep the shop afloat, although he says things have improved on that front as well. Life is on the up and up for him and his family. Still watching his pennies though, travels everywhere on an e-scooter, not bothering with a car.

He is now embedded here within DDS (Digital Data Solutions) and now looks up as well.

'Okay. I'm sorry – this can't be easy. If you feel up to it, let's hear it from the beginning,' I suggest.

We grab chairs from everywhere so we can all sit down. Suzie passes a box of tissues to Tia, who seems the calmest of all of them.

She nods and starts, 'I'm a member of the Australian Rugby Sevens training squad. I stress I'm not in the playing group, but the wider training squad. I am dead serious about making sure I have the best chance to make the team, especially for the Olympics. I do not jeopardise my chances by doing anything stupid and nothing goes into my body I don't know about. Nothing. I want you to know this upfront, so as I tell you this story, you have this as background.'

I look at her, thinking she is a good-looking lady and looks very much like an athlete. Strong, athletically built, muscular but in a feminine way. She is dressed in a t-shirt and what I would call footie shorts.

She takes a sip of water from her water bottle and starts:

'Chloe, a good school friend of mine, is getting married, so I agreed to go on her hen's night. I don't drink, so I'm used to drinking water, Coke, etc whilst friends have a good time. I don't need alcohol to enjoy myself and it doesn't faze me that others do.

'Anyway, we were at the Venu nightclub in the Valley last Saturday night and Joel Flanigan, you know, *"the next big thing"*'—(this is said with air quote marks)—'at the Lions'—(Brisbane Lions AFL team)—'was there. He hit on me, but he's not my type so I blew him off. He didn't seem to like that. Most of my friends were encouraging me to dance with him, being so, so hot – their words, not mine.

'But no, I didn't have any interest. Anyway, he insisted on buying me a drink, so I let him buy me a Coke Zero. After that, it's a bit blurry and apparently, I was dancing with him and others. My friends all thought I was having a good time. Anyway, long story short, I woke up Sunday morning in his apartment, naked in his bed. I did not go there willingly.

'Of course, he was rather smug, saying we had had such a good time and he wanted to keep doing it. I got dressed and out of there. I rang Aunt Alitia, told her what had happened and she came and picked me up and took me to the hospital and asked for me to be examined as a rape victim.

'A female doctor and nurse examined me, in their words "under the rape protocol". I can tell you it is not a pleasant experience. And that's not being critical of the staff, they did what seemed a proper professional job. Taking close-up photos and the like of my private parts, is, well, very embarrassing and demeaning. I was blood tested as well, having told them I believe I had been drugged. They even bagged and kept my underwear for DNA testing but did warn of the very lengthy delays in DNA testing currently.'

Here, she dabs her eyes and Alitia goes over and gives her a hug.

'They asked if I wanted to report it to the police and I said yes. We then had to wait over two hours for a couple of the police sex crimes unit to turn up. They met with the doctor first and then interviewed me. They were both female officers and very sympathetic, but when I named Joel as my attacker, they obviously recognised his name and, well, something seemed to change. They continued to interview me, recording it all, but seemed to try and divert me away from my claim of being drugged.'

Here, Pig interrupts, asking, 'The Venu you said?'

Tia nods.

'Is this you with your friends? he asks.

I wheel my chair over to look over his shoulder and everyone else follows, so we are all peering over his shoulders so we can see his monitors.

Tia confirms, 'Yes that's us.'

We can see Tia and three other girls standing in the queue waiting to get into the Venu.

Pig asks, 'Who's who amongst your friends?'

'That's Chloe in the white pantsuit, Maddie in the long floral dress and April in the black skirt.'

I look over and see Hoang has the same vision as Pig on his screen.

He then says to Pig, 'I'm in as well. What do you want me to look at?'

Pig replies, 'I'm going to watch the bar area. Why don't you follow the girls?'

'Will do.'

Maria and Tia move over and watch over Hoang's shoulder whilst the rest stay where we are.

'What's Joel Flanigan look like?' asks Jenny. Pig pulls a headshot photo up on his second screen. This is clearly taken from a recent *Courier Mail* image.

Pig is running the CCTV for the bar area a little faster than normal.

He is well adept at watching at this speed and whilst I can keep up, it's clear Suzie, Jenny and Alitia can't.

Suddenly, he stops, rewinds a little and then starts again in slow-mo. We watch as Joel is served a beer and a glass of Coke, moves over to a side table and very surreptitiously adds something to the Coke from a small vial.

'Shit.'

'Gotcha, you bastard.'

'What?' This is from Maria, looking over toward us.

I nod at the screen, look at Tia and say, 'You are right, he did spike your drink – we have it here on the CCTV tape.'

She quickly comes over and watches another replay, saying, 'You fucking cunt.'

Alitia, mother-like, says, 'Tia!'

Tia, looking rather upset now, says, 'Well, he is. Here is the proof he drugged me, then raped me. He is a fucking arsehole and I'm going to see he goes to prison. Don't care how embarrassing it is for me.'

The tissues are again getting a workout amongst the girls as they all take turns to console Tia.

In the background, Hoang says, 'I'm in his emails and here is an invoice for Rohypnol. He buys it online and has it delivered to a post box at Ashgrove here in Brisbane.'

'Fucker,' Maria adds her thoughts.

Then Hoang adds, 'It's a repeat order too, not the first time he has bought it.'

I look at Pig and say, 'We may have a serial rapist on our hands.'

He looks back at me, saying, 'Well, we need to sort the fucker out. If the cops won't, we will.'

We fist bump.

I glance at Suzie and yes, she is watching closely with a concerned look on her face.

It gets a bit emotional for a while as the girls all console Tia who tears up this time, now confronted with proof she was drugged and raped.

Pig and I look at each other, wishing we had some privacy so we can discuss the next steps.

We let the girls settle before Pig asks, 'When do you expect to hear from the police about your drug screening?'

Alitia answers, 'They wouldn't give us a time frame, nor were they very forthcoming about when they may interview arsehole Joel.'

I catch Suzie's eye and with a flick of my head indicate she gets them out of here.

She is looking at me with a puzzled look then says, 'Why don't we go down the road for a bite of lunch, leave the boys here to keep digging?'

They all agree, with Hoang staying back with Pig and me.

Once they have all left, I say, 'In my opinion, it's highly unlikely this is the first time he has done this. Hoang, how many orders has he received of Rohypnol?'

'That was the second one I have found so far.'

'Okay, can you check his credit cards and make a list of the dates he has received the Rohypnol and also the dates he has gone to Venu or any other nightclubs?'

'Okay, will do.'

Pig starts, 'What an absolute arsehole. Good-looking kid, should be able to get laid anytime he wants, so why's he need to drug them? We need to caution Tia and Alitia that they can't let on to the police they have seen the CCTV footage or know for sure she was drugged.

'I want to have a closer look at what's going on around the bar area too. I was only focused on what might relate to Tia, but I suspect I saw drugs being sold over the bar. Bloody dangerous practise these days,' he finishes.

I add, 'Not if you have the right protection.'

He nods whilst Hoang stops and looks from Pig to me, then resumes his searching. Maybe wondering what the hell he's got himself involved with, working for us!

I continue, 'Guess it's fair enough they – the police, I mean – walk slowly slowly, before accusing someone of his profile with rape, but we will need to monitor their investigation, just to ensure it stays on track.'

'I can do that,' says Hoang. 'I have accessed their system before.'

'What, cancelling speeding fines now, ah?' Pig teases him.

'No, no nothing like that, but I was following a case up home about a cat burglar. He was climbing the high rises around Palm Cove and that and breaking in. I thought the name sounded familiar, so I looked their files up and yeah, was a guy two years ahead of me at school. He was always getting in trouble for climbing stuff as a kid, so didn't surprise me really. Anyway, when Tia comes back, I will get the case file number off her, then we can monitor it.'

'Cool,' Pig and I say, almost in unison.

With the girls out of the way, I now ask Hoang, 'How did you manage to get into his emails so quickly?'

He looks up with a small smile, saying, 'That's a new tool I'm working on. First time I have actually used it. But it lets me trace and then access personal emails associated with social media, like Facebook, X, Instagram. I can't fault it yet.'

Pig, who of course is watching and listening, says, 'On ya. Glad you're on the side of the good guys! How easy is it to use? Can you share it with us – or at least Maria? Will make her job of tracking these delinquent fathers a lot easier.'

'Yeah, sure. Do you think it might have any value? Like, could I licence its use or something? You know, like we have done with "CatchEm"?'

Pig and I look at each other, evaluating, before I reply, 'Maybe, but the trouble is all the big value will put it in the hands of people who will abuse it. Let's test it out some more and maybe we will discuss it with Midge and Matteo, get their opinions. How's that sound?'

'Cool,' replies Hoang.

The girls all traipse back in with Suzie tossing me, Pig and Hoang a ham and cheese toastie each, plus coffee of course.

Bless her!

Tia says, 'I have to ask you guys, how can you access the CCTV footage and Joel's emails so quickly?'

It's Suzie who responds rather firmly, 'Don't ask.'

Tia, still with a puzzled look on her face, leaves it and I get in quick with a change of subject.

'Tia, Alitia I have to warn you what you have seen here cannot be used in a court of law but if we can find it, so can the police. But the critical point is, you cannot let them know you have seen it, or even know of its existence. Is that clear?'

Alitia and Tia look at each other, I suspect a little disappointed they can't use this information to demand action from the cops.

Suzie chimes in, 'He is right. You will potentially delay the investigation if you mention this, as they will then be side-tracked into investigating how you know. You don't want to bring that on yourselves.'

I then continue, 'Tia, we are here to help you get justice. Please keep us informed. You can liaise with Maria if it's easier, and we will continue looking in the background and reach out to a couple of cops we know and trust to try and ensure they stay on track. We will help you get your justice.'

Maria then chimes in, 'We have a saying here, "Mortice – Justice Mort style" and believe me, Mortice provides many different forms of justice!'

Both Tia and Alitia seem puzzled but don't ask any more questions.

Hoang asks Tia for the police case file number, which she digs out of her handbag and gives him. Then I ask for both hers and Alitia's phone numbers as I'm sure we will have more questions.

I ask, 'What about your friends, Tia? What do they say about the evening?'

She snorts. 'Some friends they are, letting me go off with him. I asked them and they thought I was having a great time, and claimed they wanted me to have a good time, saying I deserved it after all my training and the strict life I choose to lead.'

We nod as Alitia and Tia prepare to leave, getting hugs all round from Suzie, Maria, Jenny and even Pig. Handshake from me, and a simple nod from Hoang. The way of the younger generation.

Suzie and Jenny disappear back into their office after we share some consoling words.

I watch out the window and note they get into a lime green Suzuki

Jimny, the little 4x4 'cult car' that has become so popular. I note Tia is driving and think, *Somehow, the car suits the girl*, clearly a strong-willed, determined and independent young lady.

Right on cue, my computer beeps.

CHAPTER 18

I sit down and look to see what it has found.

Pig over my shoulder.

Great, a name for the male in our photo.

One Daniel Belgrave. Never heard of him. When I check, I see he has been identified from his LinkedIn account.

Quite random considering some of the sophisticated databases we had submitted his photo to.

Pig claps me on the shoulder, saying, 'Great, we have a start point. I'll see what I can dig up on him, whilst Hoang digs out dates, et cetera, from Joel's credit cards.'

Hoang adds, 'Won't be long. He has two credit cards: one a NAB Mastercard, the other a Westpac Visa. He uses the Visa for all his online shopping. I've found invoices for some kinky stuff too, by the way. Leather straps and other bondage gear. The Mastercard seems to be for his everyday stuff. I have a list of dates for Venu and a couple of other nightclubs. "Ball and Chain" and "Splendiferous" he seems to frequent. But Venu seems his favourite. I've emailed them through to you.'

'Good-o.'

Daniel Belgrave. Why did you want or need to kill my wife? I think.

I'm going to find out, and there will be consequences. Big consequences.

Knowing Pig will start hunting in his usual databases, I go left field and do a search of Daniel's name in ASIC's (Australian Securities and Investment Commission) databases, where there is a record of every company director, company name, etc.

Might seem random but let's see.

By inputting his name, I find I need his full name and date of birth. Bugger, more digging!

I leave it to Pig. No sense us tripping over each other searching for the same info.

Two urgent investigations going on together now.

Hoang sends an email, listing all the dates he has found for Joel's visits to the three nightclubs.

With Pig busy digging out details on Daniel, I take first dibs on Joel's mischief.

Leaving his most recent visit, when he had his 'date' with Tia, I look back and he seems to visit a nightclub whenever the Lions have a home game. Yes, I cross-referenced with their playing schedule.

Certainly, Venu is the most popular. I decide, seeing as we already have access to their CCTV, I will look at their dates first.

The last one is a fortnight earlier than Tia's night out, so I monitor the entrance and sure enough, around 10.15 I see him and a couple of mates walking confidently up to the bouncers at the entrance, ignoring the queue waiting to gain entrance. They show a pass or something on their phones and are immediately allowed in.

I then watch as they grab a drink and circulate the room, checking out their options, I guess.

I watch as Joel hones in on a lady, dancing with a glass in her hand. They dance a few more minutes and he moves on. He talks to a couple more before inviting another lady up to dance. They finish the set and resume their seats. He finishes his beer and leans over, I suspect offering the lady a drink. She accepts and he heads to the bar.

At this stage, the lady appears keen and willing, so there wouldn't appear to be a need to dope her.

And he doesn't.

Nor does he on the next two trips to the bar.

I fast-forward as they seem to be having a great time, and then I see them leave together arm in arm.

Shit. I suddenly remember we didn't ask Tia where Joel lived.

I ask, 'Hoang, can you dig up Joel's address, please? If he lives in an apartment complex, I want to see if there is CCTV on it.'

'Hold on.'

'He has an apartment on the third floor in Freshwater Apartments on Gray Street, New Farm.'

'Thanks. You better look out, Pig. This kid is good!'

'Better looking too!' comes from Maria. Pig just smiles.

I start digging. I find Freshwater Apartments do have CCTV footage of the entrance, both inside and out. I scroll back to Saturday night, late and yes, there is Tia and Joel exiting what I assume is an Uber, Joel having to help Tia out. When she stands, she rearranges herself, pulling her skirt down.

With Joel's arm under her armpits, he helps her into the building and into a lift.

I fast forward until I see Tia come out of the building, phone in hand, and she appears to be crying.

I let the tape roll and eighteen minutes later, I see Alitia pull up in a Hyundai Santa Fa, get out and run over to Tia. Hugs and tears as they hold each other tight.

After a few minutes, they get into the Santa Fa and sit there for a few minutes, deciding what to do and where to go I'm guessing.

They move off, I presume to the hospital as they described.

Mmm, a few questions we need to ask Tia.

1. Which hospital did she go to?
2. Contact details for her friends

CHAPTER 19

Pig comes up with Daniel Belgrave's full name, DOB and address – somewhere around Mudgeeraba, down on the Gold Coast. Along with his mobile phone number and even his driver's licence details. He is thorough, as always!

I check the phone number back against the number provided to the motel after Liz's accident and it's a match.

Bingo – or is that bugger?

I tell Pig, and then remember the phone number isn't carried by any of the networks, and I had assumed it had been cancelled.

But now, it looks like we have another 'dark web' phone number. I share this with Pig.

He replies, 'I'll try tracing his phone provider again and then, if I'm lucky, get a list of his recent calls, going back as far as the accident.'

Now armed with the info I need, I go back to the ASIC website and input his full name and DOB.

Shit, he is a director of six businesses. Some companies I even recognise, in the tourism industry on the Gold Coast, including hot air ballooning, a jetboat tour and a day tour operator. Seems he is a bit of an entrepreneur. All the businesses are headquartered in Surfers Paradise on the Gold Coast.

I give Pig the highlights and comment, 'So why does a legitimate businessman need to have Liz killed?'

Pig responds, 'Why does a legitimate businessman need a dark web phone number? You're right, it isn't carried by any legitimate phone providers. Something isn't right here.'

I now send Daniel's full details, including the phone number, to Robert at Section V and Midge, in case they have him or his phone number tagged for any reason. I also mention the phone number may be another dark web phone.

Whilst I am digging into Daniel, Hoang and Pig are tracking back through the CCTV footage at Venu and Ball and Chain, tracing Joel's movements. Seems Splendiferous only keeps their tapes for two weeks before taping over them.

A little later, Pig says, 'Shit, I now have him on tape spiking two other girls' drinks at Venu in the last three months. Fucking arsehole.'

Hoang then asks Pig, 'Can you have a look at this with me? I think I have him doing the same at the Ball and Chain a couple of months ago.'

Pig wheels over to watch over Hoang's shoulder and they converse before Pig responds, 'Yep, no doubt there's number four.'

'Fucking arsehole.'

I add, 'I wonder if the cops have had other complainants about this Joel? Did you download the police file yet, Hoang?'

'No,' he replies. 'I have been looking for any more drink spiking. Will access it now.'

A short time later he says, 'Here it is. I've set up a new investigation file in Tia's name and have added it in there. There isn't any mention of any other claims against Joel.'

I open it and read it. Really only the salient facts so far, with a note saying they are waiting on DNA and blood test results before deciding what next steps to take.

* * *

Ten days later, Tia rings in a bit of a panic saying Joel has texted her asking to meet in New Farm Park tomorrow night at 10.30.

I put her on speaker and Pig and Maria both stop and listen.

I say, 'Tia, it seems very strange he's asking to meet you at night, not at a café or somewhere. We will come with you; I don't like the sound of this. I wonder what has happened for him the reach out now. Have you heard from him since that night?'

'Well, yes, he did text me asking if I wanted to meet up but I ignored it.'

I ask, 'Have you heard anything from the cops at all?'

'No, nothing. I have left a couple of messages and Officer Ryan did leave me a message, but they haven't given me an update.'

Maria speaks up, 'Tia, I will come with you but if anything looks out of ordinary, we will let Mort and Pig handle it. Okay?'

'Thanks, Aunty M, that would be good.'

After a few reassuring words, Tia hangs up.

Pig asks, 'Aunty M, ah?'

Maria smiles and says, 'We aren't related but I've been friends with Alitia for years. She is Tia's guardian – her mum still lives in Fiji. They sent her over here to Alitia so she could get ahead in life. I've always been around, so she has always called me Aunty M. She is a good kid, dead keen and totally focused on getting to the Olympics with the Sevens squad.'

Maria wheels over to us and we chat about it. Pig quickly goes back into the police file and says, 'Well, that will be why he wants to meet. The cops have Tia's blood results back. It confirms Rohypnol in her bloodstream. They have consequently interviewed Joel. In his statement, he is adamant it was consensual sex. She went home with him happily, he claims. When confronted by the drugging claim, he became indignant, claiming he could pull any girl whenever he wanted to. Cocky shit. He even asked for his lawyer, so that stopped the interview. The comments suggest they, the police, think it will be difficult to prove rape, with the *"she said, he said"* scenario.'

Next evening and as agreed, Pig and I take the van and park in the car park near the tennis court in New Farm Park, the suggested meet point, making us even more sure this is a set up. Maria and Tia are in Tia's little Jimny, parked just up the road.

As we watch, we see Joel get out of his Tesla and then four big, older guys get out of a Dodge Ram dual cab parked behind him. They all are armed with baseball bats, which they are trying to hide behind their backs.

I look at Pig and say, 'These pricks look like they mean business. Let's go give them a lesson.' I text Maria, telling them to sit tight.

As we suspected something like this was on the cards, Pig had launched his latest drone – this one is called Freddie – before anyone else arrived. The evening's events will be recorded.

We exit the van, pulling on gloves. They will help protect our knuckles.

The four thugs are standing in a huddle with Joel standing off to the side.

We wander toward them. When close enough, I say to Joel, 'So, you can't handle the pressure. You've got to bring your bully boys along, ah?'

From the huddle comes an older voice, 'Who the fuck are you? We are here to teach that little bitch a lesson. She's not going to get away with accusing my Joel of being a rapist. Little slut.'

'We are friends of hers and for the record, there is no doubt your darling son is a rapist. We have him on tape drugging four girls now. He's going to do a long stretch in jail. We all know what happens to rapists in prison, ah.'

'Like fuck. We will beat the shit out of you, then hunt the bitch down and give her a right beating as well.'

I laugh and look at him and his three mates, all big, overweight bully boys.

'Mate, you are going to hospital. All of you, then we will take little Joel down to the cop shop and he can confess to drugging. How many altogether, Joel?'

'Ha, ha, funny man. There is four of us. We will beat the shit out of you.'

All the while, I have been slowly edging closer to him and now I'm inside the arc of the baseball bat, which will prove useless now. He just doesn't realise it.

'Hospital for all four of you. Broken bones, you will be lucky to walk when we have finished with you. We are trained killers, not schoolyard bullies like you four hicks.'

'Who you calling a hick, cunt?' And with that, he unleashes a big overarm swing of the baseball bat, aimed at my head. I'm taller and bigger than he is, so I step in front of him, reach up and stop the swing as it comes over his shoulder. Stop it dead. Then I knee him in the balls. He screams and I wrench the bat out of his hands. As he is hunched up,

I give him a tap (a not-so-light tap) on the head with his own bat. He drops like a stone.

At the same time, Pig comes under assault by numbers two and three. I turn around and with number three about to clout Pig, using my baseball bat, I connect with his swing, jarring his bat out of his hands. I reverse my action and bring the bat down hard on his arm, near his elbow. He screams in pain, dropping to his knees.

Pig has taken care of number two. Number four has come to his senses and is high-tailing it back to the Dodge Ram.

Pig, with a smile on his face, leans down and holds the baseball bat horizontally to the ground. With a flick of his wrist, he launches it like a frisbee or a boomerang.

But this baseball bat aren't coming back.

Pig stays down in the action pose, waiting to see how good his throw is.

A couple of seconds later, another howl rings out as the bat connects with the runner behind his knees, knocking him to the ground.

I look around and realise Joel has also done a runner as I see the Telsa take off down the one-way road.

I go back over to the leader, who we assume is Joel's dad. He's still out to it.

I then go over to numbers two and three and say, 'Tell your mate if Tia ever hears from him or Joel again, we will come back and finish the job. You won't be able to walk or work for months. The kid is a rapist. We have the proof, so make sure you think about that before doing anything to protect him. Now, you better round up your mates and beat it, otherwise the cops will be here to find you.'

Pig and I collect the three baseball bats lying around (number four is a little way away, where he fell so we don't bother retrieving that.)

We head to the van. Whilst Pig lands Freddie the drone, I text Mara saying, *'Get going. Suggest Tia comes to the office in the morning to discuss next steps.'*

We quietly leave, not sure if anyone will have seen or heard anything, therefore unsure if the cops might arrive soon or not.

As Pig still lives in Suzie's apartment here in New Farm, I drop him off where I had picked him up from and head home to some deserved shut-eye.

CHAPTER 20

When Maria arrives in the morning, she tells us Tia has a training session first up, so will call in later in the morning.

She arrives late morning and greets us by saying: 'I've been stood down by the Sevens team over this.' She is close to tears. 'They stress it is only precautionary, but they want the team doctor to confirm I'm all clear of Rohypnol and any other drugs. The girls and all the officials are being really supportive. They are like a second family to me.'

She pauses before continuing, 'The cops have been in touch this morning, confirming they found traces of Rohypnol in my blood, but the physical examination didn't find any evidence of forced penetration. Such a lousy way to describe it. In their words and whilst they concede it is highly likely someone had spiked my drink, they cannot prove who. I even asked if they had reviewed the CCTV from the Venu, and they said yes, the CCTV footage had been handed over, but it didn't show any evidence of drink spiking. So long story short, they have advised that unless any new evidence turns up, they don't see how they can charge him. Slimy prick.'

Maria gets up and goes over pulling her in for a hug. We see Tia's shoulders slump as she has a quiet cry.

Suzie and Jenny have heard and popped out so there are more tears and murmuring of sympathy.

Hoang, sitting quietly in the background, says softly, 'Mort and Pig, look at this. The CCTV footage the cops have on file has been doctored. The scene we have showing Joel spiking her drink has been cut out. It's not a bad job of splicing it, but any IT tech would easily see it has been doctored.'

We are all now crowding around him, and he pulls the original footage up on his second screen and runs them concurrently.

No doubt about it, someone has cut the incriminating scene out. Pig then goes back through the police footage and points out that the other scene he thought showed a drug transaction going down over the bar had also been cut out. At least implying the footage had been doctored by the Venu staff, not the police.

Shit, a brick wall.

I sit there pondering.

When the girls quieten down, I say, 'Tia, justice can come in many forms. How bad do you want justice?'

Silence. A look of concern flashes across Suzie's face, I'm sure wondering what I have in mind. I ensured Maria did not mention last night's episode to her.

Tia replies, 'He shouldn't be able to get away with it. Having seen what you can do last night, he wouldn't stand a chance but him getting beaten up wouldn't make me feel any better.

Suzie gives me a look that says, *What the hell?*

I ignore her and reply to Tia.

'No that's not what I had in mind, but we can publicly humiliate him if you would like that, and you wouldn't need to be exposed as one of the victims.'

Jenny jumps in. 'What, has he raped others?'

Pig replies, 'We have him on tape spiking drinks on three other occasions and that's only in the last three months. We can't identify the victims and for all we know, they were happy having sex with him – maybe they don't even know he spiked their drinks.'

Jenny gasps in horror before saying, 'He shouldn't be able to get away with that.'

I reply, 'No, he shouldn't.'

Maria, still with her arms around Tia's shoulders, asks, 'What have you got in mind?'

I ponder my answer before deciding to put it out there and see what they all think.

'Well, there are plenty of "true crime" podcasts out there these days, forcing the police and coroners to reopen old cases. We can provide the evidence in secret to a well-respected journalist who can then word it in such a way as to make sure everyone knows who they are talking about. He will get his comeuppance and you will have your revenge or justice, call it what you will.'

'Shit yes!' is Tia's quick response before Suzie cautions her, 'Are you sure?'

Tia replies, 'What have I got to lose? The cops aren't going to do their job, so he can keep on getting away with it.'

I butt in, saying, 'To be fair, the cops have not been given the full CCTV footage, so they may be guilty of being naïve or taking the easy option, but I am sure they would have gone after him if they had the full footage as we have.'

Tia, Maria, Suzie and Jenny are having a chat about the consequences and how it may impact Tia. But they don't dissuade her.

She comes back to me, saying, 'Mort, hell yes I like your idea. How do we go about it?'

I reply, 'Let me put together a plan but, sorry, I will need you to sign up as a client of Suzie's and give her a full statement, that way it remains confidential. Can you also ask the cops for a copy of your statement? I'm pretty sure you are entitled to it.' Suzie nods in agreement. 'The journalist will also want to talk to you, get a feel for your side of the story.'

She is already nodding her head in agreement.

'This might even be a better outcome for me. I won't have the threat of the court case hanging over my head for months. Once the podcast is done and out of the way, I can get back to my life, on my terms.'

Sounds like a plan.

* * *

When Pig comes in the next morning, his first words are, 'I need coffee, now. Make that a double strength.'

I raise a querying eyebrow. He shudders theatrically, saying, 'I just gave Stace her first driving lesson. She has never driven before. She should not be on the road.' Another shudder as I pour him a double-strength coffee.

Suzie, who had been talking to me, says, 'What? How come she has never driven before?'

Pig looks at Suzie, saying, 'You know her background. She has never had a use for a car, or the capacity to own one.'

Suzie colours slightly, realising how insensitive she had been.

'Mate, you might be best to leave her driver training to an expert,' I say.

'You betcha I will be, my nerves will be shot if I try to do it,' he says. This from the calmest, coolest man I know. I smile.

Pig continues, saying he heard from Midge overnight, relaying the message: 'He has a record of Belgrave's phone number talking to some of, get this, the Garcia cartel. Small world, ah? Anyway, he has asked if we can get his voice on tape and share it with him to confirm we have the right person. You have to wonder who he really is if he is dealing with the drug mobs in the States at the same time he shows here as a reputable businessman.'

'Well, shouldn't be too difficult to get his voice on tape. We do have his phone number, we can always just call him, posing as a call centre selling some shit. Might get Maria to do it. Sexist, I know, but most of those calls are female and he is more likely to be polite, rather than hang up on us. Solar panels. These are all the rage these days. Maria can call him with a special "season-ending" offer on a solar power system.'

'What am I going to be doing?' asks Maria.

'We want you to call Belgrave and try to sell him a solar system, so we get his voice on tape.'

'Cool, I can do that. We have been looking at it ourselves lately, so I already know some of the lingo.'

'Great, we will sit down shortly and put a spiel together with you.'

But first I want to complete my presentation for our friendly *Courier Mail* journalist Colleen Hill.

I spend the rest of the day on this, with Tia coming back in and sitting down with Suzie and making a formal statement, not dissimilar to her police report, which has been emailed to her today as well.

The presentation includes snippets of the CCTV footage not in the police file, and also of the three other ladies' drinks being spiked, along with her original police report and her statement to Suzie. We also doctor up the drone footage of the fight, ensuring that Pig and I aren't recognisable, even using a voice distorter for any of the audio we include.

Once I am happy with it, I share it with Pig and Suzie for their comments.

Suzie has signed Tia up as a client. We also do the paperwork showing that SDA (Suzie Dunn and associates) have contracted us to investigate Tia's complaint. This means we are also covered by legal privilege. I hasten to add, we won't be protected for the unauthorised accessing the Venu's CCTV footage, but they certainly won't be able to deny it.

Once Suzie is finished with Tia, she hangs around, clearly curious about what we do. We don't mind; she is easy to chat to.

Then, late in the afternoon, a thunderstorm hits and as we are teasing Hoang about how wet he is going to get, riding his scooter home in the rain, Tia pipes up, 'I'll give you a lift. We should get your scooter in the back. Where do you live?'

Hoang replies, 'Cool. Thanks. I share a flat in Kedron.' (An older well-established suburb on the northside.)

I've never asked Hoang how long it usually takes him, as he wouldn't be able to use the Clem7 tunnel or M3 freeway, the quickest way, (well, depending on traffic) from Kedron to Tingalpa.

So, I do now. 'Hoang, how long does it normally take you on your little scooter?'

'Ah, about thirty to thirty-five minutes. Keep in mind, I can go onto the footpath anytime I need if the traffic's backed up, so I don't usually stop too often,' he says with a smile.

They wait a bit and then with a lull in the storm they run out, load the e-scooter into the little Jimny and away they go.

At the end of the day, Suzie comes out and hands me a hard copy of my presentation for Colleen showing some changes in red ink. I review these and decide a couple of her changes are worthwhile and make these changes. Pig had also suggested a couple which I have incorporated into the final report before turning the lights out and heading upstairs.

Suzie is cooking, so I am looking forward to putting my feet up whilst she slaves over the stove. Or, more likely, over the microwave!

I put a call into Colleen the next morning. She answers on the first ring. 'Hi, Mort. Good to hear from you. Hope you have something nice and juicy for me?'

'Hi, Colleen. Yes, I believe I do, although more serious than juicy. I would like to sit down with you and walk you through a situation, an opportunity for you. When would suit to meet up?'

'Great, I'm tied up this morning but any time after two p.m. today or tomorrow will be fine.'

'Okay, I will book a meeting room and come back to you with a time and place. Back to you shortly.'

I check Suzie's availability then go online and book a meeting room at the Brisbane Marriott hotel for two-thirty this afternoon.

I text the details to Colleen and Suzie.

Two-thirty that afternoon and Suzie and I are waiting for Colleen. As you will recall, we have both met her previously and I have brought Suzie along for the same reason. To ensure we keep within legal parameters.

I see Colleen come in. She sees us and comes over. We shake hands all round and I lead the way to our designated meeting room. Yes, the coffee is hot and waiting!

I start, 'Colleen, Suzie here has a client that has been drugged and raped by a high-profile local sportsman. You and the rest of the state know this person. We have irrefutable evidence of the spiking of her drink. Her blood tests done the next day as part of the "rape protocol" show Rohypnol still in her bloodstream.

'As part of our investigations, we have proof of him spiking three other ladies' drinks over the last three months. We can't identify these ladies and for all we know, they had consensual sex with him. But he did spike their drinks.

'After the police interviewed the suspect, our client was asked by her attacker to meet with him and when she arrived at the meeting point, she was met by four males, all armed with baseball bats. In their words, they were "going to beat the shit out of her" for making the rape claim against this individual.'

I can sense Colleen is dying to ask a question. I'm pretty sure I know what the question is too!

'But if she has been assessed under "rape protocol", she obviously has reported this to the police. Why aren't they doing something about it?'

'Fair point,' I reply. 'They have interviewed the suspect, and he claims the sex was consensual and of course, denies spiking her drink. Their view is, they have no proof he spiked her drink. The Rohypnol could have been in her blood for days. Apparently, it can be detected for up to a week.'

She butts in, 'But if, as you say, you have irrefutable proof, why don't the cops?'

I nod, acknowledging a good point. 'We have a copy of the nightclub's original CCTV footage. The copy the nightclub provided to the cops has been doctored. The scene showing the drink being spiked has been edited out. We also have copies of invoices showing the suspect receiving two shipments of Rohypnol in the last three months.'

'Shit.'

We are silent as she digests what I have told her.

'You mentioned four guys were going to beat her up. What happened?'

'We took care of them.' I give her a hard look, letting her know no further information was going to be forthcoming.

'Alright, how did you get the nightclub's original CCTV footage?'

Here, Suzie steps in and says, 'It was dropped off anonymously to my office on a USB. We have to assume someone wanted the right thing to be done but didn't want to go to the police.'

Colleen looks from Suzie to me and back again, obviously suspecting this isn't exactly the truth.

'What about these invoices you claim to have?'

'On the same USB stick,' deadpans Suzie.

'Okay, what do you have in mind?

I respond, 'Because the police do not have enough evidence to prosecute and the threats that have been made against the victim by the suspect's family, we thought you might like to do a podcast, highlighting the case and frankly the ineffective police investigation. You know, get it all out in the open, no innuendo, no vagueness. A public appeal to others who have dated this prick with maybe a suspicion of rape. We might be surprised how many come in. Each shipment of Rohypnol has enough for ten drink spikes, and now being on his second shipment, it is fair to assume he has spiked ten to fifteen girls' drinks.'

'Bloody hell. Who are we talking about?'

'This is in confidence, right?' I ask.

'Yes, no question,' she responds.

'Joel Flanigan.'

Colleen purses her lips. 'You mean the Brisbane Lion.'

I nod.

'Mmm, I see what you mean, "the next big thing" in AFL circles. I don't follow the sport, and I certainly know who he is. Who is the victim?'

I let Suzie answer, 'Her name is Tia Lomani. She too is an athlete and a member of the broader Australian Rugby Sevens training squad. She is very disciplined about what she puts into her body and is devastated by being both drugged and raped. She is also very determined that Flanagan doesn't continue to get away with what he is doing. As the police aren't going to prosecute him, she, we, believe this is a good way to put a stop to this arsehole.'

This is a strong word from Suzie, showing she too is incensed by what has happened.

I add, 'I have prepared a presentation to show you if you're interested?'

'Sure, absolutely,' is Colleen's reply.

I pull my laptop out of my satchel and plug it into the projector, so it shows on the screen at the end of the room.

This isn't a fancy PowerPoint, merely a collection of facts.

I start the show with a face shot of Tia, and another of Joel, taken from *The Courier Mail* a couple of weeks ago.

Then a timeline, starting back at the first drink spiking we uncovered from the Venu's CCTV footage, some nine weeks earlier. I add, 'The Venu nightclub is where the spiking took place. They tape over their files every three months, so nothing further back can be traced.'

We sit silently, letting the presentation play out. We included footage of the four guys with baseball bats and then all four lying on the ground injured. Neither Pig nor I feature, but we left the audio of the threats made by who, we later found out, was Peter Flanagan, Joel's father. No idea who the others are. Not relevant.

I had scanned Tia's police report and her statement to Suzie, so Colleen asked me to pause it whilst she read these through.

At the end, I show the timeline again, starting from the date of the first Rohypnol shipment, the first spiking of drink we found and including the one from the Ball and Chain and culminating with Tia's rape.

At the end of the show, Colleen asks, 'Can I keep this?'

'No, not yet,' I reply. 'We would like you to go back and discuss this with your powers that be and come up with a plan. Then we will need to have a legal agreement, agreed and signed before we hand over this and copies of all the information we have. Tia is happy to be interviewed by you as well but does want to remain anonymous. How does that sound?'

'Sounds fine to me, and I agree a podcast is the right platform to present this, with an appeal for any others that may have wondered if they had been drugged. I would expect we would advertise the podcast widely, gaining plenty of interest.'

I interrupt to say, 'We have a record of the dates he has gone to the Venu, Ball and Chain and Splendiferous, so we can quickly eliminate any gold diggers or publicity seekers.'

Colleen again. 'I will go back to the office and discuss all this with my editor and get back to you. Are you or Tia looking for payments for any of this?'

'No, certainly not. From Tia's point of view – and ours, I guess – we just want to see this arsehole stopped.'

'Good. Let me get going and I will come back to you in a few days so we can discuss any finer points. Obviously, our legal team will want to review the agreement.'

Suzie slides across a legal agreement she has prepared, saying, 'This is a draft of what I propose are minimum requirements to protect Tia and also our anonymous source. I will email this through to you when back in the office as well.'

Colleen gives me a smirk, clearly believing I am the anonymous source. I smile back.

We shake hands, with Colleen assuring us she will be back to us as soon as possible. She leaves with a purposeful stride, keen to get going, I suspect.

I take Suzie's hand and say, 'It's the end of the day. Why don't you shout your new source dinner here?' I smile sweetly.

Of course, she can't refuse, and we have an enjoyable early dinner at Motion Dining there at the Marriott.

CHAPTER 21

Next morning and Maria is all set to give Daniel Belgrave a call. She and Pig had sorted her sales pitch yesterday afternoon and she is all set.

I give her one of my prepaid phones to call from, not wanting him to know who is calling him or to able to trace the call back.

She dials.

'Daniel speaking,' is his answer.

I'm a little surprised he answers the call – many these days do not.

'Hi, Daniel, thanks for taking my call. I am sure you, like most of us, are keen to do your bit to de-carbon our environment.'

He butts in, 'What is it you are selling?'

'Sir, we have a season-ending special on our home solar power systems. You even get to sell any surplus power your system generates back to the grid, ensuring you an even better saving on your home power needs.'

Again, he butts in. 'Thank you but we already have a solar power system at home. But do you offer one for office complexes? That I would be interested in?'

'Sir, I don't have any information on our commercial systems in front of me. Perhaps I can call you back once I collate the information?'

'No, but if you can email through your brochure, I will review it.'

'I can certainly do that, Sir. What is your email address?'

Maria is smiling like a Cheshire cat having successfully got sufficient of his voice on tape, and now he is throwing in his email address to boot!

He relays his email address, which Maria dutifully writes down, assuring him he will see a brochure in the next few days.

She hangs up and we all high-five.

Good job!

As Hoang isn't in today, I send him an email asking him to set up a trace on Belgrave's email with filters to identify any suspicious emails, i.e. related to drugs or anything out of the ordinary. I surmise he would have a different email for any shifty business stuff but you never know, we might get lucky.

Pig now crops Maria's voice out of the audio and sends the recording of Daniel talking off to Midge.

Now we need to wait and see.

Patience, we have plenty.

Time for coffee!

Whilst we are waiting for both Colleen and now Midge to get back to us on these two separate investigations, Pig and I turn our attention back to Dicky and Mo, both associated with the Melbourne-based Red Skins bikie club. Dickie with his 'dark web' phone and using a voice synthesiser when talking to Deputy Warden Thomas and where these two individuals fit into the picture.

But first, we have a date in the Family Court.

Yes, Suzie is up against her nemesis Brownlow. Maria has proof that three other clients of his have been 'playing the system', i.e. understating their earnings and delaying their alimony payments.

The judge had warned him if he was found to have other clients rorting the system he may be found in contempt of court.

We (well, me, particularly) are keen to see how this pans out, having taken an instant dislike to the man over the disparaging way he treated Suzie.

Suzie's time to shine!

Like last time we come early but court is late starting, and again, like last time, Maria does an excellent job in detailing what Brownlow's client has been spending money on whilst remaining in arrears. There is no overseas holiday this time but a clear pattern of buying toys and gifts for new girlfriends, whilst neglecting his two kids.

The judge again reserves judgement and warns Brownlow that if he has any other clients following the same practice, he is to present them to court within seven days, with a plan for each of them to catch up on their alimony.

Suzie advises the judge she has two more clients whose former partners are represented by Brownlow, and she is ready to submit to the court with similar allegations.

Brownlow again looks daggers at her, getting my gander up!

With a bang of the gavel, the judge advises Brownlow he will rule on his contempt situation when announcing his decision in this case.

I'm happy with that!

Back in the office, I decide to review our audio from Deputy Warden Thomas's phone.

I know this will be a slow and arduous task, as his file includes all conversations, text messages and even all conversations he has had.

Hot coffee and in I plunge.

This takes the rest of the day and for little gain, so far at least.

Then just as we are packing up for the night, Pig's phone starts with some random tune neither of us recognises. 'Midge,' we say in unison.

Sure enough, he is ringing to say, yes, they have Belgrave's voice on file talking to some high-level members of the Garcia drug cartel and he is intrigued how we have come across him. We explain what brought him to our attention and that we suspect he may have been the one who killed Liz. And simply because she took a photo of her meal where he and a lady were in the background.

He gives us another warning about how dangerous the upper echelons of these drug cartels are and to remain vigilant. 'Yes, Midge,' we chorus.

Then just before he hangs up, he adds, 'Seeing as you now have at least two baddies using dark web phones, I have just sent you a link where you can download a new software app. This will enable you to track all phones triangulated by tower locations across the various networks, including dark web phones. This is brand new, hot off the press, so hope it helps you solve some of these issues you're having!'

'Awesome. Thanks, Midge,' I reply, beating Pig to the punch.

He hangs up and we look at each other, with Pig saying, 'Right, we can now trace Dicky and Belgrave! That makes it a lot simpler.'

Of course, we can't wait to try it, so Pig downloads the app and we both add it to our phones. I punch in Dicky's phone number.

We get the swirling symbol for a minute or two then we can see his phone – and therefore, we assume, Dicky – moving north along Brunswick Street in Fitzroy down in Melbourne. Bonus! We fist bump and Pig sets up a permanent tracking of Dicky's phone, so we will get locations where it stays put, i.e., his home and workplace.

We agree we will monitor him for a few days so we get a feel for his movements before making plans.

A big step forward. Thank goodness for technology, ah!

With Pig about to head home, I say, 'Belgrave being associated with the Garcia cartel is strange, considering everything we have learnt about him shows him as being a legitimate businessman. We need someone to try and trace the money somehow. You know, "follow the money, honey",' I say in a false voice, making Pig smile.

Pig replies, 'Yeah, quite strange. You mean like an accountant or something?'

'Yeah, I guess so. Maybe a forensic accountant. Someone expert in digging through all these financial records to get to the heart of his businesses. To my inexperienced eye, his company structures look complex. Maybe they are deliberately that way, to make it harder to find the truth about his business dealings.'

Pig, practical as ever, asks, 'Who?'

I shrug my shoulders, saying, 'No idea yet, but I'm sure we will think of someone or something. Maybe MGC has someone like that we can use.'

Pig makes a non-committal grunt (as pigs do!) as he closes the door behind him.

Over dinner, Suzie and I discuss Pig and Stacey's exciting news. It's a subject I'm a little anxious about, as Suzie and I are also keen to start a family. She has expressed her concern as she approaches forty, that she doesn't want to wait too long, as we have agreed we want to have two kids, so they always have company.

I add, 'You know, I'm always happy to increase our practising!' getting a smile from her.

We have been trying for a little while but have not got to the stage of going 'scientific' just yet.

CHAPTER 22

It's a few days later when Colleen calls.

'Hi, Colleen,' I answer.

'Hi, Mort. I have discussed the rape case with my editor and he, in turn, has discussed with our legal department, and whilst we are all keen, we do need to clarify some things. Would you be able to meet us, say, tomorrow at ten a.m.?'

'Let me check with Suzie. I don't know her schedule and I'll come back to you shortly. Where would you like to meet?'

'The Marriott again will be fine, as I'm sure you won't want to come here.' (I can sense her smiling as she says this.)

'No worries. Let me get back to you shortly. Bye.'

I tell Pig and Maria *The Courier Mail* are keen but want to clarify a few things. I wander into Suzie's office, where she is on the phone.

I sit on the corner of Jenny's desk and chat with her waiting for Suzie to finish.

'Hi. Colleen just rang, they are keen but the editor and their legal team have some questions. Are you available to meet them at the Marriott tomorrow at ten?'

She pulls up her Outlook calendar to check. 'Yes, I can rearrange a couple of things so that will be fine.'

'Okay, lock it in and I'll confirm.'

We smile at each other. Love, ah!

I call Colleen back and confirm that we can make ten in the morning. I also suggest she send through their queries so we can discuss internally before we meet. Should make the meeting shorter.

Colleen doesn't have my email, as I want to remain a 'man of mystery', so she promises to send their proposed changes back to Suzie.

A short time later, Suzie flicks me Colleen's email, noting the changes are primarily around legal aspects. Lawyers have to have their pissing contests!

Later in the afternoon as Pig and I watch where Dicky has been, I say to Pig, 'You know, I think Marg down at Paramount would be our best chance of finding a helpful accountant. But I don't want to ask her over the phone, so I might shoot down to Sydney later in the week and have a chat with her.'

Pig nods, saying, 'I don't know of anyone else. Only other option would be to check with MGC.'

'Okay, I'll have a look at flights.'

There is a knock on our front door. I glance at the CCTV to see who is there. 'Shit, it's Hannah!' I exclaim, ensuring everyone else looks as well. As I get up to go and open the door, Pig explains to Maria who Hannah is.

I open the door, welcoming her in and giving her a friendly hug, with Pig lined up behind me. Suzie has heard us talking and sticks her head out. Nosey, isn't she? When she sees who our visitor is, they too have a hug and she introduces Jenny, with Pig introducing Maria, explaining, 'Hannah is a US Secret Service Agent, part of their VIP protection team.'

Once the excitement winds down and we are all sitting around, I say, 'This is a nice surprise, Hannah. What brings you to little old Brisbane?'

She smiles, saying, 'I'm here as lead agent on our preliminary security assessment for the vice president's visit next year for the G7 summit.'

I'm, a little confused, saying, 'Hold on, we were told an Agent Nichols may be in touch?'

Hannah smiles, doing a mini bow. 'That's me!'

'Shit, sorry, I didn't make the connection, knowing Mary's name is Cutler, I guess I assumed yours was as well. Sorry.'

She again smiles. 'No problem. No, I have always kept my father's name. So here I am.'

'Cool. How long are you staying?'

'We arrived yesterday, got ourselves settled in, met with our liaisons with both Queensland Police and your federal police this morning. My colleague Travis fancies himself as a surfer, so he has headed down to the Gold Coast to "catch a wave".' She uses air quote marks as she says this. 'We fly home on Tuesday morning.' She pulls a face as she says this. 'It's such a long flight.'

Suzie smiles, saying, 'Yes, it is but I guess we are used to it. If we want to go anywhere, it's a long flight.'

Hannah follows Suzie into her office as they continue to chat.

A little later, I pop in and join them, suggesting, 'Why don't we have a BBQ on Sunday and I will invite my cousin Judy and her family. Uncle Albert's daughter. As your mum and Albert seem to be settling in for the long haul, what do you think?'

Hannah seems excited at the prospect so I say, 'Cool, I will give her a call and see if that suits them.'

I dig out Judy's number and give her a call.

'Hi, Mort. What's wrong? Has someone died? I haven't heard from you... well, must be years?'

I laugh, a little embarrassed, as it's true. Whilst Judy and I were quite close growing up, through my years in the army I didn't maintain contact. When Mum was alive, she kept me informed, but since then really only little titbits Dad had passed on. I did know she was married and had a little daughter a couple of years ago.

I was a little surprised I had her phone number in fact!

'Hi, Judy. Yes, I am not the best at staying in touch. How have you been?'

'All good here. Harry and I are going okay. Little Aubrey keeps us on our toes, I must say.'

'She must be, what, two now?' I ask, really just to let her know I was aware she had a daughter.

Judy laughs. 'No, three going on thirteen!'

I smile before saying, 'Judy, the reason I'm calling is, you know your dad's friend Mary?'

'Well, yes, I know who she is. I have spoken to her a couple of times on the phone but never met her,' she replies.

'Okay, I'm not sure if you know but we ran into your dad, Mary and her daughter Hannah a few months ago when we were in Washington, and, well, Hannah is here on business. So, we were thinking, maybe we get together for a BBQ on Sunday so you two can meet, and we can catch up as well.'

'Hell yes. That would be great. I'm dying to know what's going on with Dad and Mary. Will be good to catch up with you as well. You're engaged, aren't you?'

'Yes,' I say, smiling. I know I know, I should be long past the soppy stage but simply, I'm not!

'Cool. Let's make it eleven-thirty for a lunch barbie. I will text you our address. We are in Tingalpa.'

'Great, we live in Karalee, out Ipswich way. Hold on. I thought Dad told me Hannah was a secret agent or something?'

'Yes, she is a secret service agent. They provide security to the president and all-important dignitaries.'

'So how can she be here on business?'

I look at Hannah, who, along with Suzie, has been following the conversation. She nods so I continue, 'She is here leading a preliminary security review for next year's G7 summit here in Brisbane.'

'Wow, that's pretty cool. I'll have to ask her who the most famous person she has met. Cool, can't wait to meet her and catch up with you. Sorry, what is your fiancée's name? I don't think anyone told me that.'

'Suzie,' I say, smiling at her enthusiasm. Same old Judy, always up for some gossip!

'Okay, look forward to seeing you all on Sunday.'

We hang up.

I look around, most are watching me, amused at my apparent embarrassment.

'Done. Eleven-thirty Sunday for a barbie.'

'Cool,' says Hannah, looking at her watch. 'I have a Zoom meeting scheduled for four-thirty p.m., so I need to get going, but Mort, Julien, I do want to meet with you, ideally at the convention centre and Rydge's

Hotel to get your take on the planned security measures. Just so you know, you are listed as "high-level security advisers".' Again, she uses air quotes to emphasise what she's just said.

'That's how I got this gig actually. I told my bosses that I know you both and had met you in Washington. They were aware of some of your exploits, so were really impressed when I told them you had been to my home! Thanks, you got me a free trip to Australia!'

Pig and I smile, whilst Jenny looks a little perplexed, no doubt wondering what she means by 'our exploits'. I will let Suzie handle that one!

'Yeah, we can meet you tomorrow afternoon, say, two p.m. at Rydge's. Does that work?'

Pig nods, as does Hannah. 'Done, Travis will be with me. We are staying at Rydge's, so if I'm not in the lobby when you arrive, just ask at the desk.'

We shake hands, then we change our minds and make it hugs.

The next morning at ten finds Suzie and I sitting in our designated meeting room at the Marriott again, coffee pot full, as is my mug, when Colleen comes in, followed by her editor Chris and lawyer Ronald.

After introductions are out of the way and everyone's coffee cups are filled, Chris, the editor, takes charge.

'Mort, Suzie, we share your concern about how this young man seems to be getting away with drugging and potentially raping these young ladies. And how or why someone is covering up his actions. We believe the best way to present this would be a live presentation on our website – that is, a video podcast. This will enable us to show the video feed and documents, making a far greater impact than a conventional podcast.'

Yes, that makes sense, I suddenly realise and with Suzie giving me a sideways glance, I suspect she thinks so too.

'That said, we have to be very careful we don't make any claims we can't support with valid proof.'

Suzie takes over, having warned me to let her do the talking. 'We are happy to provide the full extent of our proof, Chris, once we have a watertight agreement in place. If you like, we can run through the presentation again with you now.'

Chris looks to Roland, who nods, so I plug my laptop into the projector and fire it up.

I take over, providing the commentary on the slides. At the end of the presentation, Roland asks, 'And you have these physical documents as well?'

I hand them over saying, 'These are copies, obviously.'

He studies these and gives Chris a nod.

He and Suzie then discuss the variations he wants to the agreement, mainly centred around *The Courier Mail* having exclusive rights to this story and Tia not being allowed to give or sell her story to any other publication. They also want total control over the editorial side of things along with how they market it. Suzie jumps in, demanding Tia and her are to be entitled to review and agree before it goes to air. They go to and fro on this for a bit, but it's clear Suzie has no intention of accepting anything less and they concede the point. Chris then explains that they may choose to not name Joel, as the mystery and intrigue will pique far more interest, and after the video podcast goes to air, the media pack will be on the hunt, thus intensifying interest in the story. He adds that he will let it slip that he is an AFL player so the Broncos and other sports will know they are in the clear.

Suzie confirms Tia has no interest in further publicity.

The two of them go back and forward for a few minutes on other minor points, all very amicable, so maybe I was doing Ronald a disservice thinking he would want a pissing contest!

After about ten minutes, Suzie says, 'Okay I'm happy with that. I will need to explain these changes to my client but I see no reason why she will not agree. If you send me the revised agreement, depending on Tia's movements, we should be able to have it signed and back to you by the end of the week.'

Nods all-round.

My turn.

'Assuming it is signed this week, what is the likely timeline from there?'

Colleen, who seems keen to take over now the legal stuff is sorted, comes back, 'I would want to sit down with Tia for a chat. I like to do this more as a chat rather than a formal interview, and we can even do it outside somewhere if that makes her more comfortable.' Then, looking at me, she says, 'Would you be interested in presenting the facts, Mort?'

I smile, thinking, *Nice try,* before saying, 'No, that isn't happening. You are welcome to use your own man or do it yourself. Happy to give further background, off-camera, though.'

She smiles at me, reinforcing my thought, she was simply teasing me.

Suzie then pipes up, saying, 'For the record, I will accompany Tia, so I can advise her if or when necessary.'

Again, this seems to have been assumed.

'Okay but back to my question – what is the timeline?'

'Oh, sorry, got sidetracked.' Colleen continues, 'If we can get the interview or chat out of the way early next week, we can do a little further backgrounding, start building some publicity and maybe release the video podcast Friday the following week.'

With nods all round, Chris gets up, shakes our hands and says, 'Awesome. An unpleasant situation but will be good to bring it out into the daylight. Thank you for bringing it to us.'

They leave. I look at my watch but before I can make a suggestion, Suzie takes my hand and says, 'No, I can't buy you lunch. I have a Teams meeting set up for twelve.'

'Oh, what about the room I booked for the afternoon? I thought different scenery might make the little buggers swim!'

Suzie smiles and squeezes my hand, not acknowledging my crude humour. 'Don't forget, you're meeting Hannah at two, so I wouldn't have had your attention for long.'

'Time for a quickie though,' I reply with a smile!

This time, she ignores me as she heads to the car park.

Whilst I hadn't booked a room and was only teasing her, it makes me think, *Maybe I should surprise her and take her away for a weekend. Yes, a good old-fashioned dirty weekend.* Now that does sound like a plan!

I have plenty of time before our two p.m. meeting with Hannah, so I head into M Bar café. Time to catch up on emails over a decent coffee.

Pig and I agreed to meet at Rydge's at one-thirty to chat first before meeting up with Hannah, but she's in the lobby when I walk in, putting an end to that. Then with Pig and Travis, we visit the rooms the 'Veep' will be staying in and the route they will take her to and from the conference centre where the G7 summit will take place. We make our comments and suggestions.

Next morning, I catch the six a.m. flight from Brisbane to Sydney, wanting to be in the café on the ground floor of Paramount's office building when Marg stops to collect her morning coffee.

The flight arrives on time and I jump in a taxi, so I'm confident I will beat her in, as long as she hasn't changed her routine, of course.

I get there, order two large long blacks and take them to a table where she won't be able to miss me when she comes in.

Fifteen minutes later, I see her come bustling in – a little late, I suspect – digging her purse out as she comes into the café. She glances my way and literally does a double-take!

I raise her coffee in a toast and she comes over, smiling, saying, 'Hi, Mort. Lovely surprise. Good to see you.'

As we have passed the handshake stage, I stand so we can have a little hug and say, 'Likewise, Marg. Good to see you, but you are a little late this morning.'

Her face shows shock but then she realises I am teasing her, and she punches my shoulder lightly.

'Do you have a few minutes?' I ask.

'Sure,' she says, glancing at her watch.

'I'll be brief,' I start. 'Marg, we are investigating a businessman, who, from all accounts, is a legitimate businessman. He certainly has some well-known businesses. But we know with absolute certainty that he has high-level connections with some of the world's largest drug cartels. We think the best way to prove this will be the old "follow the money" and of course, that is way beyond our capabilities.

'So, I'm hoping you might know of someone or an organisation who may be able to assist us. If they can, they will also be helping to remove the scourge of drugs off the street, as well as being involved in this high-level investigation. Do you know anyone that might be suitable and interested?' I finish with a large dose of hope.

She takes another sip of her coffee. 'You know, you might be lucky. A dear friend of mine has just gone through a nasty divorce. She was deputy head of KPMG's forensic accounting division. The trouble is her former husband is senior partner, so she had to resign. She is a little lost, to be honest. They never had kids and her work has always been her focus. This might just be the fillip she needs to get her life back on track. Would you like me to call her?'

'Yes, please, if you think she might be interested.'

She nods, takes her phone out, pulls up a name from favourites and dials, putting the call on speaker.

'What are you calling for at this god-awful hour?' comes what seems to be an older lady's voice after several rings.

'Diedes, are you sober?'

Great start, I think but Marg is smiling at me.

'Of course, I'm sober. It's still morning, isn't it?' comes the reply.

'I want you to meet someone. I'm sitting with him now. You will enjoy hearing what he has to say.'

'Is he good-looking?'

'Yes, he is.'

'Don't let him go and I've got first dibs on him then. See you in thirty minutes. Don't let him go! Oops, where are you?'

Marg, laughing, says, 'At the café in the lobby of our building. I'll hog-tie him to the table and meet you here in thirty minutes. Now hustle.'

Marg's face twitches as she recounts she and Diedre had gone through university together; she was an adult student and they had always got on like a house on fire. 'You will love her. But I need to go up to the office I have a short meeting then I will be back before the thirty minutes is up. Although I'll be surprised if she isn't late. Good seeing you, Mort, and if

Diedes is interested, it will be great for her to get her teeth into something again. See you shortly.' She touches me on the arm as she leaves.

As you know, I'm a patient guy and I'm in a café, so no shortage of coffee and sweet snacks.

I'm good!

It's thirty-five minutes later and Marg appears, grabs three long blacks and heads over to where I'm still sitting.

She hands me one of the coffees, flicking her hair off her face, saying, 'Diedes is just getting out of a taxi, so should be with us shortly.'

Sure enough, a shortish woman in her early fifties, I'm guessing, comes bustling in. She totally ignores Marg, making a beeline for me, and says, 'Whatever bullshit Mags has told you, ignore it. I'm Diedre but friends call me Diedes and you must be Mort. I recognise you from the way Mags used to describe you. She had the hots for you, you know!'

This elicits a 'Diedes!' from Marg.

I'm smiling, already liking Diedre.

'Hi, Diedre. Yes, I'm Mort,' I say and offer to shake her hand. She pushes my hand away and reaches up for a hug. As she is so short, I lean down to make the hug more comfortable for her.

'How nice of you, Mort. Now, what's all the rush about?'

Marg starts, 'Well, Mort surprised me this morning when I came in for my coffee and he has a proposition for you,' she says straight-faced.

I'm sure she deliberately used the word 'proposition' to tease Diedre.

'Ooh, a proposition. Do tell, Mort,' Diedre says.

I smile at them both, clearly very close friends. 'Diedre—'

She butts in immediately, saying, 'I said friends call me Diedes, Mort, and you already qualify, so please, no more Diedre!'

I bow my head in acknowledgement and say, 'Thank you, Diedes. I am honoured!'

'Now, what is this proposition you have for me?'

'I don't know how much Marg has told you about our work.'

She again butts in, saying, 'Work – she never speaks about your work. Other aspects about you, sure, but not work!'

Marg comes back, laughing, saying, 'Diedes, you're incorrigible.'

I start again, 'Well, we have a certain skill set that enables us to find information about companies and individuals. We currently have a target of an investigation who presents as a successful businessman. He has several well-known businesses up on the Gold Coast, but we also have irrefutable proof of him dealing with one of the world's largest drug cartels. We don't have the expertise to dig into his company structure or his finances. Knowing and respecting Marg from when we worked with her last year, I came down to see if she knew anyone who might be able to assist.'

'Well, you have come to the right place. Not only can I help, but I'm available for an immediate start. But I don't come cheap. I am highly skilled and need to be renumerated accordingly. But from what you have said, surely this is a matter for the police? They do have their own division of forensic accountants, even if they are mere plodders. If they paid better money, they would get far better results. Still, I can't change the world, but I am keen to help you.'

'This case is personal. For the record, we are affiliated with government law enforcement. You would be familiar with ACSC, the Australian Cyber Security Centre?' I ask.

'Sure. Never had any dealings with them but I know of them and what they do. Why?'

'Well, we work with them and contract to other sections of the government law enforcement services as well. I am just explaining this as background, wanting to assure you we are good guys!'

'I would never have doubted that, Mort. So, tell me what you want me to do.'

I pull up my satchel, extract a folder and place it on the table. 'Diedes, I need to ask you to sign this NDA, please. What we are going to talk about and some of the information you will learn cannot be shared with anyone.'

Here, Marg stands up, saying, 'Sounds like time for me to disappear, so I don't learn anything that might get me shot!'

I get up and give her a hug, saying, 'Thanks, Marg. I appreciate your help.'

'Go on, get lost. We have business to attend to,' is Diedre's off-hand reply.

Marg ignores her and adds, 'I almost forgot, how is Hoang doing? I hear he is working for you part-time?'

'Yes, and doing very well too. He's fitted in nicely and helping us out big time. He has another new app he has developed as well. Smart kid. Also, if you haven't seen him for a while, you would hardly recognise him. He has slimmed down big time – runs, lifts weights, lost all his baby fat. Done him the world of good and he has gained a lot of self-confidence too.'

'Oh, that is good news. No, I haven't seen him for ages.'

Diedes waves her off, saying, 'Get lost. I want to start work here.'

Marg shakes her head and waves as she heads back to her office.

Diedes has been reading through the NDA. She pulls a pen from her purse and signs with a flourish.

'Now, what's a girl got to do to get a coffee around here?'

I nod, get up and go and get two more large long blacks.

When I return, she has her laptop out and asks, 'Who will I be working for?'

I tell her, 'Our company is Digital Data Solutions, DDS for short.'

'Okay, I have your website up here. Very vague, isn't it?'

'Yes, deliberately so. But it does generate a good level of inquiry for legitimate work such as digital security checks and audits,' I reply.

'Money. How much an hour are you paying?'

'To be frank, I have no idea what a good forensic accountant is worth.'

She butts in, 'Good? I'm the best – awesome, not mere good. I would expect one hundred and fifty dollars per hour plus incidentals. I have an ABN so I can invoice you and you won't have to worry about pesky things like super, holiday pay, etc. Frankly, that's cheap. At KPMG, I charged out at five hundred and fifty dollars per hour.'

I reach out my hand and say, 'Deal.'

We shake and nod.

Done.

I look around at the crowded café and say, 'Diedes, is there somewhere we can go so we can talk in confidence?'

She looks at me before saying, 'Best place would be my apartment. You will be my first male visitor, so you better behave yourself!' She is smiling of course, and we both pack up and head out to the street. She quickly orders an Uber, and we get in and off we go to her apartment.

Once there, we set our laptops up on her dining table after she clears a pile of other documents and dirty dishes off it.

'Okay, first step. With your permission, I will have my colleague Pig log into–'

'You can't call someone Pig. That's not on.'

I look at her, somewhat surprised. 'That's his name. Well, nickname, I guess. He has always been called that.'

'Well, I'm not calling anyone Pig. I would be offended.'

I shrug. 'His real name is Julien. Feel free to call him that – he won't care.'

'Alright then.'

'As I was saying, I want Pig to log in to your laptop and set up a secure portal. It is crucial that you always log in through this portal, as otherwise, you might have nasty types banging on your door. This portal will make it impossible for anyone to trace you. We clear on this?

'In fact, I would encourage you to use this portal for all your internet, emails, everything as once you start moving in the murky world of the internet, you never know who you may attract.'

'Yes, I'm good with that. We had something similar at KPMG. What info do you need for him to log in?'

'He will send you a link to a website "Logmein" and then he will take it from there. What is your email address?'

She relays her email and I flick this to Pig who is online, no doubt listening to our chat.

A minute later, the Logmein logo appears on her screen. She follows the prompts and Pig does his thing.

He then puts up on her screen her address, something we had chatted about, as I want to ensure she fully understands how sophisticated hackers are these days.

She is suitably appalled and promises to only use the new portal we have established.

With Pig now able to hear the conversation, I introduce Deidre to Pig and she butts in, saying, 'I'm not going to call you Pig, so I will be calling you Julien. My friends call me Diedes, and you already qualify as a friend.'

'Call me whatever you like, but never late for breakfast,' Pig replies!

Pig then adds another portal inside the main one, through which he has already set up access to Belgrave's company's accounting system. He, like many smaller businesses, uses Xero as his accounting software.

'Good, I'm all over Xero,' claims Diedes.

I then explain that Belgrave has six businesses run through five different companies that we have traced so far.

'Cool. What is it you expect to find?'

'Well, as I said, whilst he appears as a solid upright citizen, we know he has high level dealings with the Garcia drug cartel in the states. We need to understand how and where the two scenarios fit together.'

'Alright. You also said this was personal?'

I pause here, having hoped to avoid the long story.

'Diedes, I am a fifteen-year vet. I – well, Pig and I – have some very specialised skills. Whilst we were on a mission in Afghanistan a few years ago, my wife was killed in a car accident in Brisbane. Something seemed fishy to me so when I cashed out, I started looking into it.

'So far, we can prove it wasn't an accident, someone had deliberately rammed her car, killing her. Thus, making it murder. Belgrave is our main suspect for her murder. As I said, we also have a strong association with law enforcement here and also in the USA and through those connections, we have identified Belgrave as being an associate of the Garcia drug cartel. We suspect he has other business interests, which aren't showing up in the usual ASIC searches. That's where we hope your expertise will help us. So, whilst this is a personal crusade currently, once we prove he is a drug lynchpin, or whatever, we will flip it over and be acting on behalf of the government.'

Quick as a flash, she comes back, 'Well, the government can pay me three hundred dollars per hour when we get to that stage.'

I smile, 'No worries I'll keep that in mind.'

Silence as she digests all this.

Pig pipes up, saying, 'Diedes, we have a saying here: "Mortice – Justice Mort Style". You will learn Mortice covers a wider range of justice than the law can provide.'

'Ooh, sounds exciting! Alrighty then, let's get started. But I must warn you, I work long and odd hours. I'm no nine to fiver. If I'm down a rabbit hole, I just keep burrowing, often working all night without noticing it. Will I be paid weekly?'

'Yes, send through your invoice on a Friday and you will be paid no later than Monday. How's that sound?'

'Good. Well off you go, I've got work to do. I'll send you a report each Friday as well, unless I find anything exciting, I'll likely want to share it with you when I find it. Might be better if you turn notifications off, otherwise I might wake you at some ungodly hour!'

I'm smiling as I pack my laptop up and get ready to leave.

Pig pipes up, saying, 'Looking forward to working with you, Diedes, and hopefully meeting you too.'

'Likewise, Julien.'

I'm now standing waiting to say goodbye, but she is already busy on her laptop, I lean over, wrap my arms around her shoulders and say, 'Now, don't forget, always use the portal, please.'

I get waved away. She is already immersed!

Ah well, mission accomplished. Back to the airport and home.

Next morning, I pull up the tracking of Dicky's phone down in Melbourne.

I Google Map the location where the phone spent the night and come up with an address on Victoria Street, Brunswick East.

Paste the address into another couple of databases and bingo, I have apartment B owned by one Richard David Wilkinson. AKA Dicky, a common abbreviation for Richard.

We have an identity.

More database searches give me his licence details (three speeding fines in the last three years), plus both a Harley Davidson Softail and an Audi Q5 registered in his name. I can't see if anyone else lives at the address and Google shows it as an old-fashioned six-pack apartment building. Nothing flash.

I share the info with Pig.

Next, I follow the phone as it moves through Melbourne, eventually coming to Fitness First on Burwood Road. Stays there just over an hour and then moves on to stop in a small car park at the rear of a strip mall on Toorak Road Camberwell. Not far from the Harwell Post Office. In another database search, I see shop three is home to RDW Realty. Bingo! After a few minutes, the phone moves across the road. I follow it on Google. It seems to visit The Cake and Pie Shop – maybe he has similar tastes to us! Assuming the phone is in his pocket, he is only there long enough to grab a coffee (and maybe a cake!) before settling back in the office of RDW.

I say to Pig, 'Looks like a quick visit to Melbourne is on the cards. I have his home, and now his office. Looks like he runs a small realty business called RDW Realty.'

'Original, isn't he?' is Pig's reply.

Then into ASIC's database, checking on who the owners and directors of RDW Realty are. This comes back to our mate Dicky as sole owner and director.

He is also listed as a director of one other business, 'Harwell Maintenance Services,' so I am guessing he subcontracts property maintenance to himself and therefore is double dipping on his clients!

I check out their website and whilst they do offer residential properties for sale, it seems their main focus is on property rental, claiming to have an 'extensive' rental roll.

I therefore surmise he will have a few staff.

As Hoang has just walked in, I flick the website and company details to him and ask if he can access their system and emails.

'Sure,' he says. 'No problem.'

Sure enough, only ten minutes later, he sends me a link into their system. It appears they use Hubspot as their CRM (Client Relationship Management system) and, phew, this integrates with Xero. We do at least understand the basics of Xero. They seem to have five personal emails, but then 'sales', 'maintenance' and 'rental' may have more than one user. Time will tell. In reality, we are only interested in Dicky anyway. I'm quickly into their Xero file and a check of the payroll confirms a total of eight. However, four of these are causals. I run a Profit and Loss statement for the last three months, and he seems to be doing okay. I check the revenue lines, looking for any potential 'other' income. No sizable amounts.

A quick check of the electoral roll for Brunswick doesn't bring up any other official residents of Dicky's address. Don't worry, I don't need to do this search manually – we have access to a sophisticated search program. You simply input the name or address and poof, out spits the answer!

Technology, don't you just love it?

It is a bugger we can't access his callers but I plan on rectifying that on a quick trip to Melbourne in a week or so, once we have an understanding of his routine.

CHAPTER 23

It's Friday afternoon. My phone rings; it's Diedes. I answer it.

'Hi, Diedes. How are you going?'

'Well, Mort, I have been busy, so thought I would give you a call with my first report. Of course, I will detail it by email and send through with my invoice, but I have been a busy girl. I think you will be amazed at what I have achieved so far. I am!'

Clearly impressed with herself!

'Great, let me get Pig on the line as well.'

Pig has heard one side of the conversation and is already reaching for his phone. I add him to the call.

Once they have said their hellos, Diedes gets underway.

'As I said, Mort, you are going to be blown away by what I have dug up so far. Mind you, I haven't had much sleep; I've been having some much fun!' She takes a big breath and starts, 'Okay, you have already got all his legitimate businesses, so we will leave those aside for now. What is exciting is that he has another five businesses he is at least involved with on what I'm calling his Darkside!

'Through a few aliases, he is partners in three nightclubs: Venu in Brisbane.'

(This makes Pig and I raise our eyebrows as we look at each other.)

'Club460 on the Gold Coast and Mr Shyster in Sydney. He also has a small shipping agency – you know freight forwarder and interestingly, a used equipment and machinery business based in Archerfield there in Brisbane. Now, these five businesses are owned through various cutouts. His name does not appear anywhere. The three nightclubs each have different partners who are all the face of the nightclub, and his ownership is hidden deep, and I mean deep. Only someone as awesome as me would have cracked it open!'

I smile and glance at Pig and I suspect he, like me, finds her being so full of herself endearing not obnoxious.

She continues, 'The Venu is fifty per cent owned through his sister in her first married name. Olivia Donnolly. Club460 is actually owned by him in an alias, "Joseph Temple", and the third through a cousin, "Tim Brown". He again owns fifty per cent of these two nightclubs.

'Another alias, "Albert Temple", owns the shipping agency – called "Wacol Shipping P/L", for the record. I've got to tell you, I was a bit lucky to capture this one as it was only one document that, I suspect, used the shipping company's address accidentally, as its own, that flagged it to me. The used equipment business is owned by a third alias Murray Ball. It's called "EDA Used Equipment P/L". I have no idea what EDA stands for!

'Now, whilst I am confident these three aliases are correct, I thought you, with your broader hacking skills, would be able to prove them, as he must have licences, passports, credit cards, et cetera, in all three names to be able to open bank accounts and the like. By the way, all of his dark side businesses bank with NAB at Southport, so I suspect someone there must be on his payroll.'

'Wow, Diedes, I am impressed. That is a huge amount of info in only three days. Imagine how much you will have for us after a full week!'

This gets a snort from Diedes, as intended. Pig adds, 'I agree, Diedes. What about company accounts and bank accounts?'

'Yes, I'm getting to that. Obviously, I can't access their bank accounts, but they use Xero for all their company accounts. Interestingly, to me at least, is that all their accounts and tax returns are completed in-house, so no third-party accounting firm is involved. A Pedro Gomes is the accountant who signs all their accounts and tax returns. I have checked him out through LinkedIn and CPA – Certified Practising Accountant. He arrived from Brazil six years ago and has only worked for Belgrave, it seems. Lives at Sovereign Island there on the Gold Coast. Sorry, I forgot to mention, above all these six businesses sits a discretionary trust, with the third alias, "Murray Ball", as trustee. A bit of random info, Murray Ball is a New Zealand author, so no idea if there is any connection there. If I add up all the money in the various businesses' bank accounts, there is currently over twelve million dollars.'

'Shit!' 'Fuck'! are Pig and my responses to this number.

'Yes, a significant number. It remains fairly stable, except for when they buy used equipment, excavators, graders, big drum roller thingies – you know, machines they use to make roads. These do seem quite expensive and the overall balance dips. But in most cases, they seem to sell these machines quickly, although they do buy used machines locally as well. I have also identified regular payments to someone, or something, called JAMD.

'These go out quarterly to a bank account in the Cook Islands, which is a recognised offshore tax haven. It's also difficult to get account holder information back from their authorities.'

Silence as Pig and I absorb all this data.

Pig has the first question. 'Where do the excavators and machines they buy overseas come from?' he asks.

I look at him and nod. *Good point.*

I can hear her mouse scrolling before she comes back. 'They mostly seem to come from America but interestingly, they all get trans-shipped in Panama.'

'Why is that interesting?' I ask.

'Most shipments out of America ship direct from US ports, Galveston in Texas, Long Beach in California being the main two. I know this because my brother has an equipment hire business and I help him out sometimes with the financing of this equipment whilst its being shipped.'

'Panama is close to Columbia. It's also one of the biggest trans-shipping ports in the world,' I state, getting a smile and nod from Pig.

'Why is that relevant?' Diedes asks.

'The whole point of these fronts has to be to hide what he is really doing: importing and distributing drugs. And then laundering all the ill-gotten dollars through the nightclubs and other businesses,' I advise.

'Oh. I see. Gee, all this deceit just to hide their ill-gotten gains!'

'Diedes,' I start, 'is there any evidence of large amounts of cash being funnelled through any of the nightclubs, or, in fact, his legitimate businesses such as the jetboat tours and cruises?'

'Okay, I will put that on my list for next week, as I haven't looked at things from that angle. But I guess I need to.'

Ending the call, I get up and make Pig and me a fresh coffee and tea for Maria. With a nod of my head, I invite her over to my desk to join in.

'Okay, clearly, we have a tiger by the tail here. This looks like a serious operation. We will need to report it to MGC and no doubt, he will decide whether we pursue it or hand it over to the AFP or Border Force. It's interesting that the excavators and stuff come through Panama, not directly out of the USA. Reminds me of what Lawrence said about cutting open that big cylinder.'

Pig nods in agreement.

'We might have a look-see at this Wacol Shipping, see if we can dig past the final Bill of Lading and other documentation.'

'Okay, I'll have a look into that,' says Pig. 'Maybe we wait until I see what I can find before we report to MGC.

Another nod confirms this.

Pig then adds, 'I'll ask Diedes for the details of this bank in the Cook Islands. Maybe their security isn't too tight.'

'Good idea,' I say.

* * *

Our Sunday BBQ goes well, with Judy and Hannah both keenly quizzing each other on their respective parents. We also meet Harry, Judy's husband, and their daughter Aubrey, who, let's say, is rather reserved in her interactions with me. She's content to sit on her mother's knee, watching me with her big brown eyes!

Suzie is a different matter, happily taking her hand and wandering around the garden. Suzie says later, 'She simply has good taste!'

Judy also makes it clear she would be happy to represent her side of the family at our wedding! She is never backward in chasing anything she wants!

CHAPTER 24

It's Tuesday evening and, once again, I'm designated cook! I'm not concocting anything special, just using the microwave when Suzie comes in, having been overseeing Tia's interview for the podcast.

After getting changed and joining me at the dinner table, she explains, 'It's quite fascinating watching how the podcast is recorded. Basically, Colleen asks questions and Tia answers them. It's so obvious how keen she is to make the Sevens team for the Olympics. She came across with plenty of passion. Mind you, she was just as forceful about Joel's actions as well. I think it is going to create quite a stir when it's released on Friday. As you know, they started promoting it today and, judging by the reactions, not naming Joel will create much more attention.'

'Great, how did Tia hold up?'

'Pretty well, really. She did tear up when confronted by the tape showing him spiking her drink, so that certainly added to the story. They are also going to highlight the other dates and locations you identified as potentially drink spiking. Hopefully, other ladies will come forward for those dates as well. The cops aren't going to like it either – your investigation makes them look like rank amateurs!'

'Good. I'm keen to watch it on Friday. What time is the launch?'

'Two p.m.'

'Good-o.'

* * *

Having completed my report into Darren Belgrave and his hidden drug empire, I ask Pig to review it before I send it on to MGC.

Pig has not yet been able to access Capital Security Bank Ltd in the Cook Islands. He has asked Midge if he can confirm bank balance and any other names or entities that may be connected to Belgrave's accounts there.

In summary, we can confirm:
- He is the male identified from Liz's phone from the photo of her meal.
- He had the capacity to put together a hit on Liz in only six weeks.
- He likely drove Benson's car, which killed Liz.
- He's a proven close associate of Lancasters.
- Through various entities (companies, trusts, etc), he has six tourism related businesses on Gold Coast and Brisbane.
- On his 'dark side', he has interests in five more businesses: three night clubs, a shipping company and a used machinery business.
- He has twelve million in his various connected bank accounts.

As yet, we don't have any evidence of wrongdoing for any of the eleven businesses he has interests in.

But we are only just starting!

He is married with two children who attend All Saints College on the Gold Coast and lives in Mudgerabah in the Gold Coast hinterland.

He has a small office on Thomas Drive, Surfers Paradise, which a Google Map search shows is actually on Chevron Island.

Midge has provided audio of Belgrave talking to a high-ranking member of the Garcia Cartel.

If MGC instructs us to keep digging, our next steps will be to:
- Check out the shipping company and used equipment business and see if these are legitimate businesses or mere fronts for his drug importation business.
- Monitor his movement whilst his phone is on the dark web, through the new software patch Midge provided.
- Access his phone so we can hear what he is saying.
- Get to know his connections, both social and business.
- Quickly check into the shipment of two 40Tonne excavators currently on the water with an ETA in eight weeks' time.
- Familiarise ourselves with his routine. Being able to track his

movements by his phone is fine, but it does not help us identify who he meets and who he may be doing business with.

To date, there has been little consistency to his days except he always leaves home around six-thirty a.m. to visit Snap Fitness in Robina. He leaves there before eight and then either goes to his office or heads to various locations, often a café. Who he meets there remains a mystery.

Pig suggests a couple of changes, which I make, and off it goes to MGC. No doubt we will hear from him when he wants to discuss next steps.

It is only a couple of hours later an invite to a Pexip call with Robert and MGC comes through for Monday morning. We accept.

CHAPTER 25

It's Friday afternoon and we are all sitting around Pig's computer, waiting for Tia's video podcast to start.

Tia, her aunt Alitia and Suzie are at the offices of *The Courier Mail* – invited to sit and watch the live presentation of Colleen's video podcast.

I must say it is well presented and snappy. Joel's face is blanked out (as are others that may be too close to the camera). They have also altered Tia's voice digitally, so it is not recognisable as hers.

They replay the various footage of the drink spiking, even showing it in slo-mo to ensure everyone can see the Rohypnol being poured into the glass. Again, they blank out the name and address on the invoices for the Rohypnol, and these are very damaging.

At the end, we high-five all round, pretty pleased with the outcome.

Suzie, Tia and Alitia come in on a high, having watched the live launch of the podcast. Suzie says, 'They are pretty pumped at the size of the initial audience and will keep us posted on what the audience peaks at.'

A little later, Suzie comes out of her office to tell us, 'Colleen just called. A lady has contacted them, claiming she believes she was drugged at Venu on one of the dates we showed in the podcast. She claimed she then woke up the next morning in Joel Flanagan's bed. Doesn't remember anything in between. Colleen hasn't let on it's the same aggressor.

'She also said the police sex crimes squad have been in touch, demanding a meeting and all the data they have available. We've said that will be handled by our legal team, as we respect totally the privacy of our sources. We won't be giving you up, don't worry.'

Tia then comes to each of us in turn, giving us all a hug and thanking us all for helping her move on.

Good to finish the week on a high!

Pig and I go out into our little gym. Time for one of our regular sparring sessions, where we basically try and beat the shit out of each other but only from the shoulders to the hips, ensuring our cores remain strong and tough.

Afterward, we crack a beer each and simply chat and chill. Suddenly, I remember something I keep forgetting to ask him. 'Mate, how did you get on tracing Stacey's mum and her arsehole stepdad?'

He takes a sip of his beer (XXXX, like all good Queenslanders!), saying, 'Stace wasn't keen to know anything about them, so I haven't told her, but the arsehole is in prison in NSW for exactly what he did to Stacey. He was caught, arrested and charged, basically the same set up as with Stace and her mum. He moved in with a single mother and systematically went about abusing her daughter. The mother caught him in the act, nearly killed him with a carving knife. He got a non-parole sentence of ten years. Still two to go.'

I nod in the silence, sensing there is more to come.

'Stacey's mum lives down at South Tweed Heads. Works in aged care down there. Seems she moved up there not long after Stacey ran away.'

'Well done, mate. She's not far away if Stacey ever changes her mind.'

'No, that's what I reckon,' he finishes, swallows the last of his beer and gets in the shower.

Whilst he is in the shower, his phone rings. Keith Urban again; this time, it's *Tonight I Wanna Cry.*

Pig yells from the shower, 'You better grab that.'

I do. 'Hi, Midge. Pig's in the shower. Anything exciting?'

'Ho, Mort. Yes, more sad than exciting. We have finally tracked Dwight Brown down. Sadly, he is in an Afghan refugee camp in Pakistan with eight of his Afghan contacts, near the town of Quetta, in Baluchistan Province. It isn't an official UN camp, more a collection of tents and shanties in a field. They are stranded. Dwight is in a bad way. Apparently, he's struggling with an upper respiratory tract infection. Of course, only minimal medical facilities there. Many of his companions are in a similar condition. Poor nutrition and limited fresh water only exacerbate their condition.'

Pig has stepped out of the shower to listen. We share a look. I say, 'We can't leave him there. He is one of the original good guys.'

After a moment's silence, Midge says, 'I was hoping you would say that.'

We pause the conversation so Pig can get changed. I grab two more beers; we are going to need them.

We then discuss how and when a rescue mission can be mounted.

* * *

I watch the news on Saturday night to see what fallout there has been to the podcast.

As I get up to grab a beer, they are showing the Premier fronting the media about why the police have not acted on the evidence presented in the podcast. Standing off to one side is Mel Black, the police commissioner, watching the Premier side-on, so she is sideways to the camera.

Shit.

I freeze the image, grab my iPad and pull up the photo from Rick Shores.

Bingo!

We have a match.

Shit, Mel Black, the police commissioner, is the lady in the photo. Wearing a wig and glasses, but no doubt in my mind.

Bloody hell.

I quickly flick both images to Pig, asking, 'What u reckon?'

He rings me straight away.

'That's a match. One hundred per cent,' he says by way of greeting.

'Bloody hell. Here we have our police commissioner socialising with someone who we can now claim is a high-level drug dealer and criminal.'

I reply, 'The way she is looking at him looks far more than mere socialising. We need to find their connection. And fast! We are going to have to digest this. It certainly adds a new dimension to our investigation.'

* * *

It's Monday morning. Pig comes in late. Stacey is struggling with morning sickness, and with neither having any family, it is just the two of them. Mind you, not much I can do other than offer some sympathy!

Maria isn't giving Pig an inch, ensuring he is looking after Stacey and of course, both Suzie and Maria pop over to see her, so she knows she isn't alone.

We get stuck into trying to understand the relationship between Daniel Belgrave and Mel Black.

I check their place of birth: he's from Sydney and Mel, right here in Brisbane.

Universities next.

Bingo.

It looks like they both went to Griffith University here in Brisbane. Different courses, but their time there overlaps for three years. Daniel apparently moved to Brisbane for his high school years, having attended Brisbane Boys High School, with Mel attending Mount Maria College on the northside.

Oh dear.

I quickly update our report for MGC with this latest titbit.

At the appointed hour, we don our headphones and log in to Pexip.

MGC is front and centre. 'Boys, you seem to have a knack for digging in the right spots, don't you? A random photo and you dig in and find another nasty mess.'

Here I butt in, saying, 'Sir, not sure if you have seen the little update I sent you an hour ago. We have identified the women in the photo as Mel Black, Queensland's Police Commissioner. It appears they went to uni together.'

'Well, well, the plot thickens. The look on her face is more endearing than mere friends, which raises my level of concern significantly.'

Silence as he ponders next steps.

After a few minutes, he comes back, 'Very well, boys. I was going to have you continue digging into Mr Belgrave, and this only reinforces that position. With your police commissioner likely compromised, there is no way I can put this through official channels now. Are you comfortable pursuing Mr Belgrave, and now, seeing where Commissioner Black fits in?'

Pig and I nod and reach over and fist bump.

'Yes, Sir. We can handle that.'

'Very well then. Weekly updates, please, unless something breaks, and you can let me know immediately. Also, I am curious how you got so much corporate detail; I did not know you had that level of expertise?'

I laugh and say, 'We don't, Sir. I have contracted a very resourceful forensic accountant, just left KPMG. What we have is only three days' work. Her fees will be an add-on, Sir, at three hundred and fifty dollars per hour.'

'Mmm, best keep her efforts to a minimum at that rate then,' MGC replies.

'Sir, she tells me her charge out rate at KPMG was five hundred and fifty dollars per hour, as a reference point.'

'Mmm, maybe not too bad then. It just seems a lot to pay an accountant. Keep me posted, please.'

We hang up and Pig says, 'I thought Diedes wanted three hundred per hour for official work?'

I nod. 'That's right.' And seeing the puzzled look on Pig's face, I say, 'Well, we have to pay her weekly, cover overheads, and the like, so we need to charge her out for more to cover our additional costs.' I add with a smile, 'I run a business, not a charity!'

Time to make a plan.

'Okay, Maria, can you come over? We need to make a plan around Belgrave.'

'Sure.' She wheels across, 'accidentally' banging into Pig's chair as she does. He pushes her away. Childish, aren't they!

'Alrighty then. We need to split up the functions we need to cover. We need to check out his home and office, to see how or if we can place mics anywhere appropriate. Maria, it's time you learnt some of the skills needed for following real people. When we get back, I will get down there before he leaves home in the morning and then you can meet me at Snap Fitness at Robina, say, by seven-thirty a.m.?'

'Sure, I can manage that. Mum can take the kids to school.'

'Ideally, we need a mic in his car too. That's a point. We don't know what car or cars he drives. None are registered in his name. They must be in one of the companies. I'm sure there will be at least two: one for him and one for his wife. Maybe more. Let's have Hoang dig the car details up when he arrives.'

Pig responds, 'Okay I'll get him sorted.'

'Pig, why don't you focus on the shipping company and the equipment business? See what you can find on these, both digitally and physically.'

'On it,' he replies.

Plans made. As I won't be tailing him until after we get back from Pakistan, I review other projects I have on the go.

Then, a headline from *The Courier Mail* pops up that grabs my attention. The headline reads, 'Brisbane Lion takes time off for family reasons.'

I click through and yes, it looks like Joel Flanagan has wilted under the pressure and has been given time off. The media are already putting two and two together, trying to ask him if the police have interviewed him on possible rape charges. He runs away from the media pack, jumps in his Tesla and roars off. Leaving more questions than answers.

I wander in to tell Suzie and at the end, she puts her fist out for a fist bump. Cheeky, isn't she!

She then adds that Colleen had sent her an email saying she had been summoned by their legal team to a meeting with the sex crimes unit, who were demanding to know where they got their information. They have only said from a 'confidential source.' Apparently, the police let slip that they are threatening the manager of the Venu with obstruction of justice over the doctoring of the CCTV footage, but he is playing dumb.

Later in the afternoon, there is a knock on the door and there is Tia, loaded down with coffee for everyone.

She hands them out, saying, 'I can't thank you all enough for helping me through this. I made all these coffees myself – I work at Zarraffa's. Hopefully, they haven't gone too cold on the drive over. I'm so pleased – it now looks like he is going to be charged. The police have told me they now believe they do have enough evidence to charge him and also that one other rape victim – sorry, 'alleged' rape victim – has come forward as well. So, with any luck, he will go down for a good stretch.'

When she gets to Hoang, she says, 'Sorry, I didn't know what you drink so I bought you an iced coffee.'

'Cool, thanks,' he replies.

Tia then seems to settle down, clearly not in a hurry to leave, asking questions about what we were all doing. Of course, we have to be circumspect in our answers!

She does say to me, 'Aunty M says you were a top rugby player when you were young.'

I smile – it seems so long ago – before replying, 'Yes, I captained Ipswich Boys Grammar in the GPS competition in my last year at school. Played in plenty of rep teams in both league and union.'

'What position?' she asks.

'Number eight in rugby. Was even selected as a non-travelling reserve for the 2005 Australian Schoolboy Rugby team.'

'Really, that's way cool!' she exclaims.

I think, *That's nice*. It's been a long time since anyone mentioned my sporting prowess. After all my years in the army, I have lost interest and don't really follow any of the teams.

I continue, 'Yes, you will recognise the name of the player who kept me out of the touring team. He went on to become a distinguished wallaby.'

'Who – come on, you have to tell me now!' she exclaims.

I smile, enjoying the enthusiasm she brings.

'David Pocock. Remember him?'

'Hell, yes. He was an awesome player. Some politician now, I think.'

I nod in agreement.

* * *

When it quietens down, Pig and I sit down to recap our plans to rescue Dwight from the refugee camp in Pakistan. We are headed there tomorrow.

CHAPTER 26

Two weeks later, we are safely back from Pakistan and I'm sitting outside Clover Hill School before six a.m. Belgrave has to go past me after he leaves his home in Glenny Street Mudgeeraba, as this is the only road in and out.

At least I don't stand out parked in his street. I'm in the van, so just another tradie to most people.

Shortly after six a.m., I recognise him as he drives past in a black Mercedes GLE, the big SUV. I have positioned the van so the dashcam picks up the number plate, making it easier to confirm ownership if need be.

Knowing where he is going makes it pretty simple to follow him and as I ease down to the lights on Somerset Drive, he is still waiting to turn right. That's cool; there is another car between us.

The lights change and off he goes, following Somerset Drive across the M1 and into Robina. Then he turns right and into the car park at Snap Fitness. I keep going, taking the next left, then left again and into the Robina town centre car park. I go inside looking for a coffee, and there right in front of me is Crafted Coffee. Coffee sorted!

I wander back out and stroll over to the Snap Fitness car park. His Mercedes is parked a little way away. *Maybe he doesn't want anyone else parking next to him and dinging his vehicle,* I muse. Keeping an eye out for anyone else wandering around or taking an interest in me, I stroll in the general direction of his car, then step back onto the footpath and walk up the block. At the roundabout, I turn around and this time as I approach his vehicle, with no one around, I slip a little tracker onto the rear bumper. That will make the job easier of following him and tracking him. I head back to the van and text Maria to meet me there, not outside Snap.

Maria turns up nice and early so I ask her to follow Belgrave, and as we now have a tracker on his car, she can do this remotely – she won't need to keep him in sight. Me, I'm going back to see when his wife and kids leave the house. Dead keen to place a mic in his home office – of course, I don't know he has one but long odds he does.

Five minutes later, I am parked on Glenny Street, a few houses past Belgrave's home. At eight-fifteen a.m., another Mercedes GLE backs out of their garage, this one white. So matching cars but different colours. It is too dangerous to try and break in without further research, and the easiest way to see comings and goings from their home is to monitor it for a few days. So, I pull the van up at the closest streetlight to their home, pull the ladder off the roof and go about my business. I'm quickly up the ladder, fiddling with the bulb so it looks like I'm testing it, all the while affixing a small camera to the top of the light, directed at their driveway. I check the vision on my iPad, adjust it a little and we are good to go.

Down the ladder, remove the ladder, affix the ladder (sounds like an old nursery rhyme, doesn't it!) and I'm out of there.

I log it in and let Pig know.

Maria has texted me, saying they are on the move, currently heading down Bundall Road, heading to his office is my guess. As there is no hurry, I swing by Crafted Coffee and grab another one! Good coffee!

The day doesn't get any better. Once in his office, he stays put except to head out to a nearby café to grab some lunch. How do I know that? Easy, Maria and I had set up camp at the same café, Café Alfons, just across the road! When we saw him coming, I quickly exited around the corner so I wouldn't be noticed.

Maria tells me he hardly glanced up from his phone the whole time he was in the café anyway.

Over the ensuing days, his routine rarely changes, except for the occasional café meeting, and normally at Café Alfons. Keeping a loose watch on him has enabled us to identify some of his contacts. As we had put a CCTV camera up covering the lift access on his floor, we have a clear vision of all that comes and goes.

He seems to have a small admin team of six working from the office, including Pedro Gomes, the accountant Diedes identified.

No one that we deem suspicious at all has come and gone. We have also accessed (we don't hack, remember!) his emails, but these only pertain to his legit businesses. Clearly, he has some dark web or encrypted email addresses we have yet to identify. We have asked Midge for help tracing his dark web emails.

As part of his response, Midge shares a new tech toy with us. This is an app for our phones that will remotely unlock car doors. It apparently scans the radio frequencies of any car door within two metres, identifies the radio frequency used to connect the fob with the door mechanism and with the push of a button, the door unlocks. To then relock, you press the button again. Cool!

Tomorrow, I will use this to unlock Belgrave's GLE and place a mic, one of the mini spiders that have worked so well, in his car. He parks in an underground car park, which I will need to check out, with one of Pig's drones. Likely one of the older ones as he is rather possessive of his drones!

Pig and I decide we need to go one step further and place a camera and bug in his office, so we can hear his conversations and see his computer screen, thus seeing what he may be writing in emails.

Always more than one way to skin a cat!

As Maria isn't up for this type of work, I'm it.

No worries, I wait until the office is empty and fortunately, there doesn't appear to be any CCTV on the outside of the building.

Or in the underground car park, I find, when the next evening I send in one of the smaller drones to have a look-see. I had flown this in in the afternoon as a car was entering, as there is a roller door limiting access. I had hovered the drone on top of the car, so we're able to record his access code when he punches it to open the door. Clever, aren't we!

Again, no CCTV down here either, so I leave the drone hovering in a corner and bring it out when the next car comes out.

Around seven p.m. that evening, when the car park is empty, I drive the Camry (which fits into the scene better than either the van or Prado!), use the access code and gain access.

Over to the lifts and up I go to level three. I have equipped myself with a portable vacuum and bucket with spray bottles, and a short ladder, just in case I do come across someone.

Out of the lift, I check for CCTV. No, all clear. A quick fiddle with the door lock and I'm in.

I set the ladder up under the light, covering the reception desk, and quickly install a combo mic and camera.

Then I'm into what is clearly Belgrave's office. It is far bigger than the others with plush furnishings. Here, I again install the combo, positioned so we can film his computer screen – he uses two, plus his keyboard so I had to ensure the angle is just right. Pig, who is monitoring me online, gives me a grunt in confirmation.

Then I quickly identify the office of the accountant Pedro Gomes, placing a combo unit in his office, again positioned so we can see both his screens and keyboard.

Done and dusted.

I close and lock the office door, press the down button and the lift doors open. Clearly the lift had not moved whilst I was busy.

Exiting the car park is just as easy with an auto sensor taking the door up as I approach.

Home for a late dinner!

And what a shock when I get home. I had texted Suzie as I was leaving the Gold Coast and I walk in to a nicely set dinner table, candles and all. Suzie has also changed into a lovely dress and here I am in my casual work gear.

She greets me with a hug and kiss and I ask her, 'Do I need to get changed to keep the mood?'

'No, silly, you are fine the way you are.' With another quick kiss, she is off to the kitchen to finish serving up our dinner. There is even wine poured!

Oh, oh, she must have spent a lot of money, I'm thinking!

Once we are both seated and have toasted each other, I say, 'So, how much have you spent?' Of course, I'm smiling as I say it.

Suzie laughs but does seem a little nervous.

Curious.

After we have both eaten our meals, chatting away as always when we sit down for dinner, Suzie reaches over, takes my hand and says, 'Mort, you know I love you dearly.' To which I nod, thinking, *Where is this going?*

'Well, I don't want to wait until next year to become your wife. I am keen to tie the knot sooner rather than later. We have checked and The Loft can fit us in in eight weeks' time. It will be a Wednesday wedding but Mum, Nat and I can formalise everything by then, and I'm sure you don't mind what day of the week we get married. So, what do you say? Is that okay?'

I keep a straight face and say, 'Oh, that's a bit of a shock. Can I think about it?'

Suzie looks at me seriously for a moment, then laughing, she gently punches my shoulder, saying, 'No, you can't. You are locked in – no reneging now!'

I get out of my chair, lifting Suzie out of hers, and we kiss. I whisper, 'Love to have you as my wife as soon as possible. Happy to go to the registry office tomorrow!'

We are now in a full embrace, and we start for the bedroom. The dishes will have to wait until morning!

CHAPTER 27

Next morning, I don't say anything to Pig about the change of wedding plans, being under strict instructions that Suzie will ask him when she comes down.

This she does, asking Pig, 'Julien, Mort and I are now going to get married in eight weeks' time, on a Wednesday. Will this suit you for your best man duties?'

He looks at me with a smile and says, 'So is there another announcement you need to make?'

I laugh, saying to Suzie, 'See, I told you everyone is going to assume you're pregnant!'

She turns to Pig and says, 'No, I'm not pregnant. I just want to get it over and done with.'

'Sure, I'm delighted to rearrange my social calendar for such a great occasion! Can I let Stacey know?'

'Well, yes, of course. Official invites are already at the printers, so they will be posted within the week.'

I can't resist. 'So, you were taking my acceptance for granted were you, missy?' I advance on her as I say this, lean down and give her a kiss, just as the front door opens and Jenny walks in.

'Hi. What's going on here? Public displays of affection aren't acceptable in a lawyer's office!' She then looks to Suzie and says, 'You finally asked him, ah?'

Suzie smiles and nods.

'And he accepted.'

Okay, we've had a fun start to the day, but back to business.

I make coffee for Pig and me and we convene at my desk. I pull up the video from Belgrave's office and see he is in there, as is Gomes, the accountant.

We agree we will share the coverage of Gomes with Diedes just in case it helps her with her ongoing digging. Also, whilst Pig and I will monitor Belgrave's office, we decide to have Hoang monitor it more closely and flag anything he thinks is suspicious.

Later, when Maria comes in after doing the school run, of course, Suzie grabs her to tell her the new wedding date and in the midst of all their excitement, I say to Maria, 'Come on, we are headed down the coast. Belgrave has a couple of meetings out of the office today. Now we have a vision of his Outlook calendar, we can plan our days in advance. We don't know either of them, so might as well check them out in the flesh. He has a ten-thirty meeting at some joint called Le Vintage in Worongary, so we will head directly there. You take the Camry; I'll take the Prado.'

'Sure, boss,' is Maria's answer as she finishes making her morning cuppa before pouring it into her travel mug.

We cruise down the highway, not bothering to travel together, Maria soon out of sight in front of me – remember, I 'drive like a grandfather'!

I pull into the car park next to Le Vintage in semi-rural Worongary, just off the M1. Maria is already sitting in the Camry and of course, I get the smug grin.

I see Belgrave's Mercedes parked a few cars along. I park where the dashcam in the Prado will capture all vehicles coming and going. You never know when rego numbers may come in handy.

Belgrave is meeting a Randy Jacobson, whose LinkedIn tells us he owns and operates a competing hot air balloon business. Not sure if this meeting is collusion or friends having coffee!

I let Maria wander on ahead to check out where they are sitting, as my Google search has shown they have a nice outdoor garden setting as well as indoors.

As I approach the entrance, Maria is standing there and says, 'Let's sit inside today.'

Asked and answered!

We walk in and I detour slightly to inspect the array of cakes etc on display. Mmm, plenty of options but in the end, I go with my favourite, banana bread. I have a wedding coming up, so I do need to watch my figure!

I order and we take a seat, basically in the middle of the small café. Naturally, I let my gaze wander the room.

Shit.

I text Maria, *'Bend down and fiddle with your handbag, please. I need a good look behind you.'*

To her credit, she resists the impulse to glance behind her and bends down, fiddling with her handbag. One of these big, oversized things most mothers seem to carry.

I have my phone in front of me, positioned to take a photo over her now-ducked head of the guy sitting at the table behind. Whilst making it look like I'm typing, I take a photo of him and the guy he is sitting with, although he remains partially obscured.

I immediately send the photos to Pig, MGC, Robert and Maria, asking, *'Please confirm this is Badour. Immediate.'*

Maria sits up immediately on seeing my text an incredulous look on her face. I give her a slight nod.

I hope she understands this is going to mean a complete change of plans.

Pig comes back, *'Yes. On my way. Where?'*

Maria is copied in and at her glance, I again nod, so she responds to Pig with Le Vintage's address.

My phone rings; it's MGC. I decline it, thinking, *A bit silly ringing me when I'm obviously in a slightly awkward situation.*

He immediately texts me, *'Yes 100%. Where are you?'*

For now, I text back, *'On another case, café in Gold Coast hinterland.'*

'Keep me posted. All resources available. Do not lose him,' is his immediate reply.

I'm slightly offended MGC thinks we might lose him. I also know he will expect a phone call as soon as possible.

Just then, the waitress delivers two breakfasts to their table. Good to know, they will be there a while.

Right behind their waitress is our server, delivering Maria her tea, my coffee and banana bread.

I contemplate my next moves as I enjoy the banana bread – and coffee, of course.

Maria and I have continued chatting so patrons don't wonder why we are sitting there in silence (like a married couple!), but I have also texted her and Pig saying, *'When you finish, can you go out to your car and wait? When they are making moves to leave, I will let you know so you can identify his car and then follow, loosely. Ring me once you're on the road so I know which way you have gone, so we can alternate. We will switch to Messenger once out of here, so Pig knows what's going on as well.'*

She reads the text and gives me a nod. There is no doubting the excited look on her face either!

I also know MGC will be getting antsy with me not ringing him but I do not want to draw attention to myself by standing up to go outside to make the call.

He will just have to cope!

Maria sends me a text, *'Belgrave is leaving.'* I shrug my shoulders – bigger fish to fry!

Maria finishes her tea, but I caution her to stay a bit longer. They are only halfway through their breakfasts and I don't want Badour looking directly at me, as he will be when Maria leaves.

Once they have largely finished, I give her a nod and off she goes. Pretty excited and, knowing her, a little nervous knowing the stakes are high on this one.

I order a second large coffee, this one in a takeaway cup as our new targets get ready to leave. I take another couple of surreptitious photos of Badour's breakfast guest. Badour pays the bill. Good, we can get his credit card details. Further ways to track and trace.

They leave together and before the wait staff can clear their table, I move quickly and grab both their forks and wrap them each in the paper servettes. Why? Now we will have their DNA as proof of who they are. Unless his guest isn't in our databases.

I pay our bill and head toward the car park, noticing a black BMW735 exit and turn left, back toward the M1. I immediately call Maria to tell her they turned left. She answers, excitement clear in her voice, 'Yes on it, but I planted a tracker on their car, so we can track them remotely.'

'Awesome! Good one! Okay, wait somewhere for me. I want to know what went down.'

'Okay. There is a little convenience store here on the left. I'll pull in there and wait for you.' Just before I hang up, I hear Pig say through Messenger, 'You go girl!' I smile, thinking I can almost see him fist pump.

Five minutes later, I pull up next to Maria, who jumps in the passenger seat of the Prado with a big smile on her face.

'Well?'

She smiles again and then relays, 'When I got to the car park, I noticed the black Beemer and there was a big bloke, sort of dressed like a chauffeur, lounging against it. I assumed this was Gregor. He had a good perve as I walked to the Camry, so I flounced a bit to keep his attention.' Pig snorts as she says this, and she gets a little defensive, saying, 'What? You don't think guys like what they see when I walk past. I can tell you many do, and I sort of played up to him, doing some stretches and things. I wanted him thinking with his dick, not his head. And it worked because he was watching and smirking at me, then he glanced at his phone and straightened up and headed up to the café. I quickly ran over and attached a tracker to the rear bumper and, because he was thinking with his dick, he didn't lock the BMW, so I got a mini spider mic in the back of the car as well! It's in the pocket on the passenger side, so where Badour should be sitting! Then I got out of the car park just as they walked back down the hill. Gregor gave me smile as he saw me leaving.'

'Wow-hoo,' I say as we high-five. 'Bloody good job, Maria. We have trained you well.'

'Yes, I'll say,' adds Pig. 'Bloody good job.'

Maria is rightfully pleased with herself, so I say, 'Okay, let's get on the road. Where are they and which direction are they heading?'

She already has the app open on her phone, saying, 'They are heading north on the M1. Hold on, looks like they are exiting at Helensvale.'

'You lead,' I say as she jumps out of the Prado and back into the Camry.

We are quickly heading north on the M1, with Pig coming south on the M1 through Yatala, so fifteen to twenty minutes away. Now we are mobile and with a plan, I dial up MGC. 'Mort, hold on, I will add Robert to this call. Right, proceed.'

'Sir, we were following Belgrave this morning. He met one of his legit competitors at a local café, and when Maria and I sat down, bugger me, there was Badour and another man I don't recognise sitting behind Maria. Sir, he is travelling in a black Beemer with, we suspect, Gregor driving. We have a tracker on the car and a mic in the rear of the car as well.'

Silence.

'Well, you have done well. That is a tremendous outcome. Where is he now?'

I glance at the app, adding, 'They are driving east along the Gold Coast Highway toward Labrador currently. Sir, this was all on Maria. She managed to distract Gregor and get both the tracker and mic on the Beemer.'

'Excellent. Please pass on my congratulations to Maria. Next steps?'

'Sir, we are following at a distance. Hopefully, they are headed to an office or home, some sort of base. I also grabbed their forks, so I need to get these to you or someone for DNA testing. Badour paid for the breakfast with a credit card, so we will be able to follow that – hopefully open up a new channel to trace his funding through.'

'Excellent. Excellent. A great start to the day. Well done. Please send the forks by express post to our address here in Canberra. In plastic Ziplock bags, of course. Keep me informed, please.'

'Will do, Sir.'

Maria comes through our encrypted app, 'They have turned north on Oxley Drive now.'

'Great, you heard how happy you made MGC, Maria. High and deserved praise. You really have done well!'

'Thanks but that's enough, you are making me blush!'

I smile as I can sense the smile through her voice.

'Where are you now?' I ask Maria.

'Just approaching Harbour Town shopping centre, which is on the corner of Oxley Drive.'

'Okay I'm coming through Arundel.'

'And I'm approaching Dreamworld, so maybe ten, fifteen minutes behind you now,' adds Pig.

Then Maria butts in, 'They are turning right onto Lae Drive now.'

I grunt an acknowledgement, contemplating next steps, following them on the app now as well.

'Hold on, they are now turning right into – shit, it's only a little street. Hold on. Okay, it's called The Runaway Brace. Shit, what sort of street name is that? It's only short, they have now turned right into Pebble Beach Drive.'

We all continue in silence, then Maria says they have stopped. 'Looks like on Pebble Beach Drive. I'm turning into Lae Drive now.'

I'm looking at the map – yes, I know, naughty as I am driving but hey, we all do it!

'Okay, I'm just turning into Oxley Drive. Don't follow them into Pebble Beach Drive, Maria, it's a dead-end street. Let's meet up and make a plan. As you're leading, you find a café nearby.'

'Will do.'

Five minutes later, she comes back, 'Okay, I'm parking at the Runaway Bay Shopping Centre. There is a Café Bella, which looks okay.'

'Great, your shout. You know what we want.'

Pig pipes up, 'I'm only a few minutes out now as well.'

'Cool.'

I enter the café and find Maria has found a table at the back, away from everyone else. Good girl; clearly, she has been observing and learning!

I sit down and we fist bump. I say, 'High praise indeed from MGC. You heard it for yourself?'

'Yes, thanks. Now, can we move on? I'm proud of getting it done but I am part of the team, so always want to contribute.'

'Yes, Maria you are an integral part of the team.' I nod at our setting, adding, 'Even select the best table instinctively, ah!'

Just as the coffee is served, Pig walks in. We fist bump all round – he even gives Maria a hug, which she accepts, then pushes him off, saying, 'You don't give him'—she points at me—'a hug whenever he does well. So, thanks, but let's move on, please.'

Pig looks at her and smiles, nodding.

I check the app and the car hasn't moved. There had only been a desultory conversation in the car between Gregor and Badour.

Maria then pulls up a couple of photos she had taken of Gregor, saying, 'Almost forgot I got these photos of Gregor, so hopefully we might be able to identify him from these.'

Pig quickly says, 'Send them to me and I'll on send them to Midge as well as Robert and MGC. I let Midge know we are hot on Badour's heels again too.'

Silence as we enjoy our coffees and tea.

'Alrighty then. Pig, you got Gerty with you?'

(Gerty is his new drone. Latest model, best at everything, he has proudly told me. 'Great name,' I told him. He blamed Stacey, saying, 'I asked her for a name starting with G and somewhat devilishly, that's what she came up with.' I responded, 'Well, I wouldn't be giving her naming rights for the baby!' 'Ah, we have already agreed on the baby's name. That was easy.' I raised an eyebrow as a query but he just smiled and said nothing more.)

He nods; of course, he has Gerty. Looking at the map, I say, 'We will adjourn to the park over the road by the netball courts. That will give you pretty well direct access to their house. But first, we will do a drive-past in the van. Once we confirm which house they are at, we will check who owns or rents the property. Maybe check both neighbouring houses as well. Just in case they have a larger security team. We have to remember Badour is a highly-ranked global terrorism leader. It's extraordinary that he is hiding away anonymously here in suburban Australia.'

We start to get organised, then before we leave the table, Pig's phone rings. It's Keith Urban again; therefore, Midge.

Pig answers and puts it on speaker, after glancing around to ensure no other customers are too close to hear. He says, 'Morning, Midge – well, our morning!'

Midge comes through, saying, 'Ho boys, you do love playing at the big table, don't you! Yes, that's Badour, alright. I have done a search of your border force, and he has entered Australia a number of times, mainly to and from Asia, but also the Middle East. You might like to know he is travelling on a legitimate Australian passport in the name of Li Woo. He officially emigrated to Australia back in 2019 and the records show an address in Runaway Bay on the Gold Coast there in Queensland.'

'Shit, this bloke is in deep cover. It is not an easy process going through and being accepted as an immigrant into Australia. You do have to ask if he has had some inside help. Yes, we have tracked him to an address on Pebble Beach Drive,' is my response.

A slight pause and Midge comes back, 'Yes, that's the address on the paperwork.'

Pig asks, 'What about the image we just sent through? Do you have a name for us yet?'

Another slight pause before he comes back, 'You are keeping me busy. Another one who has been flying under the radar for a number of years – that is Gregor Jovic. Any connection to Badour?'

'Yes,' Pig replies. 'He acts as his chauffeur and, we suspect, bodyguard.'

'Okey-dokey. He is a mean dude, so know who you're up against there. He was a major in Croatia's SOA, a real badass, according to all accounts. So be wary. Also, keep a lookout for his wife/partner Nadia Vukovic. Not sure if they are legally married, but they have reputedly been together for years. She too was a major in the SOA. A dangerous couple. I haven't had time to check thoroughly but I believe they both have warrants out for their arrest from Germany. Something to do with a triple murder that went down five or six years ago.

'I am putting this together in an email, which I will spit to you shortly. As you know, Badour is on everyone's most wanted list, so will be a big feather in your caps if you nail him. Another feather, that is!'

We smile and I say, 'Thanks, Midge. You have given us plenty to think about. Are you able to send through an image of this Nadia? We have a possible connection and would be good to know what she looks like if she is around. As you know, we report directly to a high level in the Australian Government, so will be sharing this as soon as your email arrives. Any chance you can check where Gregor and maybe Nadia have entered Australia as well?'

'Okay, will do. The rest of the data is on its way. Also, a photo of Nadia, but it is five years old. That's how long they have been gone to ground. Dudes, keep me posted, please, and, as you know, I can bring some high-level support to anything you need. All three would be best behind bars, or six feet under. Oh, by the way, no record of who Badour was meeting with. No match in any of our databases. Stay safe!'

And he's gone.

I look at Pig, knowing he has accepted we are up against fearless and ruthless opposition. I broaden my look to include Maria, saying, 'Maria, no more flirting with this guy, please. He is clearly a dangerous individual; we don't need you exposing yourself to these risks.'

She nods in acceptance, and I suspect she's a little scared at what she has just heard.

I glance at my phone and notice Midge's email has arrived, 'Okay, I need to bring MGC up to speed. We will all go over to the park, and I'll update him whilst you have Gerty do her thing.'

Nods all round and we troop out to our respective wheels.

A couple of roundabouts later and we are all parked near the netball courts. Pig and Maria head over to a nearby park bench to sit and sort Gerty out.

I dial MGC and relay what we have learnt.

Silence as he chews over everything I have told him.

'Very well, Mort, huge steps. Well done to the three of you. Next steps?'

'Sir, we need to step cautiously whilst we get to know Badour's set-up. For all we know, he has an outer shield for protection as well as Gregor and Nadia. He is a highly valued terrorist, after all. We won't be taking any risks or rushing things. As long as they don't get suspicious, we are safe. Thinking about it, I'm going to ask Midge to put a flag on Woo's name so if he books any international travel, we will know.'

Robert butts in, saying, 'We can do that, Mort,' to which I reply, 'No. If I'm right and there is someone within Border Force working with these people, you flagging Woo may well alert them. Midge works at a much higher level.'

'Yes, good point,' MGC responds.

I end the call with a promise to keep them updated.

As I hang up, I see Pig and Maria walking back toward me. I get out of the Prado and lean against the door, waiting for them to reach me.

I don't have to ask, as Pig starts his brief summary as soon as they join me.

'It certainly looks like this is their base. The Beemer is parked in the drive and there is another small SUV parked in the garage. It looks like a RAV4. No sign of a woman but there is an older style cruiser-type boat moored at the pontoon on the canal, and we watched as Badour walked down there. He is still on board, and I suspect he may use it as an office. No sign of Gregor. There is a suitable streetlight near their driveway, and I would like to put a camera up to watch the canal side as well. This will be a bit trickier, but there is a channel marker at the end of their canal, so we should be able to place one on that. Will be a bit further away than normal so will use a camera with a good zoom, and a waterproof one. And a boat,' he adds as an afterthought.

I contemplate this and ask, 'What odds getting a mic and camera on board this boat?'

Pig purses his lips, saying, 'Would be difficult, but not impossible. It will need a plan.'

No worries.

We are good with plans. And enacting them!

Let's start one now.

'I will share Badour's breakfast guest with Hoang and ask him to check it across all socials as a starting point. Pig, can you do property searches on this house, plus the ones on either side? Maybe the one opposite as well, just to be safe.'

'Why?' asks Maria.

'It is possible, even probable that Badour has an "outer shield" – that is a second security team. He has Gregor and Nadia likely living with him, but he may well have another team, totally separate that he can activate if anything goes wrong.'

She pulls a face, understanding what I mean. I continue, 'These are dangerous, ruthless terrorists living in our quiet suburbia, but ruffle them and they can explode. We need to tread very carefully.'

CHAPTER 28

I dig a couple of Ziplock bags out of the glovebox in the Prado, pull the forks out of my pocket, put one in each bag and seal them, placing them on the front seat. Ready to ship when we are back in the office.

Whilst I'm doing this, Pig has been texting Hoang and asking him to access Le Vintage's system and get the credit card details from all receipts this morning, just to ensure we don't miss Badour's. I tell him, 'Badour paid at 11.18 a.m.' He looks at me and I answer his unasked question, 'Yes, I checked!'

He gets a quick reply from Hoang, *'On my way to office now. Will do first up.'*

Pig sends a thumbs up!

'Okay, let's get organised here. Pig, we won't do a drive-by. No sense now you have the drone footage but we will go and install a camera shortly. I want to do at least one other pole within their sight. Don't want to raise their suspicions by rocking up and only working on the pole outside their house.'

Pig nods, saying, 'Yes, agree. There is another light pole further back near a little cross street. This would be visible from their house.'

'Good, that sounds like a plan. We then just have to work out how to set a camera up on the channel marker you mentioned. Best done at night, I would think. Maria, not much more to be done here. Unless anything changes, we will be heading back to the office. Can you check on Belgrave? See if he is back in his office and if so, check the audio, see if anything important has come up. Mind you, with Badour back in our sites, Belgrave will need to take a back seat.'

Maria nods then adds, 'Looks like your best bet for renting a tinnie is Gold Coast Boat Hire. You can get a little 5hp tinnie or a bit bigger one with 30hp outboard. They are only up at Paradise Point. I'll flick you their link.'

'Cool, thanks!'

Maria is on the ball today!

We say our goodbyes, Maria heading back to the office, Pig and I to go climb a couple of light poles.

With Pig driving, we head back onto Lae Drive, right around the roundabout, then a quick left into the Runaway Brace (yes, weird name for a road!), right into Pebble Beach Drive, slowly across the bridge, as I try and get a good look at the target house, visible across the canal. The road wanders around and then at the intersection with The Yardarm (another weird nautical street name!) He pulls up next to the light pole. He says, 'You're up today.'

I nod, get out, open the back doors and pull out the crate holding our 'at height' safety gear, whilst Pig busies himself grabbing a couple of little wide-angle cameras for me. He then pulls the ladder off the roof and sets it up against the light pole, then sets the safety cones up around the base, designed to ensure no one comes along and knocks the base of the ladder whilst I'm up it doing you-know-what. He says, 'If we use this camera, it covers basically 180 degrees, so we will have a vision of anyone coming along the street as well along in front of their house.'

I nod, taking the camera from him. These are tiny and I slide it into my breast pocket. Of course, I have pulled my hi-viz top on and pulled the mandatory clipboard out. I check the pole ID and record this on my blank piece of paper, hand the clipboard to Pig and ascend the ladder. Up here, I have a good look around, fiddle with the bulb for show and quickly affix the camera to the top of the bulb cover. Pig has the vision up on his iPad and tells me to move it slightly to the right. Once, twice and good to go.

Down the ladder, you know the drill.

We move the van down the road and again park adjacent to the light pole just past their house. This is a little further away than the one before it but as we have a vision already from that direction, this way we get any movement from the other direction. Mind you, it is a dead-end street, so not likely to be much!

Rinse and repeat. Again, you know the drill.

Back in the van, we drive off, heading on to the end of the road, pull a U-turn and head back. We have seen no activity from the target house, even from up the ladder. As we head back toward the bridge, I say to Pig, 'What about a camera on the bridge, instead of the channel marker?'

He pulls a face before saying, 'It's a bit public. Likely, fishermen use it for fishing – it would be a bit exposed and if found, might start the locals talking.'

'Fair point,' I concede.

Back to the netball courts where I jump out and get into the Prado. Pig's last words: 'Race ya.'

Mean, aren't they!

I make a point of driving faster than normal and am sitting at my desk when Pig wanders in, seeing his mug sitting on my desk, and getting the subtle message that I had got back early enough to make coffees before he got in. Subtle or unsubtle? You take your pick.

But before taking a seat, nature calls and he heads to the bathroom.

Whilst waiting, I pull out an express post bag, address it, put the two forks in a little padded bag inside the express post bag, seal it and put it aside. Tingalpa Post Office is just up the road. Might take a walk up there a bit later.

When he is comfortably seated, he says, 'Midge replied and yes, he has found both Gregor and Nadia immigrated here at the same time as Badour in 2019. They are using the names Gregor and Nadia Johanson. So at least it seems they are formally married.'

I purse my lips in frustration. *What is going on within Border Force?*

'Will have to update MGC with this data next time we speak to him.'

I then ask Maria, 'Any update on Belgrave?'

'He returned to his office – I gather, straight from the café, judging by the timeline – and hasn't budged.'

'Thanks.'

Pig has brought up the vision from the main camera. This only activates when there is activity of a human size or larger. Not much has gone on there on our drive back.

No movement from the target house. A couple of neighbours down the street have come and gone and it looks like a house further down the street had an Amazon delivery.

'Hoang, anything on Badour's breakfast partner?'

'Yes, his name is Chen Wing. He appears to own a couple of Chinese restaurants there on the Gold Coast. One in Surfers Paradise, which looks quite large, and another in the food court at Pacific Fair Shopping Centre. He is also President of the Gold Coast chapter of the Chinese Arts council. He lives at Mermaid Beach. You might be interested to know that Li Woo is the patron of the Gold Coast chapter of the Chinese Arts Council. Also, they have their annual black-tie charity ball in just over two weeks at the Gold Coast Convention Centre. I have checked, Li Woo has accepted his invite.'

'Good work, Hoang. Thanks,' I say.

Pig chimes in, 'A bit odd, Badour being the patron of the Chinese arts council, when he is reputedly Indonesian?'

Maria and I agree.

I lean back in my chair, thinking how deeply Li Woo/Badour is immersed in life here in Australia. If only his neighbours knew the anarchy he has fostered and funded around the world. The deaths and tragedies he is responsible for. I then think, *We have to nail this bastard.*

Pig interrupts my mulling, saying, 'I'll get onto those properties now, see who owns and or rents them. But do you want to talk about how we can put a mic and camera on the old cruiser?'

'Yeah, why not? Your thoughts?'

Pig purses his lips. 'Well, we have to hire a tinnie to place the camera on the channel marker, but I don't see us getting away with using a tinnie, or any boat, to be able to sidle up to the cruiser to board it. Likewise, we have to assume that the house is pretty secure, so don't see access through there, although knowing Badour is going to that ball in a couple of weeks, maybe all three of them will be going and we can take our time.'

I butt in, 'Yes, but a lot can happen in two weeks. We need to act sooner than that.'

He nods his agreement.

I continue, 'As you know, I don't exactly have a swimmer's physique.' I pause here, hearing a snigger from the other side of the room, realising Suzie and Jenny have walked in from their office.

I raise an eyebrow and address the guilty sniggerer, Suzie. 'You have something to say?'

She puts her innocent face on, saying, 'Oh no, not at all, but I have seen you floundering around – sorry, swimming in hotel pools, you know.' Her smile is all innocent as Maria and Jenny and bugger it, Pig are all smiling. Hoang, being tactful, remains face down over his laptop.

They are most unfair in my opinion.

I choose to ignore them, continuing, 'No way I can swim there without being noticed. What we need is one of those battery-powered underwater thingies, like they had at the JW Marriott down the Gold Coast. I wonder if we could hire one for a couple of days.'

Pig joins my thought process, 'Yeah, but that was more a toy. We would need something more powerful and functional for what we are talking about.' Here, he grabs his iPad and asks, 'What do reckon you would call them?'

I shrug. 'Dunno, maybe battery-powered underwater propeller or something.'

Silence as he searches. 'Shit, you can spend over $20k on some of these. Bloody hell, top speed underwater of twenty kilometres an hour!'

'I don't want to be going that fast in a Gold Coast canal.'

Maria chimes in, 'You might have to if you have a bull shark chasing you!'

'Yeah, right,' I respond, suddenly realising Gregor and Nadia are not my only risks here.

Just then my phone rings, MGC.

'Afternoon, Sir.'

'Mort, just calling to see if there has been any developments.'

'Not really, Sir. We are sitting here contemplating how we can place a mic and camera on board the Cruiser Badour appears to use as an office. I'm not exactly swimmer material, so we are exploring underwater propulsion machines. Something that can get me to the boat and away again, hopefully unseen.'

'Well, I might be able to assist you there. I know the "Brigade", the Australian SAS division, have just got some new seagoing and underwater power units. Theirs are especially modified for surveillance work, so might be exactly what you need. I will make a call and come back to you. Anything else?'

'Well, Sir, since we spoke, we have placed a couple of cameras on light poles in their street. To cover the back of the house, we plan on placing one on a strategic channel marker in the canals, so we need to hire a boat to do that, maybe tomorrow night. We have found out Badour is patron of the Gold Coast chapter of the Chinese Arts Council. His breakfast guest this morning was one Chen Wing. He appears to own a couple of Chinese restaurants there on the Gold Coast. He is also President of the Gold Coast chapter of the Chinese Arts Council. He lives at Mermaid Beach. We have not done any diving into him as yet, Sir.

'We are currently looking into the ownership of their house and the surrounding ones, looking to see if they have an outer shield security team. This won't tell us that of course but may tell us if they are that close. Midge has confirmed Gregor and Nadia emigrated here around the same time as Badour under the names of Gregor and Nadia Johanson. The forks are packed, and I will ship these to you this afternoon. That's about all since we last spoke, Sir. Oh, Hoang, have you got Badour's credit card details from this morning?'

He replies, 'Yes, have it here for you. The one at 11.18 a.m., you said?'

'Yes, that's it. Sir, we will email that through shortly, if you can please let me know if it leads anywhere.'

'Certainly, Mort. No doubt you have been busy. Let me call my friend, the Colonel, and get back to you on what underwater equipment they can make available. I assume you need this immediately?'

'Yes, Sir, please. Want to ensure we capture all data we can, as we don't know how long they will stay put.'

'Will get back to you shortly.' And he hangs up.

I look at Pig and say, 'Well, when you summarise what we have achieved today, it's quite an impressive list, isn't it!' I include Maria in my look, so she knows her efforts are appreciated as she packs up for the day and heads home to 'feed the tribe', as she describes it!

After Hoang and Pig have left, I go up change into a pair of shorts and joggers and head off down to the post office, and post two forks to MGC!

A pleasant walk to end an eventful day.

Overnight, I get a text from Robert saying, *'Sergeant Drew Smith will arrive @ Bne (Brisbane) a/p on QF942 at 5am today.'*

I am therefore on my way to collect him. Don't know him and don't know what equipment, if any, he has brought for us. Will find out when I eventually get to the airport through peak hour traffic. I do have a phone number for him and texted him earlier when I left with an approximate ETA.

Still heading to the airport, my phone rings again. It's Deides.

'Hi, Diedes. Nice and early!'

'Hi, Mort. Yes, it is early, but also late, as I'm just about to head to bed. Have been at it all night.' Her voice turns serious. 'Mort, I have to apologise. KPMG have requested – well, in fact, one of their major clients is insisting – I do an urgent project for them. I have agreed to do this for them as a top priority. It does mean I will not be able to spend any time on your project for maybe ten days, two weeks. I'm sincerely sorry to be letting you down but I have worked for this client for many years, and their situation is urgent and critical. I am making KPMG pay through the nose as it must be pissing him off big time having to reach out to me.' (I assume 'him' would be her former husband from what Marg told me.)

'That's actually no problem, Diedes. We too have been sidetracked onto another critical case, so your delay won't cause us any issues. Thanks for letting me know. Let me know when you're free again and ready to start. By the way, we are now on the government dollar, so you can up your billing rate!'

'Cool. Thank you, Mort, for your understanding. I am dead keen to help you, intrigued where my research will lead. Yes, I will be in touch when I have finished this urgent investigation. Take care. Bye.'

I'm only ten minutes late when I pull up at the pickup point. It's not had to recognise him, standing tall, erect and alert, like any good soldier and with three checker plate machinery cases at his feet!

I pull the Prado up next to him, get out and go around the back, opening the rear door, where he meets me with his backpack and one of the cases.

We introduce ourselves, load up and are quickly on our way before any of the Gestapo-like parking inspectors notice we have come and gone.

It is quickly obvious that Drew wants to demonstrate the unit in water, so I text Pig (don't worry – I use Siri whilst driving!) and suggest he meet us on Breakfast Creek – yes, adjacent to the Brekkie Creek hotel. Just as well I had thrown in my togs and towel, ah!

On the other side of the creek, there is a canoe ramp, which should be ideal for what he wants to show us. *'On my way,'* is Pig's answer.

Good, time for coffee! Of course, just down the road is Mica Patisserie. Might even have something yummy with a name like that! Bugger, I remember my upcoming wedding.

But the coffee is good. We are still there when not only Pig arrives but he also has Maria in tow as well. She says by way of greeting, 'I'm not going to miss this swimming display!'

Drew is a serious guy, not really understanding or caring about the interplay.

As we head back to the Prado, I let Pig and Maria know Diedes too has been sidetracked from the Belgrave inquiry. We unpack the largest case first.

Wow, this thing looks a beauty. It's finished in matte black, with little ripple lines all through it. He tells us, 'These units started out as Yamaha Sea scooters but have been specifically designed for underwater surveillance work. You may need to be careful if you're working in canals – is that right?' I nod. 'Well, we have governed this down to a top speed of only five kilometres per hour, so this should work for you.'

I strip down and into my togs, and Drew does the same, removing his jeans and shoes, etc. We push the machine into the water. The machine's control panel has a GPS unit, sonar and radar and the front-mounted camera has a gradient scale, so I know the lay of the land under the water. This will be critical for us. He hands me a pair of goggles, which I fit over my fat face, and he then inserts the tiny snorkel, which is extendable, depending on how deep you are travelling. I place the bit in my mouth and clamp down on it. Pretty cool gear, this!

We spend five minutes going over the controls and he explains the slower you go, the less of a ripple you leave. He encourages me to practise on the surface before going under.

Sounds like a plan. With the unit idling, I push off into Brekkie Creek. Fortunately, it isn't low tide so there is some water! I stay on the surface, just idling along, turning left, then right, then pulling a U-ie. *I've got this,* I think and push down and head underwater. I'm hardly submerged and suddenly there is a beeping noise, so I pull back up to the surface. Drew yells out, 'You must have been close to the bottom.'

I see Pig asking him a question and Drew nods then yells, 'Yes, we can turn that down for you.'

I play around a bit more, still staying close to the surface. Once comfortable I know how to handle it, I go in and tell them I'm going to go out into Brisbane River. They nod. Drew comes over with a screwdriver and adjusts a setting before saying, 'That has muted the warning, so stay away from the bottom or any other obstacles.'

A 'good luck' from Maria, and off I go. It's only about one hundred metres from the canoe ramp to the junction with the Brisbane River, so I idle out there. I know when I am in the river as the current, an outgoing tide, pulls me along. *Good test,* I think and turn into the tide and accelerate. It jumps forward. Oops! Maybe a bit heavy on the throttle then. I try again, get it a bit smoother and third time, it's about spot on.

Now I'm moving at a comfortable speed, I decide to go under and push the control bar down. Down I go. It's murky down here but I can see the controls and have plenty of water beneath me. I had noticed a 'city cat' (Brisbane river ferry) coming toward me along the river and suddenly this flashes up on the screen, so I know I am well clear of it. The gauge tells me I am five metres down and the snorkel is working well. Must say, I'm not sure how that works but as long as I'm getting air, I don't care! I turn to the left, aiming for the other side of the river, staying around five metres down. As I close in on the shore, I can see it getting shallower on the gradient and ease up and idle down. Once I'm in only one and a half metres of water, I shut it down and stand up.

The three of them are now standing on the Newstead House pontoon and can see me clearly. Maria waves but no, Pig and Drew are too cool to wave to me. I wave back to Maria, just to hopefully embarrass Pig!

I look around, pretty comfortable with the unit now, so I turn around and head downriver slightly.

Once underwater, again maintaining my five metre depth, I turn around and head slowly toward the pontoon. When it shows up on the radar, I idle down again and go to the back side of it – that is, behind them. I surface quietly behind them; they aren't even aware I am there.

'BOO!'

They all spin round, surprised to see I have snuck up on them unseen. Good, that's what we need to achieve, so it should be good, I declare.

I head back to the canoe ramp with Drew telling us he has another surprise for us. Sounds cool!

I get back before them and have the unit out of the water when they walk up. Drew taps the second case, saying, 'You will find a wet suit in here. It will fit. We received your measurements.'

Cool, I think.

He then opens the third case and pulls out a dull green roll of something. He lets it unroll along the canoe ramp. It sort of looks like a roll of artificial turf, but it's not.

Drew explains, 'This is brand new – been tested and signed off, but not yet used live. It is a waterproof and water-resistant matt. So, if you're coming out of the water and don't want to leave a wet trail, you roll this out in front of you. Go on, Mort, crawl along this, pretending you are trying not to be seen.'

I'm still wet, so, okay, I get down and using elbows and toes, crawl along the length of the roll.

'Okay, now jump in the water, get wet again and crawl back.' Easy done. I repeat the crawl in reverse. He then picks up a slim remote, presses the button and the roll rolls itself-up behind me. And not a drop of water to be seen along the ramp.

How cool is this!

Pig and I look at each other and nod. Yes, this should safely get me in and out of the cruiser, as leaving a wet trail was a problem we hadn't found a solution for, other than having to stand and dry myself off when on the pontoon. A bit of a no-no, as you can imagine.

'I brought you two rolls so ten metres in total. Hopefully, that's enough for what you need to do?'

'Yeah, that's great,' Pig replies, getting in first. 'The pontoon is about five metres long, then he can use the second roll inside the boat.'

'Great!' I exclaim.

Drew looks at his watch, saying, 'If you're happy with that, can you run me back to the airport? I have a hold on a seat on the one o'clock flight home.'

'Sure,' I reply. 'No problem.'

We bundle the cases back into the Prado and I head off to drop him back at the airport, whilst Pig and Maria take the Camry back to the office.

CHAPTER 29

With Drew safely deposited back at Brisbane Airport, I arrive back at the office and drive into the garage, keen to ensure the wetsuit will fit me.

Maria and Pig come out when I arrive but I tell Maria to skedaddle whilst I change into the wet suit.

It does fit, although Pig does say rather unkindly, 'You might have to hold your breath to get that over your gut!' Smiling, of course.

Sadly, he isn't wrong. I seem to be developing a bit of a paunch, which I will need to do something about. I have a wedding coming up. I get the zip done up without too much trouble as Pig watches on with his usual smirk. I do a few stretches, jumps, etc to ensure the suit doesn't impact on these. I am just finishing these when not only Maria comes out but also trailing her are both Suzie and Jenny.

'What, I'm putting on a freak show, am I?' I ask, and then start doing a full set of callisthenics accompanied by numerous ribald comments from all four of them. Especially from Suzie, so I start moving toward her and she quickly disappears back inside.

Once alone again, I strip off, hang the wet suit up with some of our other equipment, get dressed and head in.

Pig has a coffee ready and he and Maria are sitting at my desk, waiting.

But first, I need to pay a visit. As we all know, what goes in, must come out!

When I'm settled at my desk, Maria pipes up, saying, 'As far as I can see, the closest boat ramp is in Howard Street, Runaway Bay. About nine hundred metres north of the canal leading into Pebble Beach Drive. It's about three k's from Gold Coast boat hire, so all quite close, really. By the way, they say their boats aren't allowed to be used at night – just so you know!'

I nod. 'Thanks, Maria. What they don't know won't hurt them. Maybe we plan on hiring one of their 30hp boats, so we can get away quickly if the shit hits the fan. Need to hire it from tomorrow for, say, three days, in case we get delayed. Need to check what the moon and weather are doing over the next couple of nights. And the tide times, I guess.'

Pig replies, 'Moon is last quarter, so it won't be an issue. Nights are meant to be clear and mild, so again, no issue, although a bit of cloud wouldn't go astray. Need to check tide times.'

Maria replies, 'High tide tonight is 12.08 a.m., tomorrow just before one a.m., then roughly an hour later each day.'

'Good-o. If we are aiming for tomorrow night, with a one a.m. high, really, anytime before three a.m. should be fine, two hours either side of high should be fine.' Thinking, *I did learn something from all those years beach camping and fishing with Dad!*

Maria pipes up again, 'They aren't very big highs, less than a metre with low of about 0.4 metres, so not a big variation.'

I look at Pig, debating and, not surprisingly, he is on the same wavelength, saying, 'We need to be in the water by twelve-thirty a.m. if we go tomorrow, or by waiting a day, it would be safer, leaving at one-thirty.'

'Yes, I agree. Let's wait a day. Twelve-thirty just seems too early to be safe. This is going to be tricky, maybe not dangerous in a lethal way, but if we stuff it up, they will run, and we will lose a massive opportunity to mine significant intel. Let's take the extra day to fine-tune our plans. Pig, we will book into a motel down there tomorrow for a few days, so we can monitor things a little better. If we are waiting a day, I wouldn't mind monitoring their evening routine, get a feel for what time lights out is, etc. Is Stacey okay on her own?'

Pig responds, a little defensively, 'Yes, she will be fine. The morning sickness has gone and other than spending heaps of money on nursery stuff, everything is pretty cool.'

'I will check with her. I'm happy to stay with her if she would prefer – if not, I'm coming with you. I'm not going to be left behind,' Maria adds.

I nod, accepting this, with Pig replying, 'Check if you like, but I'm telling you she is fine. She may even enjoy a couple of days without being fussed over.'

I look at him, thinking, *Maybe he is being overprotective of Stacey through the pregnancy and she is getting the shits with it.*

I give him a smile and get a sheepish grin in return, sufficient for me to think, *Yes, a bit of tension over too much fussing.* Note to self, *Make sure you don't fall into the same trap when our turn comes. If our turn comes.*

Maria says, 'Alright, alright then. I'm coming with you.'

Pig says, 'That's fine, but we always share a room. If you're so keen to join, you happy to share?'

'Don't forget I have already shared a room with you, put up with all your dirty habits and snoring. Bring it on, I'm up for it!'

I feel like saying, 'Children, children,' but resist.

Maria and Pig smile at each other. They do act like siblings at times, always egging each other on.

Whilst they have been having their little byplay, I find Runaway Bay Motor Inn on Oxley Drive only five to seven minutes from our action point.

'Alright, Maria, if you don't mind, can you book two rooms at the Runaway Bay Motor Inn for three nights from tomorrow? We shouldn't need the third night but let's book it in case. See if you can get an early check-in, so we can set up there in the morning.'

Before she can reply, Pig says, 'Why don't we go and check in this afternoon? That way we will get an extra night's surveillance in tonight.'

'Good idea. Let's do that. Make it four nights then. That suit you, Maria?'

Before she can answer, Pig. 'Yes, will Ronnie be able to cope alone with the kids for four days? Or you without Ronnie?' finishing with his usual smirk to ensure Maria gets his unsubtle meaning!

She ignores his second question, answering, 'Mum looks after the kids. He won't have to lift a finger but it will do him good to ferry the girls to netball training, and Junior to his footy training. Reminds me, I will have to check with Stacey how YOU'RE coping through the pregnancy!'

They smile at each other, whilst I say, 'Let's call that a draw.' We all laugh.

'That's settled. If you can, try and get adjoining rooms, please. Interconnecting would be great.'

'Will do.'

I wander into Suzie's office to let her know I'm going to be away for a few days, to which she replies, 'Do you have a guest spot at SeaWorld?' Getting a giggle out of Jenny. Mean, isn't she? I seem to be the butt of everyone's jokes these days.

I reply, 'For that remark, missy, no surprise gift for you when I get home.'

That won't do, so she quickly gets up, putting her arms around my neck, giving me a peck on the cheek, clearly thinking that will put her back in the good books. She does whisper, 'You be careful,' though.

CHAPTER 30

We arrive at the Runaway Bay Motor Inn a bit before four p.m. and check in, Pig and I in the Prado, Maria some ten minutes behind us in the Camry.

On the trip down, with Pig driving, I have booked a 'Gold Coast 2' with Gold Coast boat hire from tomorrow morning. This comes with 30hp outboard, GPS, marine radio, life jackets, etc. We have agreed Pig will go and hire it alone and I remind him he will have to show his boat licence. Yes, we both have boat licences, courtesy of the army. Don't think either of us have used them since; I certainly haven't. He will use one of our prepaid Visas to avoid leaving any more of a trail than we need to.

Hopefully, we won't need to do much other than start and steer the boat!

I also take the opportunity to update MGC.

We then formulate a plan: Pig will put Gerty up tonight and monitor the back of the house. Of most interest to us is what time Badour uses the cruiser, as that is crucial to our planning. I plan on buying a couple of fishing rods and using one, I will spend a couple of hours around dusk fishing off the Pebble Beach Drive bridge, with its view of the back of the house, I will be seeing what Gerty is filming, but I am keen to get a feel for how things operate at their house. After that, we will simply play it by ear. We have nothing specific for Maria to do, but I'm not going to banish her from the team!

Needing fishing gear as 'props', Google tells me the nearest BCF store (Boating, Camping, Fishing) is at Labrador. Off I go.

We need an early dinner and head off to the Runaway Bay Tavern where we all agree on the Chicken Parmi. Pig and I enjoy a couple of beers whilst Maria goes with a red.

We have come in separate vehicles and with Maria opting to go with Pig, they head back to the netball courts to use as their launch spot. Me, I find a park near the bridge, manfully hoping there are no other fishermen on the bridge who will see how little I know about fishing!

Good, with no one else around, I cheat and don't even pretend to bait the hook. I simply throw the line in, then hold the fishing rod. Oh, the joys of fishing!

I had also bought a little foldup stool to sit on, so I position this against the bridge railing and sit down. At least I have a good view of the back of the house and will see any coming or going at the back canal side of the house. I have the CCTV coverage of the front on my iPad as well. They get up to anything, we will know.

How to spend an evening, ah?

Over dinner, we had noted that both cars were home. We have also confirmed there is a woman living in the house but have not got any image good enough to get a formal identification. Yet.

Pig's voice comes through my ear plug, 'You've got a bite!'

'Ha, ha,' I reply. 'Not a chance, I didn't bait the hook.' I hear Maria laughing in the background.

As I lean on the bridge rail, I try to identify Gerty somewhere above me. No, I can't see or sense anything moving up there.

Darkness arrives. You can fish in the dark, so I stay where I am. I even reel the line in a couple of times to make it look like I'm seriously fishing.

Pig confirms what I see, that Badour leaves his cruiser a little after six-thirty p.m., turning the lights out. His vision is better than mine and can then see all three of them sitting down under the back patio for dinner. He takes a few photos of all of them, hoping one of the women will get us a formal ID.

I give up on the fishing gig around eight-thirty p.m. as there has been no sign of life out the back and if any of them leave, we will get it on the CCTV.

I pick up Maria, leaving Pig to continue monitoring them. We head back to our motel.

Pig stays until eleven p.m. but no one ventures back outside after dinner except Gregor wandering out for a smoke.

We will repeat this process tomorrow, hopeful that Badour doesn't need to return to the cruiser after dinner tomorrow night.

CHAPTER 31

Pig picked up the boat this morning so we decide to go and plant the camera on the channel marker. That way we can monitor the rear of the house, including who goes to and from the cruiser without needing me fishing or Gerty to be in the air.

Maria volunteers to go with Pig to do this, which is fine, leaving me to stay at the motel and monitor goings-on. I hand over the fishing rod, suggesting it was her turn to use these as props. She surprises me by saying, 'You know, I know how to use these and even bait the hooks. We take the kids fishing quite often. Junior seems to love it.' (Junior is her oldest son, also named Ronnie, so he's commonly called Junior.)

'Good,' I reply. 'You can catch our dinner then.'

'You will have to gut and bone it then – I draw the line at that. Ronnie has to do that.'

Pig adds, 'The only fish I'm eating is coming from a fish and chip shop.' I'm with Pig.

Pig's property searches on their house and their immediate neighbours have come back and I see Badour's house is owned by a company trust with a company trustee. I flick these details to Deides, asking her to see if the trust has any other assets and whether there is a mortgage on the property. And if possible, where the money came from for the initial purchase, which took place three years ago.

The neighbouring properties are both owned by couples. We have noted two kids at both these houses; therefore, we do not expect there is any connection. We are checking ownership of the cars from these properties as well, as one final check. Having grabbed the rego of the RAV4 from their house, I do a check now and find this is leased from the same company as the BMW7 series. I flick these details to Hoang to see if he can access this company's records to see who they have listed as the leasee, and hopefully where their presumably monthly payment is coming from.

Suddenly, I notice the roller door at their house going up and the RAV4 backing out.

Action time.

I grab the keys to the Camry and head left along Oxley Drive, quickly right into Lae Drive. As I approach the road to Pebble Creek Drive, the RAV4 pulls out in front of me. Talk about good timing!

The woman is driving.

Bonus!

I slow down and let another car pull between us; however, she quickly indicates she is turning right into Runaway Bay Shopping Centre. So is the car in front of me. So am I.

The car park is busy so easy to blend in; well, whilst I'm in the car, at least.

I park a little way away but where I have clear vision of her. I sit in the car whilst she exits the RAV4 and note she gives the car park a thorough check over. I'm impressed.

As she crosses in front of me heading to the shops, with my door open, I use my phone and zoom in on her, getting a couple of good close-ups of her face.

Now, time to move before she is lost in the throngs of shoppers. (Not really – it's not that busy!)

I stay fifty to sixty metres behind her and notice she pauses outside a couple of stores with angled fronts, clearly checking her back trail. She is a pro. I am certain she is Nadia; we just need confirmation.

After a short walk, she enters a hair salon: Costa and Co. As I wander past, a glance in shows her getting hugs from some of the staff, clearly a regular.

Good, I suspect she will be there for an hour or so. Time for coffee. As luck would have it, Café Bella is just ahead. I head in and manage a table giving me a view of the hair salon entrance. Coffee time. This time, I do add toasted banana bread (don't tell anyone!)

Whilst waiting for the coffee, I email both images of 'Nadia' to both Midge and Robert, asking for confirmation this is Nadia Vukovic.

Once the coffee is delivered, I call Pig to see how they are going and give them an update.

It seems the launching of the boat was a bit of an event. Pig doesn't say too much but Maria keeps interrupting to let me know he needs backing practice and that they forgot to untie the boat from the trailer before putting it in the water, getting a couple of flippant comments from 'fellow' boaties waiting for their turn to launch!

At present, they are puttering along the canal, essentially doing a little recon, with their plan to stop at the channel marker when they go back past it. Maria has both lines in the water trailing the boat but she does admit she too hasn't bothered to bait the hooks.

I let them know I have tailed Nadia to the hair salon and am sitting in Café Bella, watching for her exit. Pig asks, 'Have you sent the photos off?'

'Of course,' is my reply.

He replies, 'Enjoy your coffee then.'

'Will do!'

I wait patiently, having no idea how long it might take Nadia to have her hair done. She wears it short, so by my reckoning, it shouldn't be too long. But I'm wrong. I'm now on my third coffee when I see her exit the salon and head my way. I stay where I am, looking down at my phone, but I needn't have worried. She, like most of the world, is walking along reading her phone, oblivious to the rest of us. She goes down in my estimation of her professionalism. But I do get another good close-up photo of her as she walks past. I grab my coffee; it's in a takeaway cup, just in case, ready to leave, but bugger it, she enters Café Bella. She places her order and takes a seat at the other end of the café, looking away from me. I am able to watch her in the reflection of the glass and I see her stirring sugar into her coffee, and then she licks the spoon.

Must be a Cappuccino, I think since she's licking the foam off the spoon.

I realise I need to grab that spoon and send it off for DNA testing, which will surely prove her identity. She also paid by credit card, so I text Hoang, asking him to get the card details from Café Bella's files for the transaction at 10.37 a.m. this morning. He replies quickly, *'Will do.'*

Whilst sitting there having her coffee, she pulls a couple of Woolworths plastic shopping bags out of her handbag. Clearly, next stop is the supermarket. I don't need to know what she is buying, so I finish my coffee and head back to the car park.

I go back to the Camry and grab a tracker and mic. With no one around, I move over to the RAV4 and slip the tracker under the rear bumper. Using the 'car opener app', I open the driver's door and secret the little mini spider mic in the central air vent. Then lock it again.

In and out in seconds. I wander back taking a position outside the café, in the opposite direction to Woolies (Woolworths).

As soon as she leaves, I quickly slip back into the café, grab the spoon off her saucer and slip it into a plastic bag.

Yes, I get a couple of strange looks from people at adjacent tables, which I ignore.

I take the spoon to the post office, place it in a padded bag and express post it to MGC.

I hang around outside Woolies to see what aisle and time she checks out so Hoang can hopefully find out how she pays for her shopping.

Aisle six at 11.09 a.m. I text this to Hoang now as well.

Knowing she is heading back to her car, I head to the Camry ahead of her and exit the car park.

I proceed along Lae Drive, past her turnoff and pull over, putting my phone to my ear, so it looks like I have an excuse for stopping. I see her turn left into The Runway Brace, so head back to the motel.

As I pull up, Midge calls me. 'Hi, yes, you have now found Nadia Vukovic. Tell me so I have this right, you have Badour being bodyguarded by Gregor Jovic and Nadia Vukovic. That is a real nest of vipers. You cannot let them get away, Mort.'

'That we know, mate. We should have a DNA match for her in a day or so now as well,' I reply.

'You are thorough, as always. Tell me your plans, please.'

'Mate, still formulating those. We have set up full coverage, cars are tracked and now both mic'd, house covered but no mics. Badour seems to use a cruiser, a boat moored at their house as his office, so I'm planning on accessing that tomorrow night, which, if successful should give us significant information, which we will naturally be sharing with you.'

'Cool. Why not until tomorrow night?'

'Tides aren't really favourable tonight.'

'What, you're going in by sea?'

'Well, by canal, actually. The house backs onto a canal.'

'Got it. Just pulled the address up now. Fancy neighbourhood?'

'Middling, more upscale than down but not multi-multi-millions.'

'I didn't realise you were a qualified diver as well but nothing should surprise me about you two!'

'No, swimming isn't one of my strong suits, but we have borrowed some technology that will help us get the job done. Keep your fingers crossed. Also, Midge, we are trying to trace where the money came from to pay for the house and also their operational expenses. We expect to have more details on these in the next few days. Once we send these to you, can you let us know what you find ASAP, please?'

'Certainly will, Mort. So you know, big eyes are watching, so no shortage of resources when you need them.'

'Cool. Thanks.'

'Take care my friend and say ho to Pig – unusual only talking to one of you!'

'Will do. He is out in a tinnie at present, pretending to fish whilst placing cameras on channel markers.'

Laughing, Midge asks, 'What is a tinnie?'

'A small aluminum boat with an outboard.'

'Ha, ha, hope he is safe! Take care. Can't wait to hear the next update. Be safe.'

And he is gone. *Geez*, I think, *where would we be without Midge's help?*

Then again, he wouldn't be alive if not for us and more recently, we have once again come up trumps for them with our success against the Garcia cartel there in the States.

Whilst I have been talking to Midge, a text comes in from Maria, saying they have finished and are heading back now. I log in and check the coverage from the new channel marker camera. Good, nice and clear. I then pull up the audio from the RAV4 and hear Nadia and I presume Gregor having an argument, raised voices in a heated exchange. They're speaking in Croatian or some other language I'm not familiar with.

I immediately send this off to Robert requesting a translation, deciding not to bother Midge with this. I also tell Robert our 'Sally' has been confirmed by Midge as Nadia Vukovic. I also ask if there has been any update on the DNA from the forks I had sent down.

A quick response as MGC calls me, but I suggest we call him back once Pig arrives in ten to fifteen minutes, so he gets the complete update. He agrees.

I hear the Prado pull into the car park, so go out to watch Pig back the boat trailer into the rear car park. He doesn't do a bad job and I'm certainly not going to comment, having not had to back a trailer for many years. I would not be confident of doing any better than he does.

He confirms they placed the camera and I tell him, 'Yes, I've checked. Good vision. We can be a bit more comfortable tonight watching their routine.'

I then update him on what Midge had shared, including that 'Big Eyes' are watching. Maria butts in, saying, 'What does he mean by Big Eyes?'

Pig responds, 'It's his term for bigwigs – you know, top brass.'

'Shit, so we have the top nobs of CIA, Homeland Security, and the like all watching our progress?' she responds.

'Yes, no pressure,' I reply with a smile.

We give MGC a call and update him. No answer back on the DNA and I tell him a teaspoon is heading their way now, which should prove Nadia is Nadia.

CHAPTER 32

It's eleven p.m. two nights later and Pig and I are getting ready for our nighttime manoeuvre. We have blacked out the running lights on the tinnie. Pig and I took it down to the Broadwater again today for another test run, backing it into the water fine this time, and then we did some running, getting a feel for what speed causes the least noise and wake so we can minimise the attention we gain boating in the dark. I'm now dressed in the wet suit with the sea scooter already in the boat, along with my goggles and snorkel. We are going to meet Maria at the netball courts, where Pig will launch Gerty and leave Maria to fly it and monitor the area, not just the action point. We have agreed that I will exit the boat off Shearwater Park, which is just before we turn into the canal. (This will be interesting, I'm sure!) Maria thinks so, asking if Pig can take a video of 'the whale' exiting the tinnie.

From Shearwater Park, I will follow Pig in the tinnie to the channel marker, where he will stay on station and I will start my infiltration. It is only 180 metres from the channel marker to the pontoon and cruiser. I should be able to manage that.

At 12.45 a.m., we leave the motel, stopping at the netball courts. Pig gets Gerty in the air, giving Maria last-minute instructions, which she bats away, saying, 'You have told me a thousand times. I got it after three. Go.' She then wishes us luck. She is mic'd in with us, so she will hear what either of us has to say. Likewise, if she sees anything from Gerty she will warn us.

It's only twenty minutes to the boat ramp. There's no one around and Pig gets the trailer into the water first time. He remembers to untie the back of the boat first.

I hold the tinnie by its bow rope whilst he moves the Prado back to the car park. There are a couple of others parked here, out fishing overnight or whatever, and he parks between two of them. We never want to stand out!

I let him get in the boat before I push it out. I am in a wet suit, after all!

We putter south about one hundred metres from the shore. We see a group having a party on the northern end of Shearwater Park, so we keep going until nearly at the canal. Pig slows to an idle. I sit up on the edge of the boat, with goggles in place facing in and let myself topple backwards, just like we were taught during scuba diving training. It still feels unnatural to flop backwards into the water, but it works. Pig hands down the sea scooter. I turn it on, letting it idle whilst I fasten the snorkel in place, ensuring I can breathe freely.

Thumbs up to Pig and he moves off slowly, as agreed. I let him get ten metres in front and follow him, diving down to two metres. During our afternoon run, we had used the fish-finder to confirm the depth of the canal as far as the channel marker at least was comfortably over five metres. After that, I'm on my own.

We reach the channel marker. Pig idles down. I veer left under the road bridge, not that I can see it. I move toward the canal's right side, knowing I need the second boat moored along here.

Once I identify the correct one, I slow even more, pulling in under their pontoon. Kneeling, as there isn't sufficient room to stand under the pontoon, I check to ensure I have the right boat. Yep. I tap my earpiece twice so Pig and Maria know I have arrived. I secure the scooter to one of the pylons holding the pontoon, so it doesn't float away, retrieve the two 'carpet' rolls Drew supplied from my waterproof backpack and remove my goggles and snorkel, using the Velcro on these to secure to the scooter. Ready to rock 'n' roll!

I poke my head up the side of the pontoon, checking for any lights or movement in the house.

Nothing. I wait six minutes, just to be sure. I reach up and release the first of the 'carpet' rolls along the pontoon. The far end flops over the end of the pontoon, so yes, lengthwise, all good. I slide myself up out of the water and slither along the pontoon, feeling rather exposed whilst doing this with my back to the 'enemy'. Then again, I have Pig watching my back, and I would not want anyone else. I also know what Gerty is armed with, so I know I will be able to escape if the shit hits the fan!

We know from a close-up look we got from Gerty that there is no lock on the Cruiser door; a simple slide bolt holds it secure. I slip the bolt back and roll out the second roll. Down the steps and across the cabin. I need to reposition it a little so I can move about the cabin to affix the cameras and mics. I slip down the stairs on my tummy to again avoid standing up, ending up on the floor, where I crawl over to what is clearly his desk, with two computer screens with his laptop still plugged in.

Slack security, I reckon. No way I would allow my client to leave such an important laptop unattended. Still, that's made our job that little bit easier. I don't touch the laptop at all, not knowing what booby traps they have set. If any.

Whilst still on the stairs, I had identified a desk lamp for one camera and mic, with a second camera to go directly over his keyboard attached to the laptop. This should ensure we capture his passwords as well.

Quickly done and dusted. I have dry gloves on, so no prints or water left anyway. At the bottom of the steps, I pause and look back. No, nothing amiss. I haven't moved anything so I belly crawl up the steps, pausing before sliding the door open to see if any movement. Two taps come through my earpiece. Geez, Gerty must be giving Pig a good view if he knows I'm ready to come out! I slide out of the cruiser, winding the roll up behind me, reach up, slide the door closed and slip the bolt home.

A quick slither back along the pontoon takes me to my exit point. I slip down into the water, roll the roll up and pull it down off the pontoon, stuffing it into my backpack. Nearly ready to skedaddle.

'Twelve. Twelve,' comes through my earpiece in an urgent tone. Shit. Twelve o'clock is the house. Shit.

I slide down as far into the water on my stomach as I can, keeping my face buried in the mud under the pontoon. My backpack is also black and I have this tucked under my arm. Shit, now all I can do is wait and see what the alarm is. A whisper in my ear, 'Gregor approaching.' Shit.

All I can do is sit tight, not moving as the smallest movement will cause the water to ripple. A dead giveaway.

I hear footsteps as he comes onto the pontoon. He is walking slowly, not rushing. I take that as a big positive.

He stops directly above me. Shit. Thank goodness for my years of sniper training where I sometimes had to stay dead still for hours. My mind goes back to one such occasion where I was infiltrated six hours before my target was due to arrive, to avoid the increased security, half buried in sand, ants crawling all over me, even up my nose. Try not moving when that happens!

Back to the present. I have slowed my breathing down now, another must for snipers. He continues standing directly above me. I can smell the cigarette smoke, so I know he is having a smoke, but I also know he has not done this on any of the previous three nights we have been monitoring.

Something must have alerted him. My one saving grace may be that there is artificial grass covering the pontoon, so there is no way he can see me. But he will know if I make the slightest move with ripples in the water.

Suddenly, I feel something crawling over the back of my legs, which are just out of the water. Bloody two water rats by the feel of them. I feel their teeth nibbling the fabric of the wetsuit. I just hope they don't come up and check my face out.

Gregor moves above. The rats scurry off. Thanks, Gregor!

But he really only moved his weight from one leg to the other. I hear a lighter click, firing up another cigarette. *Take your time, mate. I'm not going anywhere!*

After what seems an eternity, he turns and walks back to the end of the pontoon. I hear the treads stop before he steps off onto the lawn. I don't move.

Another ten minutes go by. He moves off the pontoon and now I have no idea where he is or what he is doing. I am totally dependent on Pig. He whispers, 'Stay put. He is standing on the patio, just lit another cigarette.'

I can't acknowledge without moving. Pig knows that. Patience is a virtue and I have plenty.

Finally, Pig says, 'He has moved back inside, but something has made him suspicious so sit tight for a bit longer.'

Again, I don't acknowledge.

Silence. In the stillness, I realise the outgoing tide has exposed more of my body, raising my concern of being able to go underwater when it is time to leave my hidey-hole.

Eventually, Pig says, 'Okay, he seems to have moved from the window. Let's see how well you can get away without leaving a trail.'

I don't bother acknowledging but start pushing myself backwards into deeper water, at the end of the pontoon, staying on the inside of the cruiser. At the back of the cruiser, I'm in deeper water. I slip my snorkel on and push my body down underwater, feet first.

I bring the scooter out in front of me and turn it on to idle. It pulls me off my feet ever so slowly and out into the canal. I head straight past Pig but rap my knuckles twice on his hull as I go past, so he knows I'm heading straight out to the Broadwater. Once there, I veer north and surface off Shearwater Park.

Phew, that was tight.

I'm bobbing in the water as I see Pig's small wake coming toward me. He idles down as he comes alongside me. He leans down and we silently fist bump.

That was a bit tight!

I lift the scooter up out of the water and he places this in the boat. I remove my goggles and snorkel, dropping these in as well.

I then reach up and pull myself over the side, again on the seaward side, so difficult for anyone on the shore to see what we are doing. I do admit, the tinnie gets a bit wobbly there for a second with all my weight hanging on one side, but Pig had compensated somewhat by sitting on the other gunwale.

Once I'm back on board, he opens the little outboard up and we head back to the boat ramp.

Maria comes through our earpieces. 'I can hear the motor going, so I'm guessing you are away safely?'

'Yes, all clear,' I reply.

'Glad to hear it. I was bloody nervous during that, so I can only imagine how you were feeling.'

'That's what we trained for, Maria, but yes, it was a little nerve-racking, especially when a couple of water rats took a liking to my wet suit.'

'Ew, yuck. I would have squealed the house down!' she replies, causing Pig and I to smile, relieving some of our tension.

CHAPTER 33

Up early the next morning and I take myself off for a good run. Re-energising the body and mind.

Quick breakfast in the motel room with the camera and mic turned on.

We know from the last couple of days, Badour wanders down to the cruiser around nine-thirty to ten a.m.

However, it is Gregor who emerges first not long after seven a.m. He pauses outside, lights a smoke and casually walks down to the pontoon, again looking everywhere. Clearly, he's still puzzled by whatever disturbed him last night.

He looks over both sides of the pontoon and with it now being just past low tide, I am hoping I have not left any visible marks in the mud. Mind you, I was directly under the pontoon, so he will need to get down in the water to see any marks, if indeed any are still there.

He clearly doesn't see anything to raise his suspicions and continues to the cruiser, slides the bolt open, flicks on the light and stands there, looking over everything.

No, nothing out of the ordinary. He turns the light off, closes the door, wandering back to the house.

It's closer to ten when Badour emerges, coffee cup in one hand, satchel slung over his shoulder, and heads off to the cruiser. We three are all watching, keen to see if my cameras will do the job.

He enters the cabin, puts his coffee down on the desk, reaches over and opens the laptop then places his satchel on the right side of the desk.

Yes, clear vision of everything he is doing. Now, the critical part.

Will we see his password?

Yes!

He actually has two separate passwords. Pig and I both write these down, even though the vision and audio are being saved directly to our cloud. These passwords are followed by another screen requiring a scan of his right eye. Well, that's a bugger. We don't have options to get around that.

We look at each other, pulling faces.

Badour's screen comes alive and he accesses his emails with another password. We again record this. Once he has scanned through the emails received overnight, he minimises this and opens up a bank account – more passwords recorded. We look closely. Shit, twenty-four million dollars plus change.

Fuck, what are all these funds being used for? I note the name of the bank at the top of the page. First Bank of Dubai. Never heard of it.

Boom and boom!

Pig and I smile and reach out and fist bump. Maria, not to be left out, joins in also with a big smile, saying, 'We did well, didn't we!'

'Yes, Maria, we did. A good team job.' We all fist bump again.

Pig pulls his phone out, saying, 'I'm ringing Midge to let him know what we have got so he can give me a link to upload this shit to.'

He dials Midge but as usual, he doesn't pick up.

Not unusual; he will no doubt call us back shortly.

He does. This time it's The Veronicas' *If You Love Someone* he uses as a ringtone.

Pig answers, putting it on speaker.

'Yo, boys, what's happening?'

Pig answers, 'Hi, Midge, just need a link from you so we can share ongoing images we have for you.'

'Cool, what have we got this time?'

'We have Badour using his laptop, including passwords, bank account details – the works.'

'Woo-hoo. Way to go, boys, that's awesome. I'm sending a link right now. Hold on.'

Pig again. 'This time we have our colleague Maria helping us and listening in, Midge, so watch your language.'

Midge laughs, saying, 'Ho, Maria. You keep esteemed company.'

To which she replies, 'Yes, someone needs to keep them in line!'

He laughs again, saying, 'Good luck with that!'

Pig again. 'Right, have sent the link to our feed. This is live. Only problem is he uses a double password, both recorded for you, but then he has a right eye scan. So that's above our expertise level. Hopefully not yours.'

'Mmm, that's a bugger but not surprising, really. It might give me a chance to test a theory of mine out. Let's watch and collect what we can for a few days, see how it pans out. I'm watching the feed now, bloody awesome.'

'From the one bank account we have seen so far, he has twenty-four million sitting there. That can cause a lot of death and destruction,' I add.

'My oath, it can. Some of that might have to get lost in cyberspace. On it, boys. Let's stay in touch and keep monitoring. I hope you understand just how significant a breakthrough this is, boys. As I said, big eyes are watching and will be rightfully very impressed and appreciative of your work. Keep it up.'

'Right-o. So you know, we now have them under full surveillance. The feed you are watching is coming from his moored cruiser that we accessed last night. We don't yet have anything in the house – we consider it too dangerous to try and enter presently. This seems to be his main workstation, so I'm sure we will gain much from here. Let us know if you have any questions or need further info.'

'Cool, boys and girls, awesome job. Will be in touch.'

I jump in quickly, saying, 'Midge, let's keep this to as small a group as possible for now, ah. If Badour is as big a wheel as you say, we don't know have far his tentacles reach.'

There is a slight pause as he considers what I'm saying.

'Okay, Mort. I understand. You're the ones at risk here but do you have a reason to be suspicious of a leak?'

I answer quickly, 'No, Midge, but we stay alive by being ultra-cautious.'

'Cool. Got it. Stay safe. I will update you with any further data that comes my way.'

And he's gone.

Another three-way fist bump with smiles all round.

Just then, the street vision shows their garage door opening and the RAV4 backing out. I look at Maria. 'You're up.'

'Cool, I'm on it.' Grabbing her handbag, she's out the door.

'We better give MGC an update now,' I say to which Pig replies, 'Let's get coffee first. There is a little café back down the road I've seen, Harvest Bakehouse café.'

'Great, maybe something yummy to eat with a name like that – let's go.'

CHAPTER 34

It's two weeks later, a Friday. It has been a busy two weeks. The camera and mic on the cruiser have helped, gaining an inordinate amount of incriminating data from both his laptop and Badour's phone calls, which we couldn't understand, but Midge has had translated. We have captured the phone numbers of many of his contacts; apparently, many new ones that Midge and his people weren't aware of.

Midge had managed to gain access to Badour's records by logging on at the exact same time as Badour. This somehow bypassed the eye scan (don't ask me how, but Midge's theory proved correct.) Midge then changed the login procedure, making the eye scan optional. So, whilst we continue to record everything that goes down, Midge now has direct access to all Badour's records and files. Two other members of their syndicate have been identified, both living under false identities in Melbourne. They are being left alone, whilst we continue to milk Badour for all the data we can.

There was even a phone conversation with one of these Melbourne-based contacts about 'stage two of the water supply poisoning'. Badour confirmed he was keeping his 'field team' warm. Clearly, he has plans to use the O'Donnell brothers again.

Midge had also managed to divert a five million dollar payment being made by Badour to an unknown Indonesian terrorist group, which is causing consternation at both ends of the transaction!

Sniff sniff.

It's dinner time. Suzie and I are having a quiet dinner at home when my phone rings. I glance at it, seeing it is Ronnie, Maria's husband. *That's odd,* I think.

'Hi, Ronnie. How's things?'

'Hi, Mort. Sorry to bother you but do you know where Maria is? She hasn't come home yet and her phone is going straight to message bank. So, I'm hoping you can tell me where she might be?'

Shit.

'No, sorry, I don't. She is meant to ring in when she finishes for the day and sorry, I don't recall her ringing in tonight. Let me check with Pig and come back to you. I'm sure she is fine; we know where she was working this afternoon and will sort it out. I'll get back to you shortly.' I hang up, already dialing Pig and waving to Suzie as I head for the stairs.

'Not so fast,' Suzie says in a firm and authoritative tone. I pause, looking back at her. 'What's going on with Maria?'

'Not sure yet. I need to check with Pig to see if he took her call when she finished up; otherwise, I'm not sure. We can track both her phone and car, so as soon as I get downstairs, I will be doing that.'

Her response is, 'Nothing better happen to her, Mort.' Shit, I don't think Suzie has ever spoken to me like that.

I nod to her and race down the stairs as Pig picks up.

'Mate, did you take Maria's end-of-shift call tonight?' I ask.

A pause. 'No, did you?'

'No. Shit. She was doing loose surveillance on the house, wasn't she?'

Me again, 'Hold on, I'm checking the location of her phone and car.'

As I'm doing this, I notice Suzie has come down the stairs and is watching, hands on hips, with a concerned or frightened look on her face.

'Shit, her car is coming up at the Runaway Bay Shopping Centre but her phone is showing at their address.'

'Fuck. On my way,' Pig replies and hangs up.

I hang up and go to the gun safe, dial up the combo and retrieve our Glocks (we had updated our hand guns a few weeks earlier, replacing the aging HandK's with new Glocks, all courtesy of Section V), and bullet proof vests, Suzie watching silently. Before heading into the garage, I go over pull her into a hug and whisper, 'She will be fine. We will do whatever it takes to bring her back.'

She pulls away, asking earnestly, 'What do you think has happened?'

'I don't know and don't want to speculate but she should not be, and would not have, gone to their house without letting us know.'

I see she is close to tears, so I pull her close again for another quick hug before saying, 'Gotta go. Will keep you posted.' A quick peck on the cheek and I'm off.

Pig has the Prado so all I have is the iLoad.

I'm quickly through the suburban streets, onto the M1 southbound and it is Hammer Down. Speed limit be buggered. I am not driving like a grandfather tonight.

Forty minutes later, I'm pulling into the Runaway Bay Shopping Centre, following the tracking app to the Camry that Maria was driving. Pig is ten minutes behind me.

Yes, there is the Camry, parked and locked. I use my unlocker app to open it, checking it for anything out of the ordinary. Nothing. I relock it.

Pig pulls up.

I shake my head. 'Leave the Prado here. Let's go do a drive past.'

He quickly parks and locks the Prado. Before I drive off, he says, 'I checked the video and I have the RAV4 coming home and straight into the garage just after six. Both Badour and Nadia went off in a limo just after five-thirty p.m., both dressed to the nines. Then I remembered Hoang mentioning some charity ball the other day, so I checked and yes, the Chinese Arts Council ball is on tonight.'

'So, worst case, somehow Gregor has caught Maria and has her as a prisoner. Shit.'

It's, of course, dark now as we head back, turning left onto Lae Drive and quickly left again.

We circuit around Pebble Beach Drive, not slowing as we go past their house, a large two-storey home, similar to many of its neighbours.

We pull up back by the junction of the Yardarm and turn the lights off. Pig has tried Maria's phone again, as we both have throughout our drives down. I have also rung Ronnie back to say we are unsure where Maria was, but we are on our way to investigate.

We sit there quietly, discussing options, one being to swim across from beside the bridge to gain silent entry. Then, just as we agree that would be our best option, the garage door goes up and the RAV4 backs out. My phone rings. It's Maria. I put it on speaker.

'Hi, Maria. Are you alright?'

She bursts into tears, sobbing. 'Yes. I am now.'

I cut her off. 'Is that you driving the RAV4?'

'Yes. How did you know?'

'We are parked down the road. Keep coming. You're safe now. Head to the netball courts – we will follow you.'

Pig pipes up, saying, 'Maria, you're safe. We have your back.'

We hear her having a good cry as she leaves her phone on.

We wait a couple of minutes to see if anyone follows her out but no one does. She didn't shut the garage door either. No matter.

I quickly catch up to her and follow her to the netball courts, which is deserted at this time of night.

We pull up beside her. Pig is out in a flash. He helps her from the RAV4 and pulls her in for a big hug as she once again breaks down sobbing. He leads her over to a bench and they sit tightly together, Pig offering soothing words and comfort. Me? I feel like a fish out of water. As you know, sympathy is not a strong point of mine. But look out if I find out if anyone hurt her.

I reply to a text Suzie had sent some minutes ago demanding an update. *'Maria is fine. Shaken but fine. Busy now.'* Hopefully the last bit will stop her ringing or asking more questions for now.

After ten minutes or so, Pig coxes the story from Maria, by which time I am sitting beside her as well, having also given her a strong hug, bringing more tears and a mumbled 'sorry, Mort'. I pull her tight again for a moment, saying, 'You don't have anything to be sorry about.'

She starts with the story. 'Nothing had been happening, so I went to Woolies to grab some groceries to take home for dinner. As I came out, Gregor was walking toward me, so I turned right, hoping he hadn't recognised me. But he came up beside me, saying, "I would recognise those legs anywhere. Keep walking straight ahead." Up close, he is a big, intimidating man. I did as I was told, ending up at the RAV4.

'He told me to get in the back, which I did. He got in without saying anything else. I tried the door, but it must have had the child locks on as I couldn't open the door. He watched me try in the rear-view mirror, smiling at me when I couldn't open it. He didn't say anything and drove straight to their place.

'Once he had closed the garage door behind us, he opened the door and helped me out, holding me firmly by the elbow. The strength of his fingers told me he would break my arm if I tried anything.

'He took me straight into a bedroom, one I'm guessing he shared with Nadia as there were hairbrushes and make-up on the dresser.

'He pulled me to him and kissed me.'

Here, she breaks down, sobbing again, leaning into Pig for more comfort.

Shit, what happened? I'm thinking. From Pig's glance, it's clear we are sharing the same concern.

With the sobbing again subsiding, she continues, 'He was so strong. There was no way I could fight him off and escape, so I decided to play along, hoping that would improve my chances of escaping. He kissed me, and forgive me, but I kissed him back. I even undid his belt and trousers as he undid my blouse and bra, nuzzling my boobs.

'When his trousers dropped to the ground, he had no underwear on. Aaw. Anyway, as he was now thinking with his dick again and not his brain, I brought my knee up into his balls. This brought his head down and I met it with a double fist uppercut, which knocked him down. I grabbed the little Taser you gave me, Mort, and gave him a long dose.

'He is still out to it on the floor of the bedroom. I tidied myself up and got out of there. Thank you for already being here for me.'

We are both giving her a three-way hug now. I say, 'Wow, Maria, that was quick thinking. Not many would have been smart enough to play along. No question you got away because of that. Well done.' And I give her shoulders another squeeze.

'I just want to go home and give Ronnie and the kids a big hug,' she says as the tears slide down her face again.

Pig is calming her and asks, 'Would you like me to drive you home?'

'No, no, I don't want to have to tell Ronnie what nearly happened. He won't let me continue working with you if he finds out. You can't tell him or Stacey or Suzie, please.' Looking at both of us, she adds, 'I'm serious. Please, this has to remain between us only.'

I look at Pig. He nods back so I say, 'As you wish, Maria, but I am going to encourage you to talk to a psychologist or someone, so you get closure on this. I don't want your mind wandering there in the middle of the night with all the what-ifs. Understand?'

She nods, regaining strength and her composure.

'Okay. You best give Ronnie a call. He rang me asking where you were. Sorry, we didn't realise you hadn't rung in to clock off. We need to ensure we don't slip up like that again.' I'm looking at Pig as I say this. He pulls a face and nods his agreement.

She takes a shuddering breath. 'What am I going to say?'

After a pause, Pig replies, 'Let's say you had to turn your phone to aeroplane mode as our targets were sitting next to you in the café and you were recording their conversation.'

Maria and I mull this over, looking for holes, as we will both come under scrutiny from Ronnie and Suzie respectively.

'Sounds good to me. You can always claim you can't say anymore as it is confidential. We will use the same story. Believe me, Pig and I are in trouble with the girls for forgetting about you.'

She nods, looking around, perhaps only now realising where she is.

'Okay, Maria, you get in the van with me. Pig will drive the RAV4 to the shopping centre and give it a good wipe down so no clues. You can grab the Camry and head home. What happened to your groceries?'

'They should be still in the RAV4. I'll check.'

'No, don't worry about them. Pig will bring them when we meet at the Camry.'

She nods as Pig helps her to the van before she swats him away, saying, 'I'm okay now.'

We drive back to the shopping centre. Pig parks nearby and brings the groceries over with him.

Maria settles herself in the Camry, winds the window down so we can say goodbye and asks, 'What are you going to do now?'

Pig and I look at each other. We haven't spoken about this, but I say, 'Likely going to visit Gregor and if he is still out to it, capture him and hide him somewhere, maybe teach him a lesson he won't forget for a while.'

'Good,' she says and she drives off with a wave.

I text Suzie, saying, *'Maria is on her way home now. She got stuck recording our target and couldn't use her phone. All good.'*

She replies, *'Thank God. YOU better NOT FORGET to check on her in future.'*

Yes, she used capitals. I know I will hear more about this and frankly, we deserve her to break our balls. We stuffed up and Maria nearly suffered terribly because of it. Thank goodness she had the strength and fortitude to fight back.

Pig shows me his phone with a similar but even more forthright message from Stacey. I say, 'Well, we deserve it.'

He nods.

'Okay, what say we take the van over, back into the garage and extract Gregor. Badour and Nadia won't be home for at least a couple of hours I suspect, so we can plant mics and cameras in the house. We will leave the Prado here and come back sometime to collect it. Will be interesting to see how they react to Gregor missing. We need to be ready to pounce in case they decide to disappear.'

He nods. Game on.

On the drive over, he asks, 'Where can we hide Gregor if we aren't going to arrest him and put him into custody?'

I nod, saying, 'I'm keen to keep him out of the system, so I'm thinking we store him in Uncle Albert's wine cellar. It's a subterranean cellar – only has a few bottles left in it last time I looked, as he doesn't socialise much now Aunty Steph is dead. The wine is all behind bars anyway. We might have to reinforce it or secure him so he only has limited movement.'

The garage door is still up, so I back the van in. Pig dons gloves from the glovebox, handing me a set as well. I had given him his gun and we had put our vests on earlier. We now draw these. The door from the garage is closed but not locked when I try it.

Storming a potentially armed and dangerous house is bread and butter to Pig and I.

We take up positions. I'm standing tall, Pig crouched on the floor. I pull the door open. I'm aiming right, Pig left.

Clear.

Maria had confirmed the bedroom where Gregor was is to the right, but we need to clear the house first, in case he or someone else is in the kitchen area. I go right toward the bedroom, Pig left to the kitchen and living area. The bedroom door is wide open. There, on the floor, is Gregor, trousers still down at his ankles. I quietly go in and check his pulse. Slow and steady. Still out to it.

I say 'one' so Pig knows one accounted for.

We meet up at the bottom of the stairs. A nod and we both walk quietly up the stairs, each as close to the edge of the steps as possible; less chance of stairs creaking there.

We clear each room quickly. All empty.

Good. Work to do.

Quickly back down the stairs, I give Gregor's pressure point a hard squeeze to ensure he stays out to it, whilst Pig rolls him onto his stomach, zip-tying his hands behind him.

We remove his trousers and therefore his dignity when he wakes up then zip-tie his ankles together. Tightly, Pig is making sure of that.

Done. We grab him – me by the shoulders, Pig by the feet – and carry him out to the van, laying him on the floor. We then use cargo straps to secure his body to the van. I throw his trousers on top of him. He may need these at some point.

He isn't going anywhere we don't want him to.

We grab a few mini spider mics and cameras, heading back inside.

A camera and mic in the kitchen and living room each, mic only in the main bedroom and Gregor and Nadia's bedroom. We don't need to see any 'action' that might happen in either these places!

We test both the mics and cameras – good to go.

There are some official-looking papers sitting on the dining room table, so I take photos of these, glance at my watch and see it's now after eleven p.m. Time to vamoose.

Back in the van and out of there.

Next stop, Uncle Albert's.

We don't say too much on the drive to Ormeau, a Northern Gold Coast suburb of acreage living, about halfway between Brisbane and the Gold Coast. You might recall Uncle Albert's place has white picket fences all around it, from when Aunty Steph had her horses. They were her passion.

Pig does ask, 'Is Albert still away with Mary in Europe?'

'Yes, not due back to Washington for a couple of weeks yet. Not sure when he is heading home. They seem to have really bonded.'

The spare key is hiding where it always is, and being an isolated property, there are no noisy neighbours. Gregor is still out to it in the back.

We leave him there whilst we go and check out the cellar.

It's pretty much as I remember it, except there is only wine in one area of the racks and I mention to Pig, 'In years gone by, all these shelves were full of wine.' Now they are either empty or have books or files dumped on them.

The stairs down are quite steep, and he had a little pully set up for lowering a small pallet back in the day.

The lights work and we both try pulling on the secure cages set up on either side of the cellar. 'He must have kept his expensive wine in these,' is Pig's comment.

We can't budge these, good; if we can't, Gregor won't be able to.

I express my plan to Pig. 'If we run a rope across the room, from one cage to the other, then tie him to this rope with a small tether, he will be able to move a little way along the rope. We can put a bucket down so he can pee and shit in it and leave a couple of water bottles there'—I point to a serving shelf on the side—'on that shelf. Make the tether just long enough that he can reach these, but nothing else.'

He nods. 'How do we stop him moving all the way along the rope?'

'We will tie another rope across the main rope, securing it to both sides as well. This will have a double benefit of making it more difficult to pull the rope away from the cages, as he won't get any pressure on it and also stop him getting too close to either wall.'

Pig pulls a face, impressed!

'Okay, I will leave you to fashion your fancy rope masterpiece. I'll set up the surveillance camera and mic. I will add one to the front of the garage as well, in case there are any visitors.'

We carry six millimetre nylon rope in the van, along with numerous other clamps, cleats and clips that can be used to secure it. (It is a veritable mobile workshop, isn't it!) The six millimetre rope has a breaking point of over three thousand kilograms – so our mate Gregor has zero chance of breaking it.

I grab this along with a Stanley knife and a handful of cleats I will use to tie off each end after securing it to the cages. That way there are no knots he can try and undo.

Now I have a plan, it doesn't take long to set up my prison system. I again use the six millimetre rope for the shorter tether, using a pulley thing so it moves along the main rope freely – until it meets the other ropes.

I give them all a good pull. I'm happy. Pig, with a smile, then gives each point a really vigorous yank. No movement.

He says, 'I'm impressed. You didn't learn that at boy scouts!'

I smile.

Time to bring Gregor into his new digs.

He is still out to it in the van. We go back and to ensure he isn't foxing, I tickle the sole of his foot. No reaction. Even so, Pig is standing at the side door, Glock in hand whilst I climb in and remove the tie-down straps.

With this done, I go to the rear door and pull his comatose body out by his feet.

His hands and feet are still zip-tied; even so, this is one of the more dangerous moments. If he is awake, that is.

No, I did a good job of putting him into Lala Land. He doesn't stir.

We shuffle through the house and when we get to the cellar stairs, I put his feet on the top of the stairs and motion for Pig to lay him down and get down in the cellar. He does this. Once Pig is down and out of range I push Gregor down the stairs, feet first. Remembering what he had tried to do to Maria means I don't have much sympathy if he gets injured or not.

He slides down, coming to a stop in a heap on floor, his head banging down hard as it bounced off the last step.

He gives a moan, as I too step down into the cellar.

He stirs, his eyes fluttering.

We stay quietly where we are, one either side of the room, so he has to swivel his head to see us.

We wait patiently whilst he regains his senses, testing the ties holding his arms and legs before trying to focus on us.

He says, 'Who the fuck are you?'

I resist saying you-know-what and instead say, 'Your new best friends. If not for us, you would already be locked up, key thrown away. Until the deportation to Germany is approved, of course.'

I throw this in, so he knows we know who he is – that is, his real identity, not his Australian bogus one.

He looks at me and turns to look at Pig, saying, 'My head is bleeding. I need treatment.'

Pig replies, 'Not going to happen. You can bleed to death for all we care.'

(He does have a small cut on back of his head where it has bounced off the concrete floor. I would describe it as weeping, not bleeding.)

'Now, it's past our bedtime, so if you're a good boy, we will finish securing you in your new home and leave you to have a pleasant night.'

'Where am I?'

'Your own personal prison. Far more comfortable than sharing a small cell with two or three others. Our prisons are overflowing and overcrowded, so think yourself lucky.'

Whilst Pig stands guard, Glock at the ready, I approach him from behind, lift him by the shoulders and drag him toward the tether in the centre of the room. I'm a bit surprised (and disappointed) he doesn't resist. I secure the tether to his zip-tied wrists, then when I walk around in front of him, he drops his upper body, using the rope as leverage, trying to kick me. I am deliberately too far away for him to reach me, so with him now laying on the ground, with his upper body held up by the rope, I step in and bend down, right fist smashing his nose. Blood and snot go flying. I step back.

I give him a few minutes to clear the shit out of his nose before asking, 'Want to try again?'

He just lies there with a murderous look in his eyes. If looks could kill, he would need a lot more than looks, let me tell you.

Pig steps up. He points to the bucket and the water bottles. I had also added a few muesli bars with the water bottles. Don't want him starving. 'Help yourself. We will be back to check on you in a few days.'

With him still half-lying and still being held up by the rope, Pig goes to step over him and at the last minute, drops his boot into his balls, basically standing on them. Gregor howls in pain. Pig says, 'That's for trying to rape a friend of ours. I might come back and do that again in a few hours, hopefully putting you out of commission forever.'

He is still bent over in obvious agony as we climb the stairs and lock the cellar and house as we exit. I keep the key, don't want any of my extended family visiting and finding our private prisoner.

Once in the van, Pig pulls the camera footage up on his iPad and we watch as Gregor first tests his binds and then tries pulling the cages. To no avail. He slumps down onto the floor, head bowed, having to constantly wipe the blood from his nose. With his hands tied behind his back, he can't even try to massage his balls, which must be hurting something wicked.

Sniff sniff.

I look at my watch, thinking it's not too late, and dial up MGC.

I expect it to go unanswered, but he picks up, saying, 'Mort, for you to be ringing this late, you must have an update.'

'Yes, Sir. You are on speaker with Pig. Sir, tonight we took an opportunity to grab Gregor. We have him safe and secure. Badour and Nadia have gone to a charity ball tonight, so they are not aware we have Gregor. It will be interesting to see how they respond to him being uncontactable. We will be ready to go in if and when they show signs of disappearing.'

'Understood, Mort. Where are you holding him?'

'We have him in my uncle's wine cellar, quite secure and safe. I thought it better to keep him out of custody, as you just don't know who might become aware of this.'

'And your uncle is okay with this?'

'He's travelling in Europe, Sir, not expecting to be home for some weeks.'

Silence as he digests what I have told him.

'Very well, I see no harm in this development. There is little to be gained by delaying arresting the three of them as we now have full access to their records. As you say, you need to be ready to swoop should they show signs of flight. Now, tell me how and why this opportunity arose.'

Here, I let Pig relay the evening's events. The real story, not the concocted one.

At the end, MGC comes back, saying, 'Maria did well to get away from an obviously seasoned professional. And lucky.'

'Sir, we will keep you updated with any developments.'

'Thank you. Good night.' And he hangs up.

Pig says, 'I've just sent Midge an update as well, so he knows.'

He doesn't finish before his phone rings – back to a Keith Urban ringtone. He puts it on speaker.

'Ho, boys. Things must be on the up and up – you even have your own private prison cells, ah?' Midge asks, having a good laugh.

We smile and basically reconfirm what Pig told him by email.

'Clearly hotting up so looking forward to the next update. Be safe, boys.'

He hangs up.

We are approaching Brisbane when Pig says, 'Badour and Nadia have just arrived home.'

'Good. Can you turn the volume up so I can hear? Not going to be able to watch the video.'

'Sure.'

He does and the first thing I hear is Nadia say, 'Gregor is not home.'

'Where is he?' Badour asks.

'I don't know. We argued, he left.'

Silence. Then Nadia again, 'Thank you for buying this dress for me to wear tonight. It is very nice.'

I glance over to watch the screen as she says this, intrigued where this is going. I see her slide her hands over the dress and down her hips. Even I think it is a sensuous move.

Clearly, Badour does as well, as he moves closer, saying, 'It is my pleasure. You look very pretty in it. Very sexy.'

I can't resist taking another peek and yes, they are now kissing. Eyes back on the road. I hear what sounds like a zip coming down. I ask, 'Is that what it sounds like?'

I sense Pig is smiling as he replies, 'Yes, it is.'

Next, Nadia says, 'Upstairs.'

Again, I sneak a peek and see them disappearing up the stairs, Nadia's dress abandoned on the floor behind them.

The mic in the bedroom soon has the soundtrack of their lovemaking, which Pig turns down.

I can't help laughing out loud, saying, 'Of all the different scenarios I have thought through for when they got home, them hitting the sack together was not one of them.'

I'm still smiling fifteen minutes later when I drop Pig off when I say, 'Can't wait to check the footage in the morning now as well.'

He too is smiling as he exits the van.

CHAPTER 35

Next morning, I'm up earlyish. After making coffee, I'm sitting at the kitchen table. I pull up the live footage and see Nadia wrapped in a loosely tied towelling robe, sitting on a stool at the breakfast bar, drinking coffee (yes, I know it's coffee as I see her make it!)

Badour appears down the stairs. He is middle-aged, medium height, a bit on the plump side. He's nothing to look at and is also dressed in a robe with his hair still disheveled. She raises her cup to him, and he says, 'Yes, please. Is Gregor home?'

She shakes her head in the negative.

'Good,' is Badour's response as he heads directly to Nadia, leaning in and kissing her, undoing her robe as he does so.

I see she has nothing on underneath. Her robe hits the floor, as does his. I'm smiling as I watch, when Suzie, coming into the kitchen, cinching her housecoat, asks, 'What are you smiling at?'

'X-rated surveillance!'

'Show me.'

I turn my iPad just in time for her to see two naked butts rushing up the stairs.

'What were they doing?'

I gently pull her to me and kiss her and at the same time as undoing her housecoat, saying, 'This.'

Suddenly, we too are headed back to the bedroom.

A bit later, I'm now getting breakfast, with the surveillance still on, but neither Badour nor Nadia have made it back down to the kitchen.

I have heard them talking about where Gregor might be, with Nadia suggesting, 'We have been having problems, not getting on, so maybe he has picked someone up and is screwing them. I do not know what other explanation to offer.'

They do not seem in a hurry to do anything about his disappearance. Maybe the sex is so good, it is all they can think about!

I send a link to the footage to MGC and Robert with a note. *'I don't think we need to worry about them disappearing anytime soon!'*

I also pull up the coverage of Gregor in his private prison (making sure Suzie is not around to look over my shoulder). He doesn't seem to have moved, so I rewind it till when we left last night and double-speed through, just to see what he has been doing. Not much. Not much he can do.

A little later, I give Maria a call to check up on her. She answers and there are a lot of kids yelling in the background. I ask, 'Where are you?'

She replies, 'At Junior's footy game. We take turns. Ronnie is with the girls this week and I have the boys.'

'What about the youngest, Robbie?' I ask.

'He's still too young to play. He starts next year and can't wait. The boys love their footy games in the backyard. Especially when it's boys V girls, although the girls hold their own, I must say.'

'Okay, but how are you?'

A moment's pause and it seems quieter, so I suspect she has walked away from others to talk.

'I'm okay, gave the kids plenty of hugs last night and again this morning, Ronnie even got special hugs, so he is happy, and so am I. Thank you.'

'Good. My offer stands; in fact, whilst I won't insist on you seeing someone, I really hope you will.'

'Yes, Mort, I have been thinking about that and yes, I will. Thank you. I just don't know who.'

'Yeah, not sure I can help there. Normally, I would ask Suzie as she would certainly know a couple that have worked with some of her clients.'

'No. I'm not going there,' is Maria's firm reply.

'Well, let me know if you want a hand finding someone. The only other option I can think of is MGC, as we told him what happened and

I'm sure they would know a psychologist they can recommend. You will be pleased to know Gregor is locked up safe and sound, and I can assure you he is in pain.'

'Yes, Pig called me earlier and explained. The arsehole got what he deserved. It's curious that Badour and Nadia don't seem too concerned from what Pig said.'

I laugh, saying, 'Yes, they are still at it. They have hardly left the bedroom. We had X-rated surveillance there for a while!'

As I say this, I have an idea.

We say our goodbyes, just as Suzie comes up to say goodbye. She has taken up coaching junior netball now, so Saturday has become a day of leisure for me. Well, in theory, as she crushes that thought by saying, 'I have left you a list of chores on the table and I will check them off when I get home,' with her impish grin.

I prolong the goodbye kiss, asking, 'What is my reward if I get them all done?'

She uses her tongue to imply a very enticing reward before breaking the kiss and waving goodbye.

As I watch her go, I reflect. *Life is good!*

At least the kiss got me to look at the list! Mmm, not too bad. Lawns mown, edges trimmed, decking washed – where is that rain when you need it? But then I notice at the bottom, washing and vacuuming done – rain won't wash those off the list.

Ah well, I can easily put on a load of washing to get started.

But first I need to call Pig.

'Mate, you been watching the X-rated videos?' I start the conversation.

'Yeah, I have been. Stacey even caught me watching it, thinking I had taken to watching porn!'

'You know we have Gregor live; is there any way we can feed audio back to him?'

'Why, what have you in mind?'

'Well, with Nadia screwing Badour, with all the soundtrack we have of them going at it, I was thinking, if we could feed this back to him, on loop, so it just repeats. It might have a pretty big effect on him psychologically.'

Pig considers this. 'I see your point, would be pretty deflating, being captured and your wife's reaction is to fuck the boss. Not once but over and over. Good thinking. Yes, I can make that happen. Leave it with me. What do you want to do about the Prado?'

'Hadn't thought about it, to be honest. Sorry, yeah, it leaves you without wheels. You have a thought?'

'Yes. As you know, Stacey finally got her Ps the other week. Now she has to get her hours up, so if we come over and grab the van, we will go down and pick it up. She can drive the Prado home. She has driven it before.'

'Sure, that sounds like a plan. Bear in mind though, the van is my only hope of getting out of my chore list today, so have sympathy on me!'

'Cool. You're a big boy, you can win your own battles. Those you want to win, anyway,' is his reply.

'I'll set the tape up and feed it through to Gregor, then we will grab an Uber and come and pick the van up.'

'No worries, see you then.'

We hang up.

I have another thought.

Gee, that's two this morning. Things are on the up and up.

I email Midge, asking, *'As we don't talk Indonesian* (Badour's native tongue) *can you urgently get any conversations he has translated and let us know ASAP if these relate to him disappearing? Thanks.'*

Good. Now where was I? Yes, putting on some washing, then hoovering (funny how it's still called that when we mostly use Dysons these days!). Then outside in the sun.

Oh, joy.

I have hung the washing and finished the vacuuming and am enjoying a coffee when Pig and Stacey arrive. I go downstairs to see her, as she is now at thirty-two weeks pregnant and struggling a little, so I don't want her having to climb the stairs. She is in good spirits, teasing Pig about being caught watching porn this morning, so I ask, 'What's his punishment going to be?'

She smiles back, saying, 'It is nothing compared to what I am going to do to him for putting me up the duff and giving me this,' as she rubs her swollen tummy.

Pig, of course, ignores us both, saying, 'I have set the tape up and it's feeding back to Gregor. It started about twenty minutes ago. Make sure you go back and watch the start to see his reaction.' He has a smile.

As they get in the van, I say to Stacey, 'Congrats on getting your Ps. Has he bought you a car yet?' (I know he hasn't, as he is still a little scared of her being on the road on her own, often claiming 'she shouldn't be allowed to drive' and always giving a little shudder when saying this. So, I am just stirring.)

'No, he hasn't yet. He says we should wait until the baby is born.'

'Why?' I ask with my innocent face on (knowing Pig is just delaying it as long as possible.)

Stacey shrugs as Pig puts the van in gear, so I add, 'Why don't you let Stace drive, Pig? Would be good practice for her.'

I get the death stare as he pulls away!

Smiling, I head back upstairs, refresh my coffee and rewind Gregor's tape so I can watch his reaction.

Pig is right; Gregor's reaction is worth watching. Pig started the tape from when they arrived home, so with a slight lead-in before the kissing starts. On hearing their voices, he immediately is looking around, trying to work out where the voices are coming from, then, as their words sink in, his face shows, anger, frustration and defeat and back to anger. As the tape roles on, with the various instances of their interactions, he bows his head.

A frustrated and beaten man. One never to be taken lightly though. I suspect revenge will not be far away if he ever gets free.

A quick reply from Midge as well, *'Will do.'*

Now lawns and things for this suburban man!

I actually complete the list. I even have time to wash the van after Pig and Stacey drop it back and am sitting out on the deck having a beer when Suzie gets home.

Yes, she wanders around, inspecting my efforts and I even get a tick.

I am not telling you what my reward is, but we do have an early night!

CHAPTER 36

Monday morning and we are all in the office. Not much has changed at the house, although they are spending more time down in the lounge now.

We listen to them again, discussing Gregor's disappearance, with Badour saying he has reported his absence and 'they' had come back asking what his plan is. He then asks of Nadia, 'What do you think?'

She takes her time before replying, 'Well, I still don't have a better explanation than he picked up some floozy and has been screwing her all weekend.' (Pig adds, 'Just like you.')

'He should be home today if this is the case. Then again, he might now be having regrets, or be embarrassed, so he may find it difficult to come back and face me.'

Badour asks, 'Do you have any regrets?'

She smiles, saying, 'No.'

'What will we do when he does come home?'

She moves over to him, takes his hand and says, 'For now, we have to revert back to normal. We are your security team – our first priority has to be keeping you safe. Then one day, maybe we can get together.'

He kisses her, then says, 'You are right. I will have trouble keeping my hands off you though. I might have to send him on some overnight tasks, so we can get together more.'

She smiles, they kiss and suddenly head back upstairs.

They certainly are sexed up.

Good, from our point of view, keeps them distracted and avoids them making new plans.

Pig and I decide we need to go down and visit Gregor and empty his bucket, if nothing else.

It's obvious he is in agony when he has a pee, the way he throws his head back and moans. Seems to have stopped drinking, to avoid the need to pee too often.

No sympathy.

Late afternoon, Badour is in his office on the cruiser. His phone rings. There follows a rapid-fire discussion in Indonesian, and whilst we cannot understand what is being said, it is clear Badour is being reprimanded, I suspect being told to get moving and disappear, as he is very circumspect, bowing his head as he speaks in a very respectful tone.

We look at each other and Pig says, 'Hope Midge doesn't take too long to let us know what that was all about. Whoever rang him must be even further up the tree than Badour to be able to talk to him like that.'

I agree, as we watch Badour close his laptop and unplug it, pulling the power cord out and taking these with him back to the house.

Maria asks, 'Is that the first sign they are fleeing?'

'I suspect so,' I reply.

A short time later, we get our confirmation as he says to Nadia, 'We have to move. I have been instructed. Pack what you need. We will be leaving in the morning. But we still have tonight.' He comes close and kisses her.

Pig and I discuss options and we agree we need to move in tonight. Maria butts in, 'Don't exclude me. I have been in from the start and want to see it through. Please.'

'Fair enough but you will be support, outside the house. Pig and I will be the only ones going in. Agreed? Besides you don't have a bulletproof vest. We will have to organise one for you for next time,' I end with a smile.

She nods acceptance.

With a sort of plan made, we put a call in the MGC.

When he answers, I say, 'Sir, you are on speaker with Pig and Maria. It's time to bring the hammer down on these two. They are making plans to leave tomorrow, so we plan on going in tonight, arresting them whilst they are sleeping or whatever they may be doing.'

'Yes, there has certainly been plenty of promiscuous activity, hasn't there?' is his diplomatic answer.

'Your plan?'

'Sir, we will enter around two a.m. unless we see or hear anything that makes us change our plans. Will you arrange a liaison with either AFP or Queensland Police?'

'Yes, I will do that. In fact, I plan on coming up myself. I will arrange flights so I arrive there on the Gold Coast later this afternoon. I will then handle the liaison myself.'

'Good-o, Sir. Let us know where you want to meet this evening.'

'Why not book a table for dinner and we can discuss plans whilst we eat. Are you looking for any support for the arrests?'

'No, Sir, we will handle that, but ideally we want to hand them over to the authorities once we have them under arrest and out of the house. The police can then do a thorough forensic investigation, take the house and cruiser apart for any hidden documents, and the like. In reality, they will be taking the important data with them, so likely they will have this all packed, ready to go. We will also need to hand over Gregor sometime. But if okay with you, we will do that tomorrow morning. We will source a nice restaurant and let you know. Six-thirty p.m. tonight suit you?'

'Oh, as an update for you, the Irish brothers have pleaded guilty to domestic terrorism, received a suspended sentence of five years. I have arranged for them to live their life as normal but their phones are monitored twenty-four seven. This is in case they receive contact for stage two. They are back living and working in Brisbane. Thought you would like to know.'

I'm a bit surprised they haven't had to serve any jail time, and I guess Pig is of the same opinion from the face he is pulling.

'Good-o, Sir, thanks for letting us know,' I reply.

We hang up.

We look at each other and nod. I say to Maria, 'Can you book two rooms back at the Runaway Bay Motor Inn again, please? We need to find a suitable restaurant.'

Here, Pig butts in, saying, 'There is a highly recommended steak house called Cavs Steakhouse there in Runaway Bay.'

'Good, book a table for five. Please.'

'Done.'

Maria asks, 'Five?'

'I assume Robert will come with MGC; he rarely travels alone.'

I text MGC Cav's address.

CHAPTER 37

That night, at 12.30 a.m., we meet MGC, Robert and a group of Queensland police as agreed at the netball courts. As luck would have it, the Runaway Bay police station is very close to the netball courts, so they all walk over, so there is not a noticeable police presence. The water police are in the canal, staying out of sight past the bridge, just in case they try and do a runner on the cruiser. Not surprisingly, DS Chris Harris is once again our nominated liaison. She has with her six other officers. I note there is also a couple of AFP officers as well. More liaison!

We lay out the plan and whilst there is some grousing about the police not handling the assault, MGC quickly stops that conversation. Pig puts Gerty up, again allowing Maria control.

At 1.30 a.m., Pig, Maria and I head off in the van, Maria driving. We are all mic'd up so everyone will hear what goes down. She stops at the Yardarm Junction. Pig and I alight. We are armed only with our Glocks, not believing we need the EF88s. However, Maria, who will remain here, is armed with one and we borrowed a bullet-proof vest for her as well. Once we enter the house, two police cars will also converge and hold station on either side of the house, thus preventing any escape on foot.

We use our door unlocker to enter the front door. We know they did not put the alarm on when they disappeared upstairs earlier. A quick check of all downstairs room and we meet up at the base of the stairs. We pause, look at each other, nod. *Let's do this.*

Silently up the stairs, again one either side to minimise risk of squeaky stairs. We know where the main bedroom is and have no reason to think they are not in bed together. It's not that long ago we had heard them at it. Again.

At the door, I crouch down, Pig taking the high level. We both stick our eyes around the door jamb.

Bang bang.

Shit, Nadia is sitting up in bed, buck naked, her weapon held in a two-handed shooters grip supported on her knees, firing at Pig. She has not noticed me. I'm now lying flat on the floor, Glock held out in front of me. Even as I watch, she fires another shot through the wall, at where Pig may have been standing, if he wasn't the pro he is.

'Drop it or you're dead,' I say loudly.

Her gun swivels toward me.

'Don't,' I say, my finger a whisker away from firing.

She seems to sense this, raising her arms.

Badour is now sitting up in bed, randomly pulling the sheet up to cover himself. Modesty is the least of his worries now.

'Drop it off the bed. Now.'

Whilst I'm saying this, Pig has slipped into the bedroom, moving quickly along the wall, so she knows she can't escape. No way she can get us both. Fire and she is dead. They both are.

She gives up, leans over and drops the gun onto the floor. All the while glaring at me.

'Now, hands behind your heads, both of you.'

They look at each other resignedly and do as they are told.

Pig holsters his Glock and handcuffs first Nadia, then Badour's hand behind their backs.

'Now lie flat on the bed, face down.'

They again do as they are told; Pig does his thing cable tying the feet together but loosely so they can still walk.

Once this is done, I say, 'Clear. Two in custody. Wait whilst we clear the rest of upstairs.'

I'm still prone on the ground, so Pig goes and does the search of the other rooms, comes back gives me the 'all clear' nod.

'Clear. They are naked. We will let them put robes on.'

Nadia finds her voice, asking, 'Do you mind if I put proper clothes on? Please.'

I ask, 'Do you have any up here?'

She is studying me, I think already sensing we know what has been going on. She asks, 'You have Gregor?'

'Yes, we do. He is in custody. Being entertained by the audio of his wife and boss fucking themselves silly, he is singing like a bird. Very keen to avoid being deported to Germany.'

She has the good grace to bow her head, then, realising we must have mics in the room, she looks around the ceiling and dresser. Pig kindly (or perhaps unkindly) points to the mic attached to the ceiling fan. She hangs her head once more.

Addressing Nadia, I say, 'Stay where you are. Badour, slide off the bed to your right.'

He looks up, I suspect shocked we know his true name, perhaps for the first time sensing this is the end of the road for him.

He does as he is told, sitting on the edge of the bed. Pig tells him, 'Stand up and turn around. He does and Pig uses his pocketknife to cut the bindings. 'Now pull the robe there on.'

'Can't I put clothes on?'

'No.' Pig's sharp response does not leave room to argue. He pulls the robe on, cinching it tight.

Pig pulls another set of premade cable tie handcuffs from his pocket and attaches these, tightly.

He then escorts him down the stairs into the hands of the police contingent, where he is read his rights. He immediately claims he is an Indonesian national, demanding they call the Indonesian consulate. I hear MGC reply, 'Your passport says you are Australian, not Indonesian. No can do.'

Meanwhile, I have regained my feet and continue to watch Nadia closely. I can sense her desire to try something.

I wait for Pig to come back up. With him covering her, we do the same procedure. As I step in to cut her bindings, she launches herself backward, aiming to take me to the floor. I sidestep and she falls flat on her arse with an oomph.

I smile down at her, asking, 'Clothes or starkers, no matter to me. Another effort like that and we will take you into custody as you are. Imagine how you will be received in the watch house, might even accidentally leave your cell door unlocked. You know, so some of the deviates in there can come in and get a taste.'

Glaring daggers at me, she pulls herself upright. Once again, she turns her back to me so I can cut her bonds.

'Your clothes are all downstairs in your room, so let's go.'

I again get a glare, as she realises how much we know.

She leads out of the room, turning down the stairs then realising the number of police down there. They all fall silent as they watch her walk down the stairs naked.

She even pushes her chest out in an act of defiance.

Doesn't impress me!

I hand her over to a couple of female coppers who escort her into her room and allow her to get changed.

CHAPTER 38

We are headed back home, up the M1, both alone with our thoughts, Maria having headed home in the Camry earlier. I notice the cop car ahead that is carrying Badour and Nadia. It is still a fair way ahead, but we have been gaining on it slowly.

Both doing the speed limit as per our respective speedos, I surmise.

All of a sudden, I notice a couple of sets of headlights catching us from behind. Fast.

I say to Pig, 'We have a couple of Prados coming up fast behind.'

He moves his head to watch in the offside wing mirror. 'How do you know they are Prados?' is his question.

'I recognise the headlight cluster,' I tell him. He pulls a face. Impressed.

'Bugger. They have now slowed down one car back.'

Suddenly, we are both alert, suspicious.

I speed up, wanting to close the gap on the cop car, a Hyundai Santa Fe ahead. Hopefully nothing to worry about.

But.

I'm now only about one hundred metres behind the cops when one of the trailing Prados pulls out and passes both the car behind and us. I check as it passes; two in the front seats, no one visible in the back.

It stays in the fast lane, but again slows, seemingly matching the speed of the cop car. The second trailing Prado then pulls out and comes alongside us. They aren't interested in us. No one takes any notice of a white Hyundai iLoad van – that's why we drive one. Again, I glance over and see this time there are three in the vehicle.

Pig and I share a look, he mutters, 'Fuck,' and pulls up his phone – I'm driving, remember?

I glance at a road sign that shows exit 38. Yatala North is approaching.

He dials MGC, but it goes to voicemail. Shit. This time he dials 000, requesting police and ambulance service. The operator wants to know what the emergency is.

Too late.

He says, 'Police under attack, exit 38, M1 northbound. Yatala,' and hangs up.

Suddenly, the lead Prado accelerates, passes the cop car and immediately pulls in front of it, slamming on the brakes. The second one then pulls alongside the Santa Fe, forcing it off the road to the left.

The cop driving does the only safe thing to do, and swerves onto the exit. But so do both Prados, boxing the Santa Fe in, forcing it off the exit ramp where it scrapes along the barrier before coming to a halt on the sloping grass verge.

All three vehicles come to a stop. Immediately, three exit the two Prados and they are armed.

Shit.

Shit.

Clearly, Badour does have an outer security team.

I have also now pulled off the highway onto the exit ramp. Lights and motor off and am coasting to a stop fifty metres behind them.

As we come to a stop, I see one of the attackers, pointing a gun at the driver. I see the recoil. Fuck.

Two others are trying to open the back doors.

I haul on the hand brake to stop the van, open the door and standing on the sill, I aim between the open door and the frame, and fire.

I don't miss.

The shooter has lost his head and his body crumples to the ground.

Pig, meantime, is already out of the van, running and firing at the assailant trying to open the passenger rear door. I notice he goes down in my peripheral vision. My focus is the third assailant, still trying to open the driver's side rear door. I fire again, two quick shots. They hit him in the side, all I had to aim for. He goes down, out of the fight.

As the rear doors remain closed, I'm guessing the cop car has a lock button that can only be released by the driver, who I suspect is dead or seriously injured.

Suddenly, I'm being attacked by the drivers of both Prados, both firing at me. I duck back behind the open driver's door. Safe, and knowing Pig is out and will be circling around to come at them from the front, i.e. their back, I continue to fire between the door and the frame, not hopeful of hitting either of them, but keeping their attention on me.

It's not long before I hear Pig fire once, then again.

Silence.

He, like me, is a crack shot.

We both run toward the cop car, checking the assailants as we go. Three dead; two still have a pulse.

The uninjured passenger cop is slowly getting out of the front seat. He is looking both shell-shocked and badly shaken. Pig gets to him first, puts an arm around his shoulder and says, 'Call this in quick. We tried to get it in before it went down, but no time.'

He reaches for his radio, calling in an 'officer down shooting'. Then, he adds, 'Exit 38 M1 northbound,' at Pig's coaxing.

His two prisoners are still sitting silently in the rear. Handcuffed and seat belted.

Right then my phone rings. I glance at it. MGC.

I quickly move away with a knowing nod to Pig and say, 'Sir, randomly we came up behind the cop car transporting Badour and Nadia to the watchhouse when it came under attack.

'Two vehicles forced it off the road. We intervened. We have one dead cop, three dead assailants and two others seriously injured. Prisoners and second officer unharmed, as are we. Clearly, Badour did have an outer ring security team.'

Quick and succinct. Just the way our MGC expects his reports.

'Where?'

'Yatala. Exit 38 northbound on the M1. Sir, unless you want us to do anything else, we will take the two prisoners and transport them to the watch house ourselves, leaving the mess for the cops to sort out.'

Silence as he digests this. 'Very well, proceed. I will call this through so you will be expected.

'Will get moving, Sir. We will wait here until help arrives but will transfer the prisoners to the van.'

'Good luck,' and he is gone.

He too won't be heading to bed anytime soon.

Sirens in the distance.

As it's so late and Yatala is largely an industrial suburb, we have not had anyone try to use the exit.

Pig is still consoling the surviving cop, whose name is Bob, and he is now sitting on the side of the road, head between his knees. I motion Pig away with my head and whisper, 'We are taking the prisoners to the watch house as soon as help arrives. Can you cover me whilst I move them to the van?'

'Sure.'

I go over to the cop and gently ask, 'How do I release the rear door lock?' He looks at me dumbly, no doubt thinking, *Why the fuck is that important right now?* So, I add, 'We need to get the prisoners to the watch house ASAP.'

Now he nods his head, understanding, saying, 'Same as any car, either of the front doors can open them.' Duh.

I nod my thanks and choose the passenger door, which he has left open. A quick glance at his colleague and no question he is dead. Poor bugger.

I open the passenger rear door where Badour is sitting, still in his towelling robe. I press my Glock into his ample middle, hard. I don't have to say anything; I'm menacing enough. I undo his seatbelt, remove the gun and using this wave him out.

I take his arm and force him, none too gently, toward the van. Opening the side sliding door, I force him in and across to the other side, step in and secure him in his seatbelt. With his arms still handcuffed behind his back, he is secure. But to ensure he doesn't create an issue when I come back with Nadia, I pinch the choke points in his neck. He is quickly in Lala Land.

I repeat the process with Nadia, again putting her out to it as well.

The sirens are getting closer, as I approach Pig and the cop who is now in constant contact with his control, answering their questions. He looks up, saying to Pig, 'My sergeant wants a word, please.'

Pig takes his phone, looking at me. I give him a tight smile, not a humorous one, knowing the officer will be struggling to understand what happened and who the hell we are.

As I get close, I hear Pig say, 'Yes Section V, we took these two terrorists down on the Gold Coast earlier, and simply, randomly, happened to be behind your team when this went down. We took out the assailants. Yes, three dead, two with pulses.

'What, you prefer we ask nicely?' This is said with a heavy dose of sarcasm as he looks at me disgustedly. 'Leave the bullshit for later. Your man needs support now. And you have a dead officer on the scene. We will bring the prisoners to the watchhouse ourselves. Not asking for permission, just telling you.'

His tone is getting stroppier with each sentence.

With a nod, he hands the phone back to Bob, just as a cop car comes careening off the M1. One of the Kia Stingers in its fancy highway patrol livery. It comes to a shuddering halt. The two officers exit and make a beeline for their surviving colleague.

I join the little group, sensing Pig might shoot them if they start asking any more stupid questions. Not really, but you know what I mean.

I interrupt them, saying, 'Right, we have the two prisoners and will deliver them to the watch house.'

The driver of the Stinger says, 'Who the hell are you?'

Before I can answer, Bob says, 'They came to our rescue and killed the attackers.'

The two newcomers stop and look at Pig and I, and yes, I know we are an imposing sight, so I hand over my Section V ID card. He looks at it before saying, 'You better wait until the watch commander gets here.'

'Not going to happen. This has been cleared to the top. We can't risk losing these two pricks again, so we are off.'

Curt nods from us both and we walk briskly to the van as more cop cars, an ambulance and even a fire engine turn up.

I move through the crowd, getting looks from everyone. Fortunately, this exit is a simple off-and-on, just have to negotiate the big roundabout and then back onto the freeway. I notice the big Yatala Pies sign as we accelerate up the on-ramp, randomly thinking, *Must remember to come down and have one of their pies again sometime. Maybe even one of their apple turnovers.* Then I realise how inappropriate it is to be thinking of food after what has just gone down.

Then it's hammer down.

CHAPTER 39

Four hours later.

I'm sitting in an interview room at police headquarters, having been escorted there after delivering the two terrorists to the watchhouse.

MGC had kept his word, for as we approached Mt Gravatt, I saw police lights coming up behind me, fast.

I mutter, 'Fuck, just what we need, a cop wanting to give me a speeding ticket. Where the hell did he come from?'

The bike cop quickly catches up. I'm in the outside lane and not moving over. I have my hazards flashing and these have mostly worked, clearing the cars in front of me. If they haven't, a loud blast on the horn and headlights on full does the trick.

The cop pulls up beside us on the inside, nods to us, accelerates in front and keeps going. Shit, an escort, I realise. He quickly gets way ahead of us, then slows down waiting for us, with Pig commenting, 'He just realised we are already doing our top speed.'

He leads us to the police watchhouse in the city, where officers are clearly expecting us. We hand our prisoners over, even getting receipts for them. We are then asked to follow one of the officers, separated, and placed in different interview rooms.

Just as well we are patient – not sure about Pig but it's over two hours before anyone comes in. Then a DS Strange walks in, saying, 'I need to take your statement of the events tonight.'

Now a third officer has just walked in, saying he wants to go over my statement, again.

Even though I'm a patient guy, I'm getting the shits with this carry-on. Being treated like a suspect, being put through the mill.

Suddenly, the door swings open. In marches MGC.

'This is over. Mort, you are free to go. Come with me.'

'Who the fuck are you? Stay right where you are,' this latest copper says to me. I haven't bothered noting his name.

MGC steps aside and the copper can see a superior officer (I later find out it's Assistant Commissioner Watson), who nods to him and says, 'Bruce, this has all been sorted out. Both gentlemen are free to go.'

I get up and walk out into the hall, where Pig is already waiting. We fist bump. MGC, with a final glare at the copper, joins us and the assistant commissioner escorts us out. He has even had the van brought around to the front for us.

Robert is also waiting out front for MGC with some sort of limo, driver and all.

Once out of the building, MGC says to us, 'I'm sorry about that. No excuse for them treating you like common criminals, like suspects. I will be making sure you receive an apology; don't you worry about that.'

Pig and I shrug, and I say, 'Thanks for breaking us out, Sir, was bloody obvious they didn't want to let us go. That was going to be the third time I had had to go through my statement.'

He acknowledges my thanks and says, 'I have taken a room at the Sofitel. Let's adjourn there now for a quick debrief. We can order an early breakfast if you wish.'

Yes, suddenly I realise we have pulled an all-nighter. Haven't done that for a while.

CHAPTER 40

Four days later.

After all the action, we all took a couple of days off to reset.

Although Pig and I had gone and retrieved Gregor from his prison the next morning. His first words were: 'I want to make a statement. Want to make a deal. There is a lot I can tell you.'

'Way above our paygrade, mate. We will let the authorities know. You're still coming with us now.'

We unshackled him, allowed him to put his trousers on, and he came along rather meekly.

Maybe our psychological ploy had worked!

I let MGC know he wanted to do a deal. He replied, 'Get him processed and I will have AFP talk to him. Well done!'

As agreed, we delivered him to the watch house where Chris was on hand to take him into custody. She also apologised, saying, 'I'm sorry about last night. There is a small group of senior officers – you know, the types who believe processes are more important than outcomes – who resent you and your successes. They see you as out-of-control "cowboys". Major General Rutherford made mincemeat of them last night, believe me, so you will not have any further issues, I'm sure,' she finishes with a smile.

This is our first day back in the office since.

Fresh coffees in hand, Pig and I adjourn to my desk. I invite Maria to join us as she walks in.

'Right. Now Badour and co are safely out of the way, we can refocus on Daniel Belgrave. Let's refresh our list, Pig, ah.'

Pig starts a summary of the Belgrave investigation. Maria and I watching and commenting as we go:

Darren Belgrave
- Address: Mudgerabah Gold Coast. Married, two children.
- Office: Thomas Drive, Chevron Island
- He is the male identified from Liz's phone, in the background of a photo of her meal.
- Also in the photo is Police Commissioner Mel?
- Had the capacity to put together a hit on Liz in only six weeks.
- Likely he drove Benson's car, which killed Liz.
- Proven close associate of Lancaster's.
- Through various entities (companies, trusts, etc) he has six tourism-related businesses on the Gold Coast and Brisbane.
- On his 'dark side', he has interests in five more businesses: three-night clubs, a shipping company and a used machinery business.
- He has twelve million in his various connected bank accounts.
- We have audio of him talking to high-ranked Garcia cartel members in the USA.
- We have audio and video from within his office.
- CCTV footage from his home.
- Whilst his phone is on the dark web, through the new software patch Midge provided, we are now monitoring his movements.

As yet, we don't have any evidence of wrongdoing for any of his eleven businesses.

Next steps:
- Check out the shipping company and used equipment business, see if these are legitimate businesses or mere fronts for his drug importation business.
- Understand why the used equipment transits through Panama.
- How long does it stay there?
- Where is it stored?
- Who buys it on arrival?
- Need to monitor closely the next two machines coming in. Let Lawrence of AFP know as well.
- Access his phone so we can hear what he is saying.

- Continue getting to know his connections, both social and business.
- Quickly check into the shipment of two forty-tonne excavators currently on the water with an ETA in four weeks' time.
- Get to know Dicky down in Melbourne. Is there a connection between Dicky and Belgrave?
- Track down 'Mo' of the Redskins as well.

After a quick discussion, we decide, now we have identified Dicky as his 'Joe', Deputy Warden Thomas is unlikely to warrant further investigation. But maybe we should let someone know he is corrupt.

We then add a 'to-do list' for Diedes:
- How much cash do the nightclubs deposit? Can we match this to the nightly 'balancing up'? I.e. reconcile the cash they count nightly when they balance their tills to the amounts deposited at their bank.
- Any details of where and when they buy machinery out of the states (or anywhere else).
- Can she assist with supplying any of the info above for the machinery transit in Panama?
- Also the buyers of this equipment – are they legit?

Silence descends on us, as we come to the end of our thoughts and suggestions.

'Quite a list to get on with tomorrow, on top of everything else we are working on,' I conclude.

Time for a coffee!

THE END

ABOUT THE AUTHOR:

AJ Wilton, creator of the Mortice series, of which this; *Mortice: Hammer Down* is book 4, is an Australian businessman with two thriving businesses who turned to writing through the quieter times brought on by Covid.

He describes himself as a 'Hobby Author' fitting this into his already time poor days.

To date he has written four novels, in a series about Mort and Pig in what is planned to be a series of ten.

'Having two busy businesses to run, I get a real kick out of creating these stories, it is a great way for me to turn my mind off business!'

He lives in the Gold Coast hinterland in Queensland and he and his wife, both inveterate travellers look forward to continuing to explore somewhere new or returning to some of their favourite places around the world with John able to indulge his other hobby of landscape photography.

He has three adult children and three grandchildren.

Feel free to follow him @ ajwilton.com – you are welcome to ask him questions or offer feedback directly via his website.

New Found Books Australia Pty Ltd
www.newfoundbooks.au

NEW FOUND BOOKS